paper
or
plastic

D1511053

paper or plastic

Vivi Barnes

Entangled Publishing, LLC
2614 South Timberline Road
Suite 109
Fort Collins, CO 80525

Entangled Teen is an imprint of Entangled Publishing, LLC.

Visit our website at www.entangledpublishing.com.

Edited by Stacy Abrams and Tara Quigley
Cover design by Kelley York
Interior design by Jeremy Howland
Couple photo (c) Shutterstock/BlueSkyImage
Shopping bags photo (c) Shutterstock/ILeysen
Price tag photo (c) iStock/linearcurves

Print ISBN 978-1-62266-521-1
Ebook ISBN 978-1-62266-526-6

Manufactured in the United States of America

First Edition February 2015

10 9 8 7 6 5 4 3 2 1

*To Robert, Carlton, and Trish—for a lifetime of memories,
inspiration, and laughs*

CHAPTER 1

It was just a cheap tube of lipstick in a shade I would never wear, if I wore lipstick at all.

Which I didn't.

So I couldn't believe I was sitting here, staring at the frosted square of glass in the door, holding my breath every time a shadow moved past.

Court shifted slightly, but her expression was bored. Her mom had already appeared, popping her head in for a few seconds to click her tongue and say, "Courtney Ann," in that slightly disappointed way that made me wish I were going home with her instead of my own mother.

Why did I do it? All I knew was that Mom's pinched expression this morning as she looked from my superstar sister, Rory, to me, the *meh* daughter, had been fixed in my mind. Her words, *Why can't you be more like your sister,* were familiar enough by now. Then she had to add in the fact that I was *throwing away* my future on some ridiculous pipe dream when I could be so much more. And all because I asked to go to Space Coast Fastpitch Softball Camp at the end of summer instead of joining her boring League of Southern Women group. I remember my sole thought as I slipped the lipstick into my pocket: *Take that, Mom.*

Still. The first really wrong thing I did in my entire life, and I got caught.

The annoying ticks of the wall clock reminded me that we had been sitting here for an hour. I wanted to take the stapler off the desk and throw it at the clock as hard as I could.

"What's taking so long?" I asked Court, who was busy with her phone. Probably texting Bryce, her long-time boyfriend and one of my best friends. If it wasn't for Bryce, I don't know if I would've become friends with Court. She liked to live on the edge, way outside my comfort zone. I didn't even *like* shopping—that was her thing.

I wished Syd were here. As my softball teammate and forever best friend, Syd would be a whole lot better at commiserating. She'd know what to say to make me laugh instead of staring at her phone the whole time.

"I don't know," Court finally said. "I guess they're waiting for the cops."

My heart sank to my shoes. Cops? "But it was just a couple of lipsticks."

She shrugged and kept texting. How could she look so calm right now? Was it too much to hope that the store manager would talk to our parents and leave the police out of it?

"What do you think is going to happen to us?" I asked for the third time, trying to keep the shakiness out of my voice.

She sighed and looked up at me. "Seriously, Lex, stop worrying. It's not like they'll arrest us. We're only sixteen. Minors." She stuck out her tongue at the door. "My brother got in trouble for drinking vodka at a party when he was seventeen and got off with just a warning. We'll be okay."

I nodded, but that didn't make me feel better. Drinking vodka didn't exactly match up to outright theft.

The door handle turned, and both Court and I jumped to our feet. *Ha!* I wanted to say. *You're not so cool about this after all.*

The security guard stuck his head in. "Courtney?" He motioned to her. She slipped her phone back into her pocket and moved forward through the door, flipping her black curls and looking back to wink at me. Before the door closed, I could see her mother shaking her head. My throat clenched as I remembered *my* mother would be here any moment, and she'd be doing a whole lot more than just shaking her head. I wished my dad would show up instead, but I knew he was working.

Fifteen minutes later, Court still hadn't reappeared. My stomach churned and my throat was dry. I wondered if it would be okay to ask for water. Most of all, I wondered what happened to Court. Had she been arrested after all? If so, wouldn't they have taken me, too?

It was wrong.

It was wrong.

It was wrong.

If I repeated it enough times like a mantra, maybe I'd get out of this.

I'm an idiot.

I'm an idiot.

I'm an idiot.

Maybe they were using this as a scare tactic. Some kind of "freak the kid out so she'll never do this again" trick.

It was working.

The handle turned, breaking my thoughts, but instead of jumping up, I pressed my back against the wall. The perfumed air reached my nose even before the giant nest of blond hair breached the gap in the door.

Besides the heavy scent of gardenias that floated about her, the first thing anyone would notice about my mother was that she loomed above practically everyone. She could've been mistaken for a women's basketball player, except for the face so heavily made up that it was a wonder the foundation didn't slide off her face. I'd rarely seen her without makeup myself. I doubt my father ever had, either.

The balding, pudgy store manager who followed seemed in awe of her. Or maybe he was just afraid.

"Alexis Jasmine Dubois!"

I cringed. I hated when she said my full name, especially in front of others. It always sounded like a bunch of crappy princess names thrown together. And it was a constant reminder of what she had expected me to be and what I most definitely was not.

She glared at me before turning her sweetest pageant smile on the store manager. "I don't know where she gets these crazy ideas. I'm sure it's all on her father's side. But we really appreciate the opportunity you're giving her, Mr. Hanson."

Opportunity?

Mr. Hanson blinked. "Oh, of course, Mrs. Dubois. I'm only too happy to extend a second chance to Alexis. My own son got in trouble when he was sixteen, so I know how having a record can damage a person's future."

Wait, what?

My mother nodded, still smiling, though it had an edge as she glanced at me. I knew she was going to let me have it later, but I almost didn't care. I wasn't going to get arrested. He was just letting me go. The "Hallelujah" song was reverberating in my head, and I felt like hugging him.

As my mother and Mr. Hanson talked, all I could focus on was the fact that no sheriff was being called in and no handcuffs were being snapped around my wrists. I was happily oblivious to their conversation.

Until a few words yanked me back to reality.

"Just bring her in Monday morning for the paperwork and uniform shirt, and we'll be good to go," Mr. Hanson said, smiling at me.

The happiness I felt inside whooshed out of me as if someone had punched me in the stomach. I stared at him. "Um, what?"

"Mr. Hanson understands that you were acting like a

stupid teenager," my mother said. "He has kindly agreed to allow you to work your summer here at SmartMart. In return, you'll get to keep the incident off your record, not to mention a paycheck. That'll be a change."

"But I'm already working this summer. Remember Let's Have a Ball? And I'm supposed to go to softball camp in August, too."

My mother's eyes narrowed slightly. She definitely remembered, and I could see she cared about it as little as if I had said I was going to get a drink of water.

I turned to Mr. Hanson before she could answer. "I'm sorry, Mr. Hanson. I really appreciate the opportunity, but I already have plans this summer."

My mother took my hand in one of hers in what would look like a loving gesture if she weren't digging her fingernails into my skin. I tried to pull away, but she had a grip of steel. "Don't be silly, Alexis. You have plenty of time before your camp, and you don't make money playing ball with little kids." She laughed lightly. She seemed to have missed the point of volunteering. "SmartMart is offering an excellent opportunity here, and I think you need to take it."

"But—"

"Mr. Hanson," my mother said without lifting her eyes from me. "Would you give me just a moment alone with my daughter?"

No, don't leave me with Crazy! I wanted to shout. But I just watched, helpless in her grip, as the store manager nodded and bowed out, giving me a sympathetic look before shutting the door behind him.

As soon as the latch clicked, my mother's pretense at charm and grace dropped. "I'm going to say this once, Alexis. If you don't accept this man's offer, you'll end up with shoplifting on your record that will follow you around the rest of your life. And think about what everyone will say about my parenting skills."

"This has nothing to do with you—" I started, but she pulled me closer. I got a strong whiff of her perfume and tried not to choke.

"This has everything to do with me, not to mention your sister. Can you imagine if this followed us through the circuit? I'd be criticized for being one of those mothers who can't control her kids, and Aurora's career would be over."

Aurora's career? It was true that my mother loved pageant life more than anything else—her claim to fame was being runner-up in the Miss Florida pageant when she was young. Pictures of her glory days hung in pride on our wall, and we endured story after story about how she should have won, and how the judges just felt sorry for the girl who actually won because of her poor background. She had even tried getting me involved in pageants when I was too young to know better, except I hated every single moment of it and finally refused to do it anymore. So yes, I knew she took the whole pageant thing seriously. But a seven-year-old's *career*? I knew better than to roll my eyes, but in my defense, they kind of moved on their own.

They could've at least waited until my mother's back was turned.

Her lips pressed together in a cold line. "Control yourself," she hissed. "Now, you are going to take this job and be glad about it. And if you don't, you can spend your entire high school career taking the bus instead of that car you want so badly, got it?"

She had me now. I needed that car, and my mother knew it. "Wait a second, that's not fair. I've been saving up—"

"Not even enough to fund the tires," she finished. "You're expecting us to foot the rest. Which we won't do if you don't get serious and take this job. And by the way, your camp is at the end of summer, so *if* we agree that you can go, it shouldn't interfere."

"But Let's Have a Ball camp—"

"You put in what, five or six *unpaid* hours a week there?"

"Eight," I mumbled. It would be more if I had a car to drive myself, but I didn't want to go there.

"Exactly. Plenty of time left for a real job."

"Dad won't—"

"Your father will agree with me. You have your choice. Take it or leave it."

Some choice. I knew I would have to do what she said. The car and my softball camp were the only things she could really hold over my head. "Fine," I whispered.

She turned on a heel and opened the door. "Mr. Hanson?" Her voice sounded musical again.

He entered the room, his face politely inquisitive.

"She'll be delighted to accept the position."

Hanson clapped his pudgy hands together. "Wonderful! Welcome to the team, Alexis."

I reached out to shake his extended hand, trying to

smile. I sucked at acting. My eyes dropped to the floor while he and my mother chatted.

SmartMart—Where Everybody Farts. That's what everyone called this place ever since some guy posted a People of SmartMart video on YouTube. It was a contest for whoever could take the funniest video or picture with their cell phone and post it on his blog. I sent in two—one of a woman walking around with a dressed-up dog in a stroller and another of an employee talking animatedly to herself. I didn't win, but the one that did showed a guy bending to pick up something and farting really loudly. The woman's puckered face behind him was priceless.

I felt sick to my stomach as my mother and I left the store. The fact that I wasn't going to jail should've made me feel relieved, but at the moment, all I could do was feel sorry for the situation I'd gotten myself into.

Grandma opened the front door as soon as my hand touched the knob. "Well, well, well," she said as my mother breezed past us into the house. Grandma looked unusually grim, her short red nails clicking against the wood frame. "I understand you've been doing time."

I swallowed hard, my stomach knotting inside me.

She held out her hand. "What I want to know is why you're holding out on your grandma. I could use a little more color in my lips."

I moved past her into the house as she laughed. "Funny.

Mom told you, huh?"

"Well, I overheard her conversation with whoever called earlier. Let me tell you, I'd be surprised if the whole neighborhood didn't hear, loud as she was jabbering."

In the other room, I could hear my mother ranting on the phone to my dad. I could picture him on the other end, sighing and saying, "I know, dear, yes dear."

"She's pretty mad," I said.

"What were you thinking, Lexie? That's not like you to steal. Gamble and drink, maybe, but not steal."

"The gambling and drinking got old."

She cocked her head at me, one penciled eyebrow raised in a perfect arch. I sighed. "Court wanted to see if we could get away with it. It was stupid, I know."

She wrinkled her nose. "Oh, that girl. She's going to find herself in jail one day if she's not careful."

Grandma didn't really dislike Court. She even said she saw herself in her. Grandma considered herself a hell-raiser—being the only one out of her five brothers and sisters to have both a college education and a criminal record. If standing up for human rights during the civil rights movement in the sixties could be considered hell-raising. I was proud of her for it, though.

"I'm going upstairs," I said, kissing her cheek. "Try not to get in trouble while I'm gone."

"Party pooper."

My phone buzzed in my pocket as I walked up to my room. It was Court.

You okay?

I typed my response. *Yep. C U at SM Monday?*

SM?

SmartMart.

Um I got out of it.

My heart sank. I scrolled through my contacts to find Court's name, but before I could call her, the phone buzzed with an incoming call from Syd. I pressed the answer key and before I could even say anything, Syd said, "Oh God, Lex, are you okay? Court told me what happened."

I sighed. "Yeah, I'm okay."

"Girl, I can't believe you let Court talk you into stealing. Why do we even put up with her?"

"Because she's Bryce's girlfriend," I said, still annoyed at Court's text. It was true—I liked Court, she was usually a lot of fun—but crap like this made me wonder why I even liked her, other than the fact that she was dating one of my best friends. And now she somehow got out of working at SmartMart—figures. "But it was my fault, too. I didn't need to do it. And now I'm stuck working at crappy SmartMart for the rest of the summer." I explained about the deal my mother made with the manager. To which she had the obvious response: "Oh my God, you're going to be like those people on that video."

"Shut up, I am not."

"I think my great-grandma has some old slippers and a muumuu you could borrow."

"Shut up, Syd." But I was laughing now. Syd always made me feel better.

"You could've at least stolen from a better store," she

joked. "Seriously, though, is there a way we can get you out of it? Cole and Ryan are gonna be in town, and I thought it'd be fun to hang out."

I rolled my eyes, glad Syd couldn't see me. Cole and Ryan were twins from our neighborhood who attended a school for the arts in New York. They'd always been obnoxious, but it'd gotten worse since they'd been accepted to that school. Syd had a thing for them since forever. "I don't know that I want to spend the summer watching you drool over those jerks," I said.

"Well, last summer Cole told me Ryan was totally into you. I thought you'd at least want to, you know—"

"No thanks. I don't speak imbecile," I said, inwardly gagging. Syd and Court had been trying to set me up with someone since I broke up with my last boyfriend several months ago. Most of the guys I knew were totally immature with a one-track mind. "I might consider making out with him if it'd get me out of this stupid job, though. It's not fair. Court said she didn't have to take the deal. How'd she get out of it?"

"Because Court does whatever Court wants. Her mom's easy like that."

I spent a few more minutes on the phone with Syd before hanging up. I had looked forward to summer so much—I adored the kids at Let's Have a Ball camp, and with college only two years away, volunteering was really important. Not to mention things I took for granted every summer, like playing volleyball at the beach with my friends and working on my pitch. Now that most of my friends had cars—except me, of course—it would've been an awesome summer.

I grabbed my pillow and pressed it to my face. Good-bye, fun summer. Beginning Monday, I'd be working at SmartMart. Alone.

I was going to be one of the People of SmartMart.

CHAPTER 2

On Monday morning, Mr. Hanson wasted no time getting me set up with a trainer. I'd barely finished signing the application when I was introduced to gray-haired, fragile-looking Bessie, who was probably about a hundred years old. She sure could move, though, and I found myself almost jogging to keep up as she showed me around the store.

SmartMart was what Mr. Hanson proudly referred to as a superstore for one-stop shopping, where customers could buy milk, jeans, DVDs, and fishing lures all in a single trip. There weren't very many shoppers in the aisles yet, so there was a peaceful, kind of pleasant vibe in the store, something I sincerely hoped would be more than just the calm before the storm. A couple times we stopped to help customers—a cute little boy who lost his mother and a woman who needed help finding a list of cold medicines.

As Bessie talked to the woman, I noticed a tall, dark-haired guy organizing an endcap display of cans a couple aisles away. His long-sleeved shirt and tie screamed *manager*, though he didn't seem to be much older than me. He was kind of cute, too, at least from this distance. His eyes lifted to meet mine, widening slightly as if he recognized me. Yeah, no. I totally would've remembered this guy.

With his gaze still fixed on me, he absently placed the can in his hand on the display, but it crashed to the floor, taking out several others with it. He quickly scrambled to pick them up, looking completely flustered.

I turned back to the customer, trying not to giggle. By the time I looked around again, he was gone.

The rest of the employees greeted me as we passed their locations, their smiles warm and friendly. The old man who Bessie introduced as Jake pretended to be startled by me, straightening up and bowing deeply, making me laugh. Another woman gave me a hug as she welcomed me to the team. It wasn't a bad morning at all.

When a person is naive enough to believe things are starting to look up, that's exactly when they begin falling down. And that very moment was when I learned about Code B.

"Code B," Bessie called into her radio as we hurried toward a guy on his hands and knees. Too late I realized that the *B* must stand for Barf. I jerked to a halt at the sight of the mess in front of the guy, but Bessie went over to see if he was okay. Another employee soon appeared, pushing a bucket and mop to the scene, while I was busy straightening the sunglasses on the nearest display. Okay, so maybe they were straight already. But Code B my ass—more like Code Screw This.

I noticed the cute manager from earlier walking toward me—or toward the mess, more likely. He was tall and fair-skinned—my guess was that he didn't spend time out in the Florida sun as much as I did. He was definitely hot in a "nice guy" kind of way, his wavy dark hair a striking contrast to his deep blue eyes. As he got closer, I noticed just a hint of a shadow around his jawline that kept him from looking too much like the boy next door, which might've helped to explain the fluttering in my stomach. I'd always found myself a lot more interested in the tall, dark, and dangerous type.

There was something strangely familiar about him. Maybe I had seen him briefly during a shopping trip with my mother. I couldn't remember. I turned back to the sunglasses, my arm knocking over some of the display.

"Crap," I muttered, bending over to pick them up. Manager Guy hurried over to pick up a pair that had flown under one of the jewelry racks. "Thanks, um…" I glanced at his nametag as he stood up to place the pair back on the display. "Grayson." Of course he'd have a hot name, too.

His eyebrows pinched slightly as he glanced down at the nametag. "Oh. Yeah, no problem," he said, frowning. Maybe I should've sounded more enthusiastic or something. Or maybe he was still embarrassed about earlier.

"I'm normally not this clumsy," I said. Lame. "Well, I am, but I usually save it for huge displays of cans."

I grinned, and he laughed. "Yeah, that's what I get for not paying attention. Anyway, I should probably thank *you* for giving me an excuse to avoid that mess a little longer." He nodded toward Barf Guy, who was now moaning on the floor.

"I'll just make it a point to throw sunglasses around whenever there's a Code B."

"I'll keep an eye out for them," he said, winking. Maybe he wasn't my age after all. Guys I knew didn't wink. I kind of liked it, though.

Grayson's radio buzzed with someone calling for backup at the disaster zone. "Guess I'd better go."

"Good luck," I called as he walked away. He glanced once over his shoulder at me, rolling his eyes as the guy retched again.

Bessie poked my shoulder from the other side, making me jump. Her knowing eyes were amused.

"How can you stand that?" I asked, knowing that my cheeks were burning. "So gross!"

She laughed. "Honey, I had two kids who used to get sick all the time, not to mention grandkids." She glanced around at the guy who was still on the floor. "Probably drunk. I don't know how people do that so early in the morning."

"I wish they'd be drunk outside," I said, shivering. I drew the line at puke.

I considered asking her about Grayson but couldn't figure out how to do it in an offhand way. My dad had gotten fired from a job a long time ago because he was dating one of his employees—who later ended up being my mother.

So I figured an employee/manager relationship wouldn't exactly be encouraged here.

Get a hold of yourself, Lex. You talked to the guy once— you're not exactly swapping phone numbers.

Bessie and I walked toward the front of the store, stopping at one of the displays to pick up a couple boxes of cereal off the floor and place them back on their shelf. "This gets messed up constantly because it's the first thing people see when they come in and it's what's on sale. You'll have to keep an eye on it whenever you pass by, and when you're greeter, keeping it straight will be part of your responsibility."

I nodded, picking up a box of Ex-Lax from the floor and placing it back on the shelf with the others. Right next to the cereal. Guess that made as much sense as everything else. Noticing a quarter on the floor next to the display, I bent down to pick it up, but my fingers slipped as it stayed put. I slid a nail under and tried to gently pry it up. It didn't budge.

"Bessie, this quarter is stuck."

She looked down at me and started laughing. "Well, if that's not an official welcome to the team, I don't know what is."

"What do you mean?"

Still chuckling, she explained how someone put it there as a joke. "But the interesting part is that we don't know who it is. Some think it's a customer, but others believe the prankster might be an employee."

I stood up and nudged the quarter with my shoe. "What do you think?"

"I think the devil walks among us." Her expression was grave as I stared at her. Then she laughed. "I'm kidding. I really have no idea."

"Such a weird thing to do."

She handed me a box of hair color that had fallen. "Honey, I wouldn't think too hard on it. We have a prankster, that's all. He or she pulls quite a few shenanigans around here—all harmless. But be sure to let me know if you figure it out."

"Hi, Bessie!" someone shouted right behind me.

I whipped around to see—*oh, no*—the very girl I had filmed for that YouTube video, the greeter who had been talking to herself. But I wasn't laughing now. As she yelled a cheery "Hi!" at me, her dark hair bobbing across her cheeks, I wanted to cry. I never thought I'd actually be working with her. I was suddenly glad I didn't win that contest and that the video didn't actually end up on YouTube.

"Ruthie, this is Alexis, the newest member of our SmartMart family."

"Hi, Ruthie."

Ruthie clapped her hands and jumped up and down. "Alexis? My daddy drives a Lexus! My daddy drives a Lexus! Do you know I rode in my daddy's Lexus? Do you have a Lexus? My daddy has a Lexus."

Her voice was piercing, and a headache that had just started pressing against my temples worsened, but I tried not to let it show. I just nodded and said, "Uh-huh."

"Where are you today, Ruthie?" Bessie asked.

"Right here," she said proudly. "Greeter. Here, I can

fix that," she said, ripping the box of hair color out of my hands and setting it on the shelf. Her rough hands became gentle as they moved other boxes to their proper spots, a big game of Tetris that she was clearly an expert at. The smile on Ruthie's face was dreamy—she liked her job.

"Have you ever used a POS?" Bessie asked when we ended the tour at an unoccupied register.

"Um...a what?"

"The POS is short for point of sale. We use a touch screen. We just upgraded from our old system last year, and some people are still having trouble with it. But I'm sure you'll pick it up in no time."

While Bessie was explaining how to weigh fruits and vegetables, a customer walked up and put his basket of groceries on the conveyor. I glanced up at the unlit register light, but he failed to catch my subtle hint. He cleared his throat when Bessie didn't stop and turn to him right away. It was probably only ten seconds, but his expression suggested he'd been waiting hours.

"Hey, miss," he snapped. He didn't bother looking at me, only Bessie.

Bessie looked over to him and smiled pleasantly. "I'm sorry, sir. This register is closed right now."

He dumped the contents of his basket onto the conveyor belt and crossed his arms. "I have ten items. This is a ten-item-only lane. It's the only express lane that you people have. So are you going to check this stuff? I'm thinking of a word. Do you know what that word is?"

The word that came to my mind was *dick*.

"Yes, sir. I understand," Bessie said without batting an eye. "I can try to call up additional cashiers, but I don't have this register set up, so I can't—"

"You have two hands, right? So don't tell me you can't ring me up."

Bessie waved toward another cashier who was signing in. "Sir, this young man will be happy to assist you at the next register."

She attempted to help the man put the stuff back in his basket, but he raised his hand slightly as if he would slap hers away. He threw the items back in his basket and turned to the other register, grumbling the whole time about senile old ladies. A roll of Mentos rolled away from him, unnoticed. I was tempted to pick it up and chuck it at his fat head.

Bessie shrugged. "Sometimes you get angry customers if they've had to wait too long. You just have to stay calm and smile, and that's usually enough to relax them."

I didn't know about that. The guy didn't look relaxed to me—like an asshole, yes, but relaxed, no. "You were just trying to help him. And this lane wasn't open. The stupid light is off."

"I know, honey. But never, ever lose your temper with a customer. Trust me, you won't win. Not only that, you'd probably end up without a job. Mr. Hanson has a zero-tolerance policy for disrespecting our customers."

A zero-tolerance policy? I had a zero-tolerance policy for someone treating Bessie like crap. The thought of someone like that coming through *my* lane formed a pit of anger in my stomach.

"It's about time for your break now," Bessie said brightly, as if she wasn't even affected by the jerkwad. "Fifteen minutes, and the break room is just inside that door to the left, past the time clock."

I nodded and headed into the employee hallway, turning straight into the women's bathroom. I put the faucet on full blast and splashed the cool water on my face, as if it could help erase the angry man's face or, at the very least, the image of puke all over the floor. One thing was for sure — no way was I ever going to have a career in retail, or in any job where I had to deal with crap like that. Ever.

I pulled my ponytail out, letting the hair fly around my face, and glared at my reflection. Awesome. Getting closer to looking like one of the People of SmartMart.

My mother expected me to fail, I knew it. The way she looked when she dropped me off this morning, that sigh that said she knew I wouldn't last the week, if even the day. That I wouldn't be anywhere near my perfect seven-year-old sister's standards — not that Rory would ever be forced to work here, even if she stole a freaking car.

Screw it. I swept my hair back into its ponytail. I was going to make this work. It was just two months of stupid. I could last two months. I'd play this grocery game of Tetris better than Ruthie. I'd even spew rainbows and sparkles if it would lift me above my mother's low expectations. I'd smile so hard it'd hurt.

I stopped at my locker on the way back out, checking my email and responding to Syd's and Court's texts asking how my day was going. *Meh except for uber-hot manager.*

My grandma had texted me a similar question, so I copied and pasted the same response for her. I knew she'd get a kick out of that.

"Did you have a nice break?" Bessie asked as I walked toward her at register five. My heart flipped as the guy she was talking to turned to look at me—it was Grayson, the bright spot in this hell called SmartMart.

"Sure," I said cheerily. "Everything's great. Hi, Grayson!" I grinned at him, but his slight return smile was hesitant as he looked from me to Bessie and back again.

"Alexis, this is Noah," Bessie said. "I believe you two have already chatted. He's a supervisor in training. You could say he's our boss the next few weeks until he heads back to school. In fact, he says you go to school together." Her expression was expectant as she looked from me to him and back again.

"Noah…?" My smile slowly slipped from my face as the pieces came together. Noah from school. Grayson wasn't his first name—it was his last.

Oh no…no, no, NO!

CHAPTER 3

Noah Grayson was a grade higher than me and known by pretty much everyone at school for ratting out my friend Bryce for vandalizing the rival school two years ago. I had already gone home from that baseball game, but from what I heard, Bryce and a couple of his friends had sneaked around the rival school, spray-painting "Ospreys Rule" over their Manatee mascot. Noah caught Bryce in the act and told the principal. Bryce got suspended from school for three days, kicked off the baseball team, and even got suspended from his tournament team for the rest of the season.

Everyone had been outraged. And without Bryce pitching, both the school's and the tournament's baseball teams lost their games, not even making it past the first round of the playoffs. Not only that, the school he vandalized had the most horrible, loud-mouthed players of any school, and they delighted in rubbing our losses in our faces whenever they could. Still did, actually.

Bryce took a lot of shit for it from everyone. And when they discovered who'd ratted him out, pretty much the entire school ostracized Noah. Bryce despised him with a passion.

The only thing I really knew about Noah now was that he was a loner, always sitting by himself with hair hanging in his face, eyes to the ground. He definitely didn't look like *this*.

Now he was my manager.

Noah nodded, his blue eyes tightening at the edges slightly as he took in my change in expression. "It's okay, Bessie. I think she remembers me."

I tried to smile again, but I'm sure he could tell that it wasn't genuine. "Yes, I do." My voice sounded weak.

"Wonderful!" the oblivious Bessie said, clapping her hands together. "You two should have a lot in common."

She excused herself and walked away. Noah's eyes followed her all the way to the door. I shifted from one leg to the other, waiting for him to say or do something. The air between us had definitely chilled, and I was pretty sure it wasn't just on my end.

"So...Noah Grayson." Brilliant, but what else was I supposed to say? I despised this guy on behalf of my best friend—was I supposed to fake being nice now?

"Yep," he said, stretching out the word so it sounded more like "ye-up." His eyes hardened as they met mine again, like he was challenging me to spill about exactly how I remembered him, and it certainly wasn't as this tall, good-looking guy. But hot or not, I couldn't like him. No way.

I pointed at his shirt and said, "Why just the last name?"

He shrugged. "Why not?"

I gritted my teeth. And to think only minutes ago I was stoked to be working with him. "Worked here long?" I asked, keeping my voice light.

"About a year. Started when I was your age."

My age? Oh, this was going *so* well. "So they made you a manager, huh?"

"No, I'm not a manager. I mean, kind of. I'm on a supervisorial training program. It's what they offer to high school and college kids who have promise."

"Ah, okay. Well, good for you." I hadn't meant to say it condescendingly—well, maybe just a little—but his furrowed brow made it pretty clear that he took it that way. His eyes cut over to the doorway again as Bessie walked toward us.

"Okay, well, I'll leave you guys alone," he said in obvious relief as he backed away. "I'm sure I'll see you later." He nodded at Bessie but didn't even glance at me.

"Well?" Bessie asked as she signed into the register.

"Well what?"

She winked at me. Ugh, Noah Grayson—was she kidding me? But I didn't say anything. Instead, I mentally ticked off the highlights from my first day.

A drunk guy puked all over the floor.

The first customer was an asshole.

The girl I had submitted a video of for YouTube was now my coworker.

My boss was a (unfortunately hot) loner kid from my high school who clearly remembered that we were *not* friends.

Fantastic day. And by fantastic, I meant kill me now.

The only thing that could save today from being a complete disaster was a visit from my friends right at lunch break.

"Lexie!" The squealing came from Syd as she and Court ran up to tackle-hug me at the cash register where I was shadowing Bessie. Bryce was behind them, grinning.

"Aw, you guys," I said. I glanced at Bessie, who winked and waved us away with a smile, though it wasn't yet my break time. I looped my arm through Syd's and walked with them toward the deli. "Today was really sucktastic till you showed up."

"Oh? Can't be all bad." Syd glanced over her shoulder and leaned in. "Where's this hot manager you mentioned?"

"Oh, oh, *yes!*" Court said, her voice rising. "Where is he?"

I shushed her, looking around quickly and praying that Noah was in the back of the store.

"What's going on?" Bryce asked, his arm automatically wrapping around Court as we stopped at the deli counter.

"Lex has a thing for this manager guy here. Where is he, Lex?"

I stared at Bryce, who I'm sure was thinking *chick stuff*, though he was grinning and waggling his eyebrows at me, an expression that would certainly drop as soon as he caught sight of Noah. I *really* wished I hadn't sent that text to Court and Syd. They'd never leave me alone about it if they knew who the hot guy was.

"I don't know where he is," I said. "I think his shift's over."

My friends' faces fell. "Damn," Court said. "We were hoping to check him out."

I shrugged. "He's okay. I mean, compared to other SmartMart employees, you know. Nothing special. Not like super hot or anything. Just average."

"All right, leave her alone," Bryce said to Court, tickling her side and making her giggle. "She obviously doesn't want to talk about it."

Court switched gears and started hugging all over Bryce as he ordered their sandwiches, but Syd kept her eyes on me. I knew she didn't believe me—I'd talked way too fast and too much—but I also knew she wouldn't push me for details. It was what I loved about her. She seemed to know when to speak up and when not to ask questions—so unlike Court, who'd blurt out anything. I had no idea how long I could keep the fact that Noah worked here a secret. I also had no idea why I even wanted to. I wasn't his biggest fan, either.

"Hey, is that him? Your hot guy?" Court asked, pointing behind me and causing everyone else to look. I turned to see Noah talking with another employee. He was still far enough away that it was hard to make out his features, I hoped. He glanced over at me, his eyes just catching mine before I turned my attention back to my friends, my face burning.

"No, not him." I grabbed a salad out of the counter and shoved it toward Syd a little too hard. "Here, have a chef's salad. Want one, too?" I asked Bryce, who was holding a foot-long sandwich in his hands and now staring at me like I had two heads. It worked to get his attention away from Noah, though, and by the unchanged expression on his face, he hadn't recognized him. Good thing Noah cut his hair this summer.

Bryce tilted his head. "You okay?"

"Yeah, sure. Just gotta get back to work." I smiled at him, tapping my fingers nervously against my pants leg. I was hungry and actually was on my lunch break, but it didn't matter. I needed to get away from my friends as fast as I could. *And damn you, Noah, for stressing me out like this.*

"You practicing tomorrow?" Bryce asked as Court and Syd went to sit at a small deli table. "Or do you have to work?"

"Not sure." I glanced over my shoulder and noticed Noah still watching me. "I'll just, um, meet you at the field?" I didn't even know what we were talking about anymore.

"Okay. Call me if you need a ride."

"Uh-huh." *Is he still watching me? Should I look around or is that too obvious?*

"What's wrong?" Bryce asked. "You're acting weird."

I laughed the most fake laugh in the world. "I'm fine. Really."

He watched me for a moment as I tried to smile and look completely relaxed, though my heart was racing. I wanted so badly to turn and see if Noah was still staring at me, but I didn't. Bryce knew me better than almost anyone. I didn't want him fishing around anymore about why I was acting like a maniac.

A shrill alarm suddenly rang. I jumped and stared around at the different employees, including Noah, racing toward the back of the store. I turned to Bryce—whatever it was, I was grateful for the interruption. "You guys should go—I think something's set off the alarm and I need to go help figure it out."

"Yeah, no problem. I'll see you tomorrow." Bryce waved to Syd and Court, who got up and followed him.

"Cole and Ryan get in today," Syd said as she passed me. It was funny how she rarely said one name without the other, like the twins really did come as a set. She always said she didn't care which one she ended up with, since they were so alike. "I'm going to stalk their house later if you get home early and want to join. Oh, and snap a picture of your hot guy, okay?" She grinned, and I smiled back with what I hoped looked like enthusiasm.

As soon as they were gone, I headed to the back. The alarm wasn't sounding anymore, and most of the employees who'd run to check it out were already walking back to their original positions, including Noah.

"What was that?" I asked him.

"Some kids thought it'd be funny to open the back door. You know, the one that clearly says 'Don't open or alarm will sound.'" He shook his head, but his eyes stayed on mine. "Stupid kids will do anything for attention."

"Ah." I moved away quickly as a customer stopped him

to ask a question. My face burned as I thought about the shoplifting from last week. Did Noah know what I did to cause me to end up working here? I hoped Mr. Hanson hadn't said anything to him, because if he did, I wondered if Noah meant that "stupid kids" remark to include me.

And if he'd seen Bryce here earlier, I had a feeling he did mean exactly that.

CHAPTER
4

The rest of the day was spent in a small training room completing the online POS training. Easy enough, and I didn't have to deal with Shoppers From Hell. Finally, Bessie came in to tell me my shift was over. I clicked save on the training module and shut down the session. She complimented me on how great I did for my first day and told me tomorrow I'd be greeting customers. I glanced at the front door and, as if on cue, a customer sneezed in his hand and wiped it on the handle of his cart. Lovely. I made a mental note to bring a big bottle of hand sanitizer tomorrow.

I clocked out at exactly five and grabbed my bag from my locker. Noah rounded the corner just as I slammed the door shut. He stopped short and gave me a tentative smile.

"Hey," he said.

"Hey," I said back.

Long pause. Then, "How'd the first day go?"

"Okay, I guess."

"Good."

We stood there staring at each other for about five seconds, which translated to about twenty-five minutes in standing-around-while-trying-to-find-something-to-say time. I'll admit, the boy still had killer eyes and a hot bod, but talk about major conversation fail. I wanted the guy back from earlier—the one who'd given me that confident, flirty smile and made me laugh. The guy I'd thought was just some randomly hot manager named Grayson. Now I had a hard time seeing past the fact that he was, to sum it up, a rat. Not that I agreed with spray-painting graffiti everywhere, but Noah didn't have to go tell on Bryce. I didn't care how long ago it was. And if he was going to hold it against me for being friends with Bryce, yeah, that was not going to work.

"So, your friends…" he started as if he'd read my mind, his eyebrow lifted like I was supposed to know what he was going to say.

"What about them?"

"I saw them earlier."

I put my hands on my hips. "And?"

He stared at me for a moment, then huffed and shook his head. "Nothing."

Yeah, that's what I thought. I gave him a half wave. "See you tomorrow."

"Okay."

As I walked out to the parking lot, I breathed a sigh of relief to see the black BMW and not my mother's Escalade.

I opened the door to my dad's warm smile and a wink. "Here you go, sweetheart," he said, handing me a cold can of Diet Coke. Dad always knew how to make things better. "So, how was the first day on the job?"

I groaned and slouched down in my seat, throwing an arm over my face and making him laugh. I loved that I didn't have to pretend with him. He had tried arguing with my mother on my behalf, knowing the whole time that it wouldn't work and that I'd end up at SmartMart. We both knew who ran the show in our family, and we knew better than to expect to win a fight with her.

Dad stopped for ice cream on the way home. "Okay, so tell me, what's the worst thing about the job?" he asked as we dove into bowls of Chocolate Avalanche.

My day flashed before me. Where could I begin? But all I said was, "Rude customers."

"And the best?"

"Best?" I shook my head.

He frowned. "Come on, Lexie. There's got to be something good."

I glanced at the worker behind the counter who was handing an ice-cream cone to a wide-eyed little girl in pigtails. Her mother was smiling at the guy and thanking him. The couple behind them was also smiling. Maybe people were nicer in a shop that sold ice cream instead of toilet paper.

"There's a lady named Bessie who is training me. She's really nice."

"Good. And?"

"And what?"

"And what else?"

I tilted my head to consider that. I knew him—he wouldn't relent until I answered. "Well...I'll get a paycheck."

"And?"

I sighed. "Dad, please."

He leaned back in his chair, giving me a fatherly look that gave me warm fuzzies rather than annoyance. "Lexie, is that all this job is to you? A paycheck?"

"Isn't that all it's supposed to be? I mean, it's a *job*."

"That is part of it, yes. But come on, have you gotten to know any of your other coworkers?"

"I was there for one whole day. Not exactly programming everyone's numbers in my phone just yet."

That made him laugh. "Okay, well, don't hate the place because it's SmartMart. There's plenty of time for you to get a more trendy job." He made air quotes with his fingers when he said that. "Some of the best jobs I ever had seemed menial at the time."

"Okay, okay, I get it." I had to change the subject before he launched into his story about when he was a janitor in college and saved a man from choking in the school's cafeteria. It was one of his favorite "lesson" stories to tell whenever Rory or I did something that warranted a lecture.

"All right, so here's another good thing," I said. "Mr. Hanson is nice. He's the manager." I thought of my other manager. I wasn't sure what to make of Noah. He seemed nice, but that "stupid kids" remark still bugged me. Maybe he didn't know what I'd done and it was just intended for the kids who set off the alarm. I decided to assume he didn't.

"Good." Dad glanced at his watch. "Oh, shoot, it's later than I thought." He stood up and gestured for me to follow. "Your mother is going to hang us out to dry if we don't get home."

My mother. The first words out of her mouth when we walked in the door were aimed at me. "Well? You didn't quit or get fired, did you?"

Nice.

"No, Mom. It's a great job. Really great."

My voice was unenthusiastic, but still she nodded, satisfied. She wrinkled her nose at my shirt. "Red is definitely not your color." She leaned forward to give me a hug. "I'm so proud of you for hanging in there," she whispered. My mother was one of the few people I knew who could smoothly follow an insult with a compliment. It was like getting punched in the face and then kissed. "Now go change. Dinner's in fifteen minutes."

Upstairs, I changed out of the musty-smelling black pants and fire engine SmartMart shirt. The thought of putting them on again made me feel kind of queasy. I gathered up clothes from my hamper and dirty towels from the bathroom and ran downstairs to put them in the washing machine, even though Mrs. Gentry would be here tomorrow. My mother paid her to come to our house twice a week to clean and do laundry, but I didn't like anyone except myself washing my clothes.

Rory was in the laundry room, laying a fluffy pink dress on the drying rack. My clean bra and silk shirt were on the tile floor. "How many times do I have to tell you to leave my clothes alone?" I asked her.

She didn't even look at me. "Put your stuff away, then. You can't hog the rack."

I snapped my bra at her leg like a whip, causing her to run out of the room screaming, "Momma! Momma! Lexie hurt me!" She brushed a couple books off the bookshelf as she tore through the hallway. Of course, stopping to pick them up would never occur to her. I picked up the books and started to place them back on the shelf, hesitating when I noticed my high school yearbooks from the past couple years. I carried them to my room, shutting the door and flopping on the bed.

I flipped casually through my freshman yearbook. I had tried everything that year—racquetball, softball, dance. Dance squad was not my thing, but it did earn me some great friends, especially Court, who had just started dating Bryce. My favorite picture of us was displayed in one corner—arms slung over each other's shoulders, laughing like we just heard the funniest joke.

That was the year my hair went through various evolutions of wavy-poof. The dance group picture presented my blond hair frizzed out a bit under the top hat—probably from the humidity. My softball picture featured my ponytail that I always wore when playing. Turning to my individual freshman photo, I shook my head at the perfectly curled long blond hair that wrapped over one of my shoulders. My mother had styled it that day. I think that was the last day I let her touch my hair. It made me look like freaking Rapunzel.

My finger trailed along the pages to find others—Syd

with her smooth, straight brown hair—the same style she wore every year. Court's dark curls and bright grin. Holly, our school's resident Mean Girl, pictured in her usual last spot as if she owned it and not just because her name was Zelner. Her smile was almost sweet. You'd never guess she was so bitchy by this angelic picture.

Flipping to the pages for the baseball team, I noted the large photo inset of Bryce, featured as "Rising Star." He was standing straight and tall, the bill of his hat pressed down to his eyebrows, ball in glove, eyes slightly off-camera as if he was focused on a batter with a full count. It was how I always thought of him, the serious consideration he gave every batter when pitching, as if every game were part of the World Series. He'd helped me tremendously when I got into softball, especially since we were both pitchers. Of all people, I credited Bryce with the fact that I had the fastest pitch of any girl in my division and that I made it into the State All-Stars this spring.

We'd always been good friends, but years of playing softball and volunteering at Let's Have a Ball camp quickly turned him into one of my best friends. In fact, we both had similar blond hair and light blue eyes, so people always thought we were related.

I wondered if he was over being angry at Noah. It happened a long time ago, so maybe I was worried for nothing. But if he was still mad, I couldn't risk losing the guy who really was like a brother to me. One thing I knew—there was no way I could be friends with Noah *and* Bryce, and of the two, I'd choose Bryce any day. Noah was just my manager at a job I hated, that was all.

Okay, clearly I was stalling. I flipped to the sophomore pages and ran my finger down the *G* names until it landed on *Grayson, Noah*.

Noah's image was smiling, his teeth showing in the "say cheese" grin we all had before they blinded us with the flash. I peered closer. His dark hair fell past his ears, almost to his shoulders. His face was thinner than it was now, and it appeared to be smooth and clear, unlike Bryce, who had the telltale zits of puberty all over his freshman face.

I tossed it aside and flipped through my sophomore yearbook, skipping my grade and heading straight to the junior class. Noah's hair was much longer than in the picture before. This was how I remembered him—hair almost blending with his black shirt, long layers hanging over one eye, almost goth-like. His current hairstyle was so different—so much shorter. Older, too. I wasn't sure which one was better. Maybe an in-between cut.

Noah wasn't smiling in this picture. His face was serious, almost brooding, like he just found out he got an F or broke up with his girlfriend or something. I tried to remember if I'd ever seen him with a girl. I couldn't remember anyone saying she had dated Noah Grayson.

My phone buzzed. I checked to see a message from my grandma.

Hows ur day?

I typed, *Ok I guess.*

U 4get sumping?

Sumping? I snickered. Grandma was always trying to

use what she called "text lingo" and frequently got it wrong.

I typed, *Don't think so.*

REALLY? The word was followed by a bunch of open-mouth emoticons.

I laughed out loud and went to the door, yanking it open. Grandma was on the other side, her cell phone in hand. I gave her a hug, breathing in the familiar light scent of cedar that clung to her clothes from the chest she kept them folded in.

"That's better," she said. She moved past me to sit on my bed, clasping her hands on her lap. "So tell me about your first day, and don't skip over this uber-hot manager you mentioned in your message."

I sank down on the bed and told her—starting with dear Bessie and ending with the visit from my friends. I explained what happened two years ago with Bryce and Noah. "So what am I supposed to do if Bryce or even Court and Syd realize Noah's working there?"

"Why do you care? It sounds like their problem, not yours."

"Because I might've, um, sent that same text to Syd and Court and now they're expecting to meet him." I could feel my face heating up, and my grandma, always the most perceptive one in the family, could tell. She tilted her head at me.

"So this uber-hot manager is Noah, and now you're afraid Bryce will be upset that you considered his enemy date-worthy." She smiled gently. "Honey, like I told you, that's his problem. Just because he had a falling-out with Noah years ago doesn't mean you're not allowed to talk to the boy. Bryce is your friend, and he should understand."

Grandma didn't know the whole story, that Bryce lost his position on the varsity team when he was finally allowed back, that his coach still referenced the incident and mentioned how much better he could've been whenever Bryce was having an "off" day. And that his traveling tournament team blamed him for the rest of the season's losses and pretty much hazed him for it. Yeah, Bryce forgiving Noah would be more shocking than a blizzard in summer. But all I said to her was, "I guess."

"Do you think Noah will ask you out?"

I gaped at her. "Grandma, we are *not* going out. We just work together. And he's not my type, trust me."

"Why not?"

"Just…no." Not after finding out who he was, at least. Which sucked again that he had to be *that* guy instead of just some cute dude at work.

"Fine, fine." She reached up to gently tuck my hair behind my ear. "What are you reading?" she asked, glancing at my open yearbook where Noah's face stared moodily up at me.

I quickly shut the book. "Nothing. Just an old yearbook."

She sighed heavily. "Sweetheart, be careful not to get so caught up in the past that it affects your future. That's no way to live your life." She leaned forward to kiss my forehead. "Now why don't you come downstairs and have a cookie with me?"

"Mom said dinner's almost ready. She'd be pissed."

"Exactly." Grandma grinned wickedly and I laughed,

following her. Grandma loved her daughter-in-law, I guess, but theirs was definitely a strained relationship. Grandma liked doing things that made Mom nuts, and my mother in turn enjoyed nagging Grandma about everything. I was just glad she lived here. When my mother upset me, I'd run to Grandma. She was always full of hugs and smiles and jokes and everything that turned the world right-side-up again. Sure, she'd forget things here and there or repeat herself, but didn't all older people? I didn't care what my parents said about her being sick. Grandma was fine—better than fine.

And she would help me get through this nightmare of a job.

CHAPTER
5

Tuesday at SmartMart wasn't too horrible, though my feet were throbbing from being on my feet all day. Noah and I didn't talk much, but at least there weren't glare daggers being thrown in either direction. Once he even smiled at me—a shy smile that made my stomach flip. I even caught myself looking for him on occasion. I wasn't sure if it was because I hoped he'd be nearby or that I hoped he wouldn't. One thing was for sure—the guy made me uncomfortable, and I hated that feeling.

After I clocked in on Wednesday, Bessie had me take a test on what I'd learned on the point of sale. Unfortunately, I passed, so she set me up in the front of the store for the second part of my training: The Greeter Position.

"Lexus, are we working together all day today?" Ruthie asked, clapping her hands as I joined her.

"Looks like it." Weird how she had dropped the *A* from my name and was just calling me Lexus. Made me feel like a car.

The Greeter Position mostly involved pasting smiles on our faces and pushing carts toward customers who entered the store. In my opinion, it was easily the most boring job ever created. But Ruthie seemed to love it more than breathing. She had a big grin on her face, and her "welcome" as customers entered the store was enthusiastic, to say the very least.

"Hi there! Welcome to SmartMart!" she yelled at one man who looked startled at the cart flying his way, but he caught it and thanked her politely.

Working with Ruthie actually made The Greeter Position much more interesting, since watching the door through her eyes meant seeing customers in a whole new light.

"That lady's name is Carol," she said after she walked a cart over to an elderly woman. I noticed that she was careful about giving the cart to Carol, not shoving it at her as she did to everyone else. "Her husband died last year, so she comes here every week and puts a bunch of stuff in her cart and talks to people about the stuff and then leaves the cart in the aisle and goes home."

I watched as Carol proceeded to the produce section, stopping to put a large bunch of bananas in her cart. She did the same with apples and peaches, smiling the whole time at other employees and customers, who all smiled back at her. "Wait, she just leaves a full cart in the aisle and takes off? Doesn't Mr. Hanson get mad about that?"

"Oh, no." Ruthie shook her head. "Mr. Hanson said we have to be understanding because she's sad and needs friends. We're her friends."

This didn't surprise me at all about Mr. Hanson. I wondered if he had a single mean or even slightly annoyed bone in his body. I somehow doubted it. And after watching Ruthie with the woman, I doubted she did, either.

As she shoved a cart at another incoming customer and shouted her greeting, I smiled at her. "Know what? You're a really nice person, Ruthie. I bet Carol is glad to have you as a friend."

Her eyes lit up in delight. "You are a nice friend too, Lexus."

I shifted, an uncomfortable feeling settling in my stomach as the stupid video I had made of her resurfaced in my mind. What the hell had I been thinking, anyway?

A few customers later, I got another update. "That guy is with a new lady every week," Ruthie told me, pointing to a huge muscle of a man who walked in with his arm around a woman in a bikini top. "Do you think he keeps them in a house and takes them out one at a time for a walk?"

I don't think I've ever laughed as hard in my life as I did at that casual observation. Ruthie joined in, though she seemed to be laughing more because I was than because of her own statement. We were laughing so hard that Bessie stopped by to ask us to keep it down, though she chuckled when I told her what Ruthie said.

Even with Ruthie's fascinating observations, time passed slowly in the Dreadful Greeter Position. I did snicker a couple of times as I watched people struggle to pick up the glued quarter on the floor, but it quickly got old.

By the time lunch came around, my nerves were growling as much as my stomach. I took my break alone, ignoring the conversation Jake was having with the vending machine and relishing in the blessed half-hour of alone time. When I returned to my shift at the door, Ruthie had a new idea to pass the time.

"Hey, Lexus! Want to play the cart game?"

"Ruthie, you can just call me Lex."

"I like Lexus!" she said loudly. "Like my daddy's Lexus!"

I cringed as several people sorting through vegetable bins turned around to stare at us. "What's the cart game?" I whispered, mostly to change the subject and get her to lower her voice.

She seemed to catch on. "Oh," she whispered. "It's where I stand on the end of the cart and you push me around and around and around."

"Um, that doesn't sound like a good idea, Ruthie."

"Oh, it's so fun! You'll love it! I can push you, too. But me first."

She went to the end of a cart and stepped up over the wheels, holding tightly to the basket. "Ready!"

I was grateful for the onslaught of people coming through the door at that moment. Ruthie seemed to forget about the cart game immediately, jumping right back into Overenthusiastic Greeter Position.

Another hour and I finally caved to pushing Ruthie around in the cart a couple times, just to break up the boredom, though I declined my own special ride from her. Her laughter as I spun the cart around was contagious, though, and I found myself laughing along with her. In a way, she was like Court—someone who could make the best of any situation and didn't care what anyone else thought. Definitely not like me, who worried way too much about what people thought.

Dizzy, I slowed down, still clinging to the cart until I could get my balance back on track. My eyes landed on Noah, whose lips were parted slightly in a weirdly awed expression as he watched us. Oh, I got it—clearly he was surprised I was actually having fun with Ruthie. I straightened and smiled as big as I could at him, one eyebrow lifted as my eyes stayed fixed on his, daring him to say anything. Then I deliberately turned my back on him.

By Thursday, I was ready to beg on my knees for Bessie to put me somewhere—anywhere—other than Greeter Position From Hell. I could *not* understand how Ruthie enjoyed it so much. I was fed up with the never-ending task of cleaning the front display (its own special kind of nightmare, since the display got messed up almost as soon as I finished organizing it), pushing carts at people, and smiling until my cheeks ached. I was more than happy to go collapse in the break room for fifteen minutes, though someone apparently thought it was funny to put some disgusting goo in the snack machine's coin return slot. Trying to retrieve my quarters in the snot-like substance made me lose my desire for the Twix bar that appeared below.

Prankster 1, Lex a big fat 0. I tossed the bar in my locker for later.

Another hour into my shift, I was willing the clock hands to move faster and whining to myself about how this was now my life when a loud, high-pitched squeal reached my ears. "Oh my God, this is awesome!"

Holly Zelner and a couple of her friends—including Maggie Martin from my softball team—were staring at me, their eyes moving up and down my body like I was wearing a clown suit instead of a SmartMart uniform. "I'd heard you were here," she said. "I just wanted to see for myself."

"Hey, Maggie," I said calmly, ignoring Holly. Maggie smiled and returned my greeting. My relief pitcher for the Falcons, Maggie was actually a nice person, so I never understood why she hung out with Holly, the most spiteful girl at my school. I had a feeling their parents were friends or something. At least, that was the only reason I could come up with.

As for Holly, I knew her issues with me started with the fact that I was best friends with Bryce, the guy she'd had a crush on for years, regardless of his dating Court. She'd show up at his baseball games wearing ridiculously high heels and butt-hugging jeans. She even tried volunteering at Let's Have a Ball last summer but spent the whole time ignoring the kids and bitching about the heat. It was Florida, so I didn't know what she expected. One of the highlights of my summer was when Bryce asked her why the hell she volunteered if she didn't like the sun. She never came back, and because I laughed when he said it, I became Public Enemy Number One.

So I had one guess as to why she was here today.

Holly jumped as Ruthie shoved a cart right into her, which made me snicker. *Way to go, Ruthie.* "Do you mind?" Holly snapped. She opened her mouth again, but I held up a hand.

"Ruthie, why don't you go take your break. I'll watch the front."

"Okay." Ruthie walked toward the employee door without turning back.

Holly looked over as a woman with skunk-like hair walked in, then grinned at me. "You know, Lex, I couldn't imagine a better place for you to work. You fit right in."

"So you're here to shop?" I asked cheerfully. "I hear there's a sale on that designer imposter perfume you like to wear."

Her face fell as her friends giggled. Holly prided herself on having the best fashion sense in school, but Court was once friends with her and said she used the little sprays that said, "If you like <insert real designer name> then you'll love <insert dumb imposter name>." True story.

"Stop it," she told her amused friends, then glared at me. "I just wanted to see if the rumor about you working here was true." She looked at her friends again. "Y'all, remind me to show you this awesome People of SmartMart video on YouTube. It's hi-lar-i-ous," she said, emphasizing each syllable. Her face relaxed into a smile as she eyed me. I yawned dramatically. "Too bad you missed the softball game today," she added. "Maggie was great out there. She pitched a no-hitter."

Maggie frowned and shook her head. "No, I didn't. I—"

"Well, just about. Didn't you say that Coach Santiago said he was thinking about replacing Lex anyway?"

I stared at Maggie, who flushed as she scuffed her sandal against the tile, her eyes not meeting mine. "Well, I think he just meant over the summer, Lex. Not in season or anything."

My stomach plummeted. Switching me out of my coveted starting pitcher's position for Maggie Martin? No way. Seriously, there was *no way*—last season I had to stay after almost every practice and work with her on her pitching. She had improved, but no way enough to replace me. But then…Coach Santiago had been disappointed, to say the least, when I told him I couldn't play today, since I was scheduled to work. It was just a scrimmage, but to our coach, every game, practice or not, counted. He didn't tolerate excuses. And Holly looked way too sure of herself.

My fingers itched to grab a cart and shove it at Holly myself—as hard as I could. But my internal Grandma took over. *Take the high road, Lex. Smile the hell out of your face and let it go.* So I just said, "I'm glad you had a good game, Maggie." And smiled.

Her eyes met mine again in relief. "Thanks. I'm sure you'll stay as primary pitcher."

Holly snorted. "Not if Lex keeps skipping practice and games. I mean, that's according to your coach, not me."

I gritted my teeth and wished for a Code B right now, right on Holly's faux jeweled sandals.

"So is it true, Lex? You wanted to work here because you applied everywhere else but no one would hire someone with your"—Holly looked me up and down again—"obvious disregard for anything resembling style?"

I shouldn't have caved. I normally wouldn't have let her get to me—especially over a comment as ridiculous as that. But the threat of being replaced with Maggie loomed over me with a pressure so heavy it felt like I was sinking into the tile floor. So it was without thinking that I said, "For your information, I was forced to take some stupid deal the manager offered because I stole something, okay? So no, I did not *want* to work here. You'd have to be a loser to actually want to work here." The words slipped off my tongue before I could catch them.

Holly's gaze lifted above my shoulder. I whipped around to see Noah behind me, his eyes wide.

Oh, no…

Of course he'd been listening. Of course he looked annoyed. Even hurt.

Of course I felt like the biggest bitch of all.

I turned around, but Holly was already stepping away, grinning. "See you later, girlfriend." She waved as she led her friends out of the store, because they certainly weren't there to shop.

Holly 1, Lex 0.

I pivoted slowly back to Noah, but he was already walking away.

"Noah," I called out weakly, but he didn't turn around.

CHAPTER
6

The rest of the day, I didn't see Noah. I kept an eye out, but either he was on the sales floor or hiding in the office. When my break started, I peeked in the assistant manager's office and even Mr. Hanson's office, but he was nowhere to be seen. I stopped to check my phone and saw a text from Syd—*Whattup buttercup?*

I responded with a *Meh* text. Then I added, *Holly showed up she's a bitch* and set the phone back down in my locker.

How could I have let Holly get to me like that? She meant nothing to me. Her words should have meant nothing. But here I was, offending Noah Grayson already. Why did I say that? Why couldn't I have just told her it was a decent place to work or something like that? Or even ignore her—who cared what she thought, anyway? If she hadn't been trying to rub Maggie as replacement pitcher in my face, I wouldn't have caved.

My dad would be so disappointed in me. So would my grandma. Syd would've said Holly wasn't worth the trouble.

I sucked.

I was busy drowning my guilt in Diet Coke and Twix during the few minutes of my last break in the employee lounge when Noah walked in. He stopped short when he saw me, his eyes narrowing slightly. I tried to smile, but he shook his head and turned to walk back out.

"Hey, Noah."

His face turned slightly so I could see his profile, but his hands stayed pressed against the door. "What?"

"I'm sorry about earlier. You know, with Holly and all."

"Forget it," he said, pushing the door open and leaving me alone.

Mr. Hanson appeared as I rejoined Ruthie at my shift. "Good afternoon, ladies. How are we today?"

"Mr. Hanson, do you know A-lexis?" Ruthie asked, bouncing on her heels.

"Why, yes, Ruthie. I had the pleasure of meeting her the other day. In fact…" He turned to me. "Can you come to my office, please, Alexis? Just for a few minutes."

He smiled, but I felt nervous flutters in my chest. I couldn't be in trouble already, could I? Unless…maybe Noah said something to him about my rude comment. Maybe he was going to fire me. Maybe that wasn't such a bad thing. Ruthie gave me a thumbs-up sign and grin as I turned to follow Mr. Hanson.

Mr. Hanson's office was just past the security office

where I'd awaited my sentence almost a week ago. It gave me the chills. If I had gone over to Syd's house or to the fields or anywhere else instead of shop(lift)ing with Court, I would probably be on the beach right now, laughing with my friends, instead of following the manager of SmartMart to his office.

"How is everything, young lady?" Mr. Hanson asked as he sat down and gestured toward an empty chair on the other side of his desk. He began shuffling through some papers.

"Fine, thanks." I sat down on the edge of the seat and rubbed my sweaty palms on my pants.

"That's good. I wanted to see... Let me see... Ah, yes, here it is." He handed me a half sheet of paper with a small map printed on it along with a phone number and the name of some clinic. "I know you filled out the rest of the forms earlier, but this is for the drug test."

"Drug test?"

He held up his hands. "It's just a requirement for every SmartMart employee. In fact, you should've taken it before starting here, but sometimes we don't get around to it right away." He raised an eyebrow. "This shouldn't be a problem, right?"

Was he kidding? "I don't take drugs. So, no."

He nodded. "Sorry, you just looked worried. The map will show you how to get there. You don't need an appointment, but you do need to have it done by the end of next week."

I folded the paper and slid it into my pocket. I wasn't sure whether to feel annoyed or relieved.

Mr. Hanson rested his chin on steepled fingers. "You know, Alexis, there's a lot of potential in this store for upward movement."

I kept my face politely interested as I inwardly gagged. He continued. "You probably think of this as just a summertime job, nothing more. But for so many of our employees, this is a stepping stone in their career. Especially for young adults like yourself. In fact, it's never too early to ask yourself the question, 'What do I want in life?'"

What did I want in life? Easy.

- My summer back.
- To stop sticking my foot in my mouth.
- To not lose my pitching position.
- A manager who knew better than to ask me what I wanted in life.

Obviously, all I could do was nod and smile. As nice as he was, the guy was delusional if he thought I considered SmartMart a stepping stone in my career.

"Do you know why I offered this opportunity to you?" he asked.

Don't you mean offered to my mother? But all I said was, "No, sir."

He lifted a small wooden frame off his desk and stared at it. "My son wasn't much older than you when he got into trouble a couple years ago. He and some friends thought they'd see if they could get away with shoplifting from a store. But the manager where they were caught called the police. Now every time he fills out a job application, he'll have to check 'yes' that he's been arrested. This will follow him around for the rest of his life. All for a pair of headphones he didn't even need."

Mr. Hanson turned the frame around to show me a picture of his family—wife, daughter, and son. Considering pudgy and balding Mr. Hanson, his son was a lot more handsome than I would've guessed—thick, wavy dark hair and broad shoulders with kind of a sly grin. I nodded politely as he turned the frame back around.

"You know," he said, placing the picture on his desk, "Vincent is a great kid, but he's had a very difficult time staying out of trouble since that incident. I thought if you could have the chance to avoid what Vincent had to go through, why not give you that chance? SmartMart may not seem like the shining star on your résumé, but it will give you a good start in life. A good, honest start, because I know you're a good, honest kid. You just need to make better choices. I hope you'll gain something from your experience here."

As I left his office, I felt a mixture of pity and relief. From the sound of it, Mr. Hanson had a lot of trouble with his son. But that wasn't my problem. I wasn't headed toward trouble—the lipstick was just a stupid mistake. And Court only got a slap on the wrist for it, thanks to her lawyer father. The idea that kind Mr. Hanson would have had me arrested was doubtful, and I wished for the hundredth time that I had figured another way out of this deal.

My mother showed up when the end of my shift finally came. I was surprised it took her this long to pay a visit. I was sure she wanted to see for herself how I was working out. Her smile was warm as she walked toward me holding Rory's hand.

"Hey, Lexie!" Rory's soprano voice rang out. She skirted by one of Ruthie's flying carts and ran up to me, blond pigtails flying, my mother trailing behind her. One of my mother's eyebrows shot up as Ruthie shouted her greeting.

"Hey, Ruthie," I said quickly, "this is my mom and my little sister, Rory."

"Hi, Rory! You look like a princess," Ruthie said. Rory giggled and curtsied.

I pulled on one of Rory's pigtails. "What are you doing here?"

"I wanted to come with Momma to pick you up. She's buying me some of that cotton candy nail polish that Katie Carducci had at the last pageant," Rory said, her voice chirpy. She could be so cute when she was happy, and nothing outside of pageants made her happier than shopping. My mother, incarnate.

Mom touched my ponytail, shaking her head slightly. She hated when I pulled my hair back. "Your sister and I thought we'd take you to dinner tonight to celebrate your first week at your new job. Dad's working late and Grandma is having dinner with a friend."

"Sounds good. I still have another fifteen minutes, though."

"That's fine. There are some things we need anyway. Come, Aurora."

Rory was giggling at Ruthie, who was making silly faces at her. "Go on, Rory," I said, pushing her away.

"She's so pretty!" Ruthie said. "She really is like a little princess."

"You've no idea," I mumbled.

As the minute hand slowly swept the short hand to the five o'clock hour, I turned to Ruthie.

"That's it for me. I'll see you Monday."

"Okay, bye Lexus!" she said as she pushed a cart into an unsuspecting woman entering the store.

I hurried away.

In the employee hall, I punched my code into the time clock, noting that it marked the time at 5:03. I was staring at the numbers, wondering if the extra minutes would add up to overtime, when Noah appeared. He punched in his code.

"You're done, too?" I asked.

His raised eyebrow shouted, *Duh*, considering he'd just clocked out. But he only nodded and turned away. I followed him. "Wait, Noah."

He turned, stepping closer to the wall as a girl with platinum blond hair breezed past us toward the time clock. "What?" His voice was short, but his expression wasn't angry. It was indifferent, and somehow that was even worse.

"I'm sorry about earlier. I didn't mean to imply that, well, you know. I mean, I know this is a great job for you."

Wow. Someone should just cut off my foot before I could shove it further into my mouth.

"For me?" Noah's expression switched from passive to irritated. "I get it. You think you're too good for SmartMart. Fine."

The girl at the time clock snorted. I ignored her. "No,

that's not what I—"

Noah turned toward the lockers before I could finish, opening one of the little square doors. I clamped my mouth shut and followed, taking my bag out of my own locker. His hand dipped behind the door, reappearing with a black T-shirt and jeans that he slung over his arm.

He slammed the metal door and turned to me, scowling. "The truth is that I *like* working here. My mother didn't *make* me. Mr. Hanson promotes people who get the job done. And I know I get paid a hell of a lot more than you. So cut out the 'I feel sorry for you losers' bullshit. You aren't above us, 'kay?"

He went toward the men's room, leaving me to stare after him with my mouth hanging open. Quiet Noah Grayson— angry. It was weird.

And, I hated to admit, kind of hot.

I seriously needed to get antibacterial gel for my brain.

The blond girl was still at the time clock, staring at me with a smirk on her lips. Ignoring her, I went into the ladies' room. I changed out of my nasty SmartMart clothes into jeans and a T-shirt, noticing as I did the smell of cigarette smoke. Was someone smoking in here? As I walked out of the stall, the platinum-haired girl stood there, smoking a cigarette and watching me. "Everything okay, honey?" she asked as I washed my hands. She didn't look more than a couple years older than me, but the way she said "honey" wasn't exactly endearing.

I ignored her.

She rested her cigarette-holding hand on the sink and

blew smoke toward me. "So, Mommy couldn't get you a job at Abercrombie?"

I stared at her. "Excuse me?"

"Must be hard for a princess like you to work with people like Noah and me. You know, people who don't get money from Daddy and actually need a job."

She went to the toilet to flush what was left of her cigarette, then walked past me without another word. Great. *Who else could I offend today?*

I walked back out, almost colliding with Noah coming out of the men's room. He was wearing black jeans and a black T-shirt that had "Cooper's" printed on it, and his hair was damp and slightly spiked up.

"Um, have a good night," I told him, not liking how my voice shook. *Damn it, Noah should* not *look this good.* He nodded and turned away. "A Bitchin' Good Time" was printed on the back of the shirt in bold white letters. He seemed so different in those clothes—maybe because he looked like a regular guy instead of a manager.

But he was no regular guy. Hot or not, Noah Grayson was a pain in the ass in the truest sense. But then, so was I, so where did that leave us?

CHAPTER
7

I dreaded going to work on Monday. The entire weekend I slept, hung out at the pool with my friends, read books I'd already read, and slept more. Everyone kept asking about my week, but I was too mentally exhausted to even talk about it, even to my grandma. I did curl up on her queen bed with her on Sunday night and watch episode after episode of *Bonanza*. She loved game shows and old western TV series—both of which I knew I'd love for the rest of my life just because she did. When I awoke the next morning, I was tucked under the covers in her bed. She was already awake but had left me to sleep.

I dressed and went downstairs. I could hear Mom's and Dad's voices in the kitchen. Grandma was in her flowery satin bathrobe in her usual chair in the living room, watching TV. Except she didn't watch TV in the mornings, and she always changed out of her bathrobe before going downstairs.

"Still in your robe?" I asked. "Isn't it kind of late?"

She looked up at me, her eyebrows furrowed slightly as if she was trying to figure out if I had spoken. "My robe?"

I pointed at it. She glanced down, running her hand over the smooth satin.

"Oh. Oh, yes. I just felt like wearing it." Something about her flat, faraway words made my stomach flip. She looked up at me again. "Are you going to school today?"

My chest felt like someone was squeezing it as hard as possible. "It's summer, Grandma. No school in summer." The words cracked as I barely managed to get them out.

"Oh. Sorry. Summer. Right." She turned her gaze back to the television. I knelt next to her, covering her cool, slender hand with mine.

"Grandma?" I said sternly, swallowing as tears threatened to slide around my eyeballs. "Grandma, don't you dare mess with me like this. It's summer, and I'm working at SmartMart today, remember?"

"Of course I remember, silly." But her voice was still far away.

I stood up and walked to the kitchen. Grandma had seemed fine since she moved in. She'd forget small things, like where she put her glasses, or leave the milk out after using it, but she always knew what day it was. And she never, ever got confused when it came to me.

I headed straight to my dad. "Grandma doesn't remember..." I couldn't finish my sentence over the lump in my throat. I didn't have to. Just one look at my face was enough to make him reach out to pull me into a hug.

"Honey, we talked about this when Grandma moved in."

"But she's been fine," I wailed. "And now she thinks I'm in school."

He patted my hair. "I know. But this is why she's here, so we can take care of her."

"She'll get better, right?"

"Better?" My mother, of course, had to have her say. "Oh, sweetheart, there is no getting better."

"Hush, Meredith," my dad said.

"She's on medicine, right?" I asked.

Dad hesitated. "Well, the doctor has her on a clinical trial, but—"

"Okay, cool," I said, pushing away from him and walking out of the kitchen and up the stairs. Anytime someone said "but" it meant "walk away fast." Dad needed to stop listening to my pessimistic mother. Clinical trial or not, the medicine was supposed to help. It would help.

It had to.

Grandma was still in her chair when I left with Dad for work. My heart ached to see her staring at the TV like that. *Please let her be okay when I get home,* I prayed silently over and over on the way to work. I kissed my dad on the cheek and got out of the car when we arrived, staring at the brightly lit SmartMart sign affixed to the tan stucco. *Week two, here we go.* I shoved all worries about Grandma to the back of my mind, pasted a smile on my face, and set my shoulders.

My second week of work started with training in bagging groceries. It wasn't quite as boring as greeter, and at least I could use half a brain to sort out frozen items from pantry items. Noah asked Ruthie to train me, and he never so much as looked at me. I guess he was still mad. I couldn't blame him.

Ruthie cackled loudly every time I mixed items that weren't supposed to be mixed. It made me learn a whole lot faster, since I couldn't stand the constant tee-heeing when I'd get something wrong. And unfortunately, I seemed to get a lot wrong in the beginning. Sometimes she'd take over and I'd watch her. One thing was for sure—Ruthie could organize items into bags faster than anyone I'd ever seen. All the frozen food together, boxes together—never a mistake like putting a can on top of a loaf of bread like I did. But even the fact that Ruthie laughed every time I'd screw up wasn't the worst part.

No. The biggest pain in the ass about this position was that I had to ask every single customer if he or she wanted paper or plastic.

"Most places don't ask anymore," Bessie had told me on my first day. "But at SmartMart, we want to offer our customers every possible convenience."

Convenience? Some of the customers looked annoyed at even having an option. They'd sling their environmentally friendly reusable bags at me, scowling as if the offer of evil plastic or foul paper was offensive. I even stopped for a while, until Mr. Hanson passed by once and said quietly, "Don't forget to ask about paper or plastic, Alexis."

Bessie stopped by at one point while I was placing a guy's frozen pizza and ice cream in a paper bag. "You're doing great, Lex!" I smiled at her, glad that she finally started calling me Lex instead of Alexis.

Ruthie, though, still felt the need to start each shift by telling me that her daddy drove a Lexus. If I ever met her daddy, I'd probably throw a can of beans at his stupid Lexus.

I was surprised how sore my feet were by the time I was relieved for break. I wasn't used to standing in one place for so long—not even when I was pitching. How long would it take to get used to this? Bessie told me she could "rustle up a fatigue mat" for me to stand on if I needed, but it was a little too late—invisible knives were already slicing into my arches. The platinum-blond girl walked by as Bessie offered that, snorting. Yeah, yeah, okay. Poor little pampered girl and her precious tired feet. "Bessie, who is that?" I asked, nodding toward the girl who had stopped several registers down to talk to a customer.

Bessie looked over her shoulder. "That's Roxanne. Why?"

"I had a conversation with her last week, so was just wondering."

"Oh, fabulous! You're making friends already."

Friends? Yeah, no. Roxanne hated me—it was obvious I just needed to stay out of her way.

Ruthie followed me to the break room with a never-ending stream of chatter.

"So, do you like it, Lexus? You're doing a great job. Really great."

"Thanks, Ruthie," I said wearily. I had checked my

phone, and there was no text from Grandma like I'd hoped. Or even from Dad telling me not to worry, that she was fine. I almost texted him, then changed my mind. If things hadn't changed, I didn't want to hear about it at work.

"Do you like it here?" she asked hopefully.

"Sure," I said dully, my mind still on Grandma.

We watched the Twix bar churn through the circles and drop to the slot below. Ruthie got on her knees and stuck her arm through the slot, emerging with my candy. She proudly offered it to me with two hands.

"Thanks."

The break room was completely empty, but she sat across from me at a small table, watching me eat my Twix and sip Diet Coke. Her eyes followed every bite. My eating seemed to fascinate her. And it made me lose my appetite. I offered her the second bar in the package, and she took it excitedly, thanking me over and over.

"Forget about it," I told her, giving her a little smile. Ruthie could make the smallest thing exciting. I just wished she'd take a breather every once in a while.

"Hi!" Ruthie shouted at someone behind me, crumbs falling from her lips.

"Hey, Ruthie."

I went stiff at the voice. Noah walked over to us but didn't sit down, even when Ruthie pointed to a chair. "How are you doing?" he asked her, completely ignoring me.

"Good! Lexus gave me her candy bar, so I'm eating it. She's nice."

Nice? Getting Noah to believe I was nice was like trying

to convince a fish it could breathe out of water. He finally looked my way, frowning.

"What?" I asked, irritated. I hated the way he made me feel, like he was ten years older than me instead of one.

"Nothing. That *was* nice of you," he said. He had the nerve to sound surprised.

I stood and picked up my half-empty soda can and the Twix wrapper. "Yeah, well, maybe you should buy next time. You get paid a hell of a lot more than me, remember?"

I marched past his gaping expression and threw the trash in the container before leaving the break room. I had to admit, it felt good to give a little crap back to Noah. I felt like high-fiving Ruthie for putting me in a position where I could say that.

I joined Bessie at the register again and cheerfully helped bag the items until she turned off her register light and told me she was going to show me how to work the floor in the grocery section. I remembered seeing other people on the floor my first day following Bessie around. It didn't seem like a bad job at all, because at least I wasn't right in the customer's face like at the register and I didn't have to see Roxanne glaring at me. By the time Bessie walked away, I figured I pretty much had a handle on everything.

Wrong.

"Hey, miss! Where's the toilet paper?" one old lady asked as I was arranging paper towel rolls right next to the toilet paper.

"Excuse me, do you sell extra-large condoms?"

"You people don't do a very good job stocking this store.

You don't carry any of the brands I want."

"Someone just opened a bag of chips in the next aisle and threw them all over the floor."

"I slipped on a puddle over there and could've hurt myself. You better hope I don't have any back problems tonight."

"Hey, this jar of pickles is already open. Does that mean I get it for free?"

"Someone threw up over here."

This last one was yelled by a woman as she ushered her sick-looking kid away. It totally threw me over the edge. Without a radio, I had to call out in the nearby aisles for Bessie. Code B my ass. I was about to run to the front and beg to be allowed to bag the rest of the day when Bessie finally appeared. The store was too busy for someone to come running back immediately with a bucket, like with that drunk guy on my first day, so she showed me some weird sawdust-like powder they tossed on puke to make it dry up fast until someone could come sweep it away. Lovely. I wasn't going to do that. Ever.

The hours dragged by.

Finally, it was just forty-five minutes until my shift was over. All the aisles were straightened, I'd gotten the once-over from some sleazy guy who looked like he got lost on the way to the porn store, and no other employee was in sight. Of course, that's when a woman dropped a jug of water on the floor, causing it to burst. She stepped away, an apologetic grin on her face, and left me alone with the spill. Another customer clicked her tongue and shook her head at me like it was my fault.

I grabbed the towel from my belt loop and dropped to my knees to wipe up the mess, ignoring the commentary from a bystander about how I wasn't going to soak up much with just that tiny towel. The towel did get saturated too quickly, but I kept mopping the floor with it. All I accomplished was to push the water around more. Brilliant. Grandma would find this situation funny. She always liked to quote, "If something can go wrong, it will." I pictured her sitting in that chair, her eyes far away, and wondered if she was still in her robe.

I ducked my head to hide the stupid tears that were starting to roll down my cheeks, one by one. Thinking about my grandma was *not* helping.

Someone dropped a yellow caution sign next to me. "Want some help?"

I glanced up at Noah, whose expression changed from amusement to concern when he saw my face. He dropped to his knees next to me and took out a small white towel from his pocket. I was afraid he might give it to me to wipe my tears, but he placed it on the floor to soak up some of the water.

"Hey, what's wrong?" he asked.

Nothing is what I meant to say. *Go away.* But what came out of my mouth in a shaky whisper was, "I can't do this. I hate it."

He didn't need to know about my grandma's condition. It was none of his business. Anyway, admitting how I felt about this crappy job actually felt good, so screw it. I did hate it. Not enough to cry about it, but who cared, anyway? I. Hated. SmartMart.

He stretched his hand toward me but then pulled back. "It's okay," he said, his attempt at comforting me kind of awkward. "It's not an easy job. It was tough for me, too, at first."

"Really," I said numbly, not even making it a question. I didn't want him to sympathize. I wanted him to walk away or even fire me. Maybe my mother would understand if I got a job somewhere else. I think she mostly wanted to see if I could do it in the first place.

"It gets easier. I promise. And the people here are great. There's Bessie—she's like a grandmother to most of us."

Wrong. The tears rolled faster now. Noah gave me his hand to help me up and escorted me to the employee area, calling on someone else to clean up the water spill. I knew I should be embarrassed, but I was way beyond that point.

In the bathroom, I splashed water on my face and stared in the mirror—the very same one I'd stared into only a week ago. The firm promise I made to myself was broken. But not really—I could do this. Grandma was going to be fine—she was just having a bad day. And why couldn't I handle this? It was a stupid summer job. Just a waste of a couple of months, that was all. And how ridiculous that I was this stressed out over a summer job when there were real problems in the world. Grandma would agree.

I just wondered for how long she'd be able to agree.

Noah was waiting for me outside the restroom when I emerged. "Feeling better?" he asked.

I nodded, trying for a smile and failing miserably.

His smile was stronger and surprisingly genuine. "Why don't you go home? There's not much left of your shift anyway. I'll make sure you get paid for the full time."

I nodded again and let him walk me to the front doors. I mumbled a good-bye and walked out into the Florida humidity before realizing my mother wouldn't be here for another half hour to pick me up. No way was I going back inside, so I sank to the hot pavement to wait.

Suck it up, Lex. If Noah can do it, so can you.

Why was that so hard to believe?

CHAPTER
8

I was grateful that my work schedule this week was only four days. Four very, very, very long days. Grandma didn't ask if I was going to school again, but she started wearing her robe more. She also kept leaving things around. Mom said she'd been doing it and I just hadn't been noticing, but I was noticing now. I'd close the refrigerator door behind her, take the remote back to the living room, turn off the coffee pot when there was no coffee left. I stayed as close as I could to her when I wasn't working, even turning down offers to hang out with my friends. The only time I went out was for softball practice. By the end of the weekend, I was exhausted.

At work, Noah and I seemed to come to an understanding. At least, we weren't ignoring each other anymore. We only worked one day together this week, since he took two days off for his SAT prep classes. We didn't talk much, but sometimes I'd catch him looking at me and I'd smile. He'd give me half a smile back. Progress, I guess.

On Friday morning I slept in, not moving when my mother knocked on the door. She poked her head in. What was the purpose of knocking if she was just going to barge in anyway? "Get up, Alexis. We're taking your sister to Forever Princess."

I didn't bother moving. "Can't I skip this trip? I have to be at camp at three."

"No. The least you can do is come support your sister while she prepares for the Coastal Princess Pageant in a couple weeks. We'll be back in plenty of time for you to go volunteer."

I pushed myself up and raised my arms above my head in a stretch. "Okay, fine. Just don't get any ideas about putting me in those dresses."

She grimaced. "Don't worry, I believe you made your point perfectly clear last time." She had tried to convince me to try on a dress "just for fun," which turned into a big argument with me yelling at her to stop trying to get me back into pageants and her yelling about how I'm letting my good looks go to waste. That was the last time we talked about it, and I really hoped she got the point.

"Hurry and get dressed," she said. "We can't wait for you to primp." She left, pulling the door only half closed.

Me? Primp? I was the cheetah next to Princess Aurora's sloth in the bathroom. Still, I got up and threw on shorts and my rattiest T-shirt. To emphasize my point about pageant wear in case Mom still felt the need to push it on me, I brushed my hair into an unflattering ponytail, shoved it under a ratty baseball cap, and completely ignored my makeup drawer. I chuckled at my plain reflection in the mirror. Perfect.

My parents were in the kitchen arguing when I went downstairs. "It's the only pageant we're going to this summer," I could hear my mother say. "I told you about it months ago. You need to stay home with your mother for once."

"I have to work, Mer. This is what we agreed when we took Mom in."

I turned to Grandma, who was standing in the living room, staring out the French doors at the pool. "Want to go for a walk?" I asked her. She loved going for long walks around the neighborhood, sharing her knowledge of trees and plants from her days as a professional landscaper. If my mother got angry about me not going to Forever Princess, screw it—they couldn't just argue like this as if she couldn't hear them.

Grandma smiled slightly, reaching over to squeeze my hand. "I'm a little tired," she said quietly, and it sucked to hear the hurt in her voice. "So what do you have planned today?"

"I'm supposed to go shopping with Rory and Mom, and you know how much fun that is. We're buying these crappy dresses for some stupid pageant. Want me to pick you up something frilly and pink, too?"

"Oh, sure. And while you're at it, I'll take a tiara. Extra large."

We laughed, but not loud enough to drown out the conversation in the kitchen.

"So that means I don't get a life? She'll be fine here, and this is important, Jackson."

"I know, but—"

"No buts."

I yanked open the patio door, and Grandma and I stepped out into the sweltering heat. "I am *so* glad I'm not working at SmartMart today. Maybe we could go swimming," I said, eyeing the bright blue water of the pool.

"And get you into trouble with your mother? No way," she said. I nodded, cringing at her defeated tone. Grandma normally loved doing things that made my mother nuts. I guess she didn't want to push her luck. She pointed at the darkening sky. "Besides, it's going to rain."

"It's summer in Florida. It rains every day."

"True. It's supposed to be a pretty nasty season. So didn't you say you work at SmartMart?" she asked as we sat in the patio chairs.

I smiled gently. "Yeah, I do. It's not a bad job, I guess." I noticed that anytime I said "work" I had to add "at SmartMart" for her to understand. I reconciled myself to the fact that she wasn't going to remember on her own. But I found if I did most of the talking, she'd be able to carry on a conversation just like the old days. She still had her sense of humor and her sense of compassion. I prayed that the disease wouldn't steal that, too.

"Not a bad job? Really?" She cocked her head, her red lips twitching as if she was trying to hold back her smile.

Grandma always saw right through me. I slumped in my chair, throwing my arm over my face dramatically.

"No," I wailed. "It sucks. Big time." I whipped my arm away and glared at her. "Seriously, what would you do if in just two weeks you were subjected to the torture of seeing *two* Code Bs?"

"Code what?"

"Sorry. Code B, which I can only assume stands for Barf."

Grandma laughed out loud, the kind of laugh that started in her stomach and required the participation of all her respiratory organs. It was one of my favorite sounds in the world, a reminder of how healthy she really was. She leaned forward and chucked me under the chin gently. "Baby, I'd think that would be awful. But you're going to stay strong and get through this, aren't you." She didn't say it like it was a question.

"Yeah, I guess."

"That's my good girl," she said. "The place would go downhill if my Lexie wasn't there to keep it in line."

"I think it's more likely to do that if I *do* work there, Grandma."

I got up, kissed her on the cheek, and headed back inside before my mother decided to go looking for me.

My parents were still arguing.

"I think you could miss just one pageant, Mer."

My mother's voice went up another octave. "Don't you care about Aurora's future? About college?"

That's when I knew my dad had lost. He couldn't hold

his ground when it came to a question of how much he cared about us. Really pissed me off, considering Dad made it perfectly clear that he put us above everything else in the world. I could almost hear him sigh. "Fine, Meredith. Fine. I'll have Patty check on Mom."

I walked into the kitchen and cleared my voice. "Hey, you know Grandma's just in the other room, right? And that she can hear every word?"

They stared at me like I had two heads. I directed a look at my mother. "Let's go." Not that I was in a hurry to get to Forever Princess, but I needed to shut her up.

"Fine. We'll continue this later," she said to my dad. He shrugged and picked up his newspaper. I knew it didn't matter. My mother always got what she wanted. Always.

Forever Princess. Probably my least favorite place in the entire world. It was never a short trip. Not with my mother. Not with anyone, actually. Ms. Frick, the snotty saleslady, seemed to know exactly how pageants worked. Or how pageant moms worked, at least. She kept a running list of sizes and favorite colors for each kid who was a regular in the store, like Rory. Ms. Frick was always prepared with plenty of dresses and accessories for Rory to try on. She immediately went to a rack that was "special, just perfect for the beautiful Aurora," and pulled out one pink dress after another.

My mother and sister oohed and ahhed at each, especially

the ones that looked like they were nothing but ruffles. It was like decorating a birthday cake, the way Mom and Ms. Frick held each dress up to Rory and squealed appreciatively. Rory, of course, started whining about how she wanted all of them, and my mother beamed like it was the greatest thing in the world.

About ten frou-frou dresses in, I started to bitch about it. I normally read a book in a corner, but this was not how I wanted to spend my precious day off.

My mother ignored me as long as she could, but when the saleslady took Rory back for yet another fitting, she turned to me and snapped, "Stop complaining and go take a walk, damn it! Because we aren't going anywhere right now."

The clinking bell over the door suggested new customers, but my mother wasn't done. She looked pointedly at my ball cap. "You know, it really makes me sad—you're so beautiful, Alexis. If you would only just pay more attention to your appearance instead of trying to dumb down your looks." She sighed and headed back toward the dressing rooms.

Woo-hoo—dumbed-down looks for the win! I turned to leave when I saw the customers who were walking in.

Wha... No! No!

Noah had the look of a guy who'd just been caught trying on dresses. After what my mother just said, I'm sure my face mirrored his shock. We stood there for a good minute or two, staring at each other like idiots.

"Noah?" the woman with him asked, nudging him.

He jumped slightly. "Oh. Lex, this is my mother."

"I am Adrienne," she said in a French accent. She held out her hand and I shook it. She was much shorter than Noah and even me, with a smooth, gentle face and beautiful smile. Obviously Noah got his dark hair and deep blue eyes from his mother.

The cutest little girl with dark ringlets twisted in yellow ribbons and the same big blue eyes gripped her mother's leg, her face buried in her skirt.

"And this is Belle, my sister," Noah said, patting the little girl's hair fondly. "She's three years old. Belle, this is Lex."

"Hi, Belle," I said softly, smiling at her. Belle peeked around shyly. "Your name is like a princess, just like my sister's." I pointed to the walking pink fluff that had emerged from the dressing room and was now twirling around in front of a huge mirror. "That's my sister, Aurora."

My mother gave us a quizzical look as Adrienne and Belle wandered over to a clothes rack, but she didn't say anything.

Noah tilted his head as he watched his sister squeal over a yellow cupcake dress. "What's up with parents naming their kids after princesses, anyway? It's like they planned for all this, you know?" He waved his hand around the shop.

I nodded, but my stomach flipped. I hoped he never learned that my middle name was Jasmine. Noah's mother was sorting through the dresses on display, smiling at her daughter's gleeful cheers at each one.

"So Belle does pageants, too?"

"Yes. She loves them," he said, smiling at his sister as she twirled around with the yellow dress tight against her body.

Doting big brother. I looked over at Rory, who was now yelling at my mom to buy her the pink fluffy nightmare. I was pretty sure in a couple years he'd be over it, too.

"What does your dad think about it?" I asked.

Noah frowned. "He's not around much."

"Oh. Sorry."

"Trust me, it's fine."

"I thought you were going for a walk," my mother said as she strolled over to us. She looked at Noah and held out a hand. "Hi. I'm Alexis's mother, Meredith."

He smiled and shook her hand. "I'm Noah. I work with your daughter."

"Oh!" She winked at me. "I hope she's been behaving herself at her job."

I rolled my eyes at Noah. "I'm leaving." I turned to push the jingling door open and emerged from the potpourri dress shop from hell. I walked down the sidewalk, letting the sun warm my face.

Noah soon caught up to me, and we walked in silence for a few minutes past shops filled with antiques.

"So how long do you think they'll be in there?" Noah asked. "My mom usually handles this stuff."

"At least another hour. Maybe two. They don't let you get out easy in that shop."

"I'll bet."

More silence. We walked past a coffee shop and Noah stopped, mumbling something I couldn't understand. "What?" I asked.

He cleared his voice and glanced at the shop. "Want

some coffee? My treat."

His treat? I stared blankly at him, wondering if he was considering this a date. I had to think not—we were only just now on speaking terms. All I could think of to say was, "I don't drink coffee." *Brilliant, Lex.*

"Oh, well, never mind then." He started to walk on.

"I drink tea, though."

Noah swung around with a grin on his face. Damn it, he knew I'd change my mind. *Noah 1, Lex 0.*

"Okay." He moved as fast as he could to get in front of me and held the door open. I made sure to get in front of him and order at the counter so he wouldn't attempt the misguided heroic act of paying for me. This was *not* a date and I didn't want to pretend like it was.

The clerk handed me a steaming cup of chai and rang it up. I reached for my purse and then realized I'd left it at the shop with my mother. *Crap.*

I quietly told the clerk to cancel the order, but Noah caught on. "Hold on, wait a minute, I've got it," he said, handing over a couple bills.

"It's okay, you don't have to—" I started, but he laughed.

"For God's sake, Lex, it's a dollar fifty. I think I can handle that." Noah sighed at my hesitation. "Look, if it bothers you that much, buy me one next time."

Next time? I thought about that. *Next time* suggested he was interested in hanging out with me again. Maybe that wasn't such a bad idea. As he ordered his coffee, I looked around the café and chose a small table with two chairs. It was weird at first to be sitting there, sipping tea and chatting with Noah. With his plain navy T-shirt and jeans, hair mussed a bit, he looked so different than when we were at SmartMart. Much more relaxed. Of course, he wasn't in a tie and playing the part of a manager. I decided to consider, for the moment at least, that we were just friends hanging out in a coffee shop.

"What are you smiling about?" he asked.

I frowned. "Sorry, I didn't realize I was smiling."

His eyebrows arched, and we both laughed. "So does your sister do a lot of pageants?" he asked.

"Yep."

"Is she going to the big one in Tallahassee in a couple weeks? The Coastal Princess Pageant," he clarified when I didn't answer.

"Oh, yeah. I think that's what it's called." I tried not to smile at the fact that he knew the actual name of the pageant. "Your sister is, too?"

He nodded. "In the three-year-old category. My mom took her to the first one just last year, and Belle loved it."

"Your mom—is she European?"

"French Canadian."

"Canada to Florida? How did she end up here?"

"She and my dad moved here when I was born. It hasn't exactly been paradise for her." He stared off into the distance for a moment, frowning.

I decided to change the subject. "So why are you so in love with SmartMart?" I asked.

"I never said I was in love with it." He took a sip of his coffee. "I like working there because I have a better chance at getting experience that most places don't offer to people our age."

"Yeah, but why do you care? I mean, are you planning to stay at SmartMart forever? Or do you want to be a grocery store manager when you graduate?"

His eyebrows pinched as if he thought I was making fun of him, but I wasn't. I really wanted to know.

"No," he said finally. "I'm working to get money for college. But I was serious about the experience. It's good that Mr. Hanson's letting me learn management—it might come in handy someday. At the very least, it'll look good on a résumé."

I stirred my tea. "What do you want to do? I mean, when you go to college?"

He smiled, a nice, faraway kind of smile. "Architecture. I love drawing, outlining plans for buildings. Sketching." He was silent for a moment, his gaze drifting to the small black and white pictures of various landmarks on the wall. "There's something to be said for structural lines, the way they converge. Beautiful."

His eyes were soft as they moved over the images. For the first time, I saw him as someone more than the shy SmartMart manager who tolerated me, more than the reclusive kid at school whose gaze never lifted above the ground or the guy who'd snitched on Bryce. Noah seemed so much older than his age. As he talked about his passion for architecture, something deep inside me stirred—a complicated, twisting knot that I had a feeling was going to unfurl painfully, frustratingly slowly.

The clanking of dishes behind the counter broke the spell, startling us both. "So what do you want to do?" he asked, raising his cup to his lips for another sip.

I hesitated. The truth sounded ridiculous, and I knew it. I wanted to play softball in college, plus I'd wanted to be in the Olympics since I was five years old. There was an Olympic girls' softball event that was disbanded, but the rumor was that it was soon coming back to the games. I wanted to be a part of that more than I wanted anything else. But the one time I was stupid enough to mention it to my mother, I got shot down. Big time.

Even my dad—the very man who introduced me to the delights of hockey, baseball, football, jai alai, and signed me up for my very first girls' softball league—was confused by it, though he tried to be supportive. He attempted to talk me into actually playing one of the other Olympic sports, since softball couldn't be guaranteed to make a comeback. Bryce was the only one who didn't tease me or look at me like I had a horn growing out of my head. He even scheduled extra practices with me after school to work on my pitch. Court would sometimes grumble that he spent more time with me than with her, but she knew Bryce was like a brother to me.

Maybe it was a dumb dream. Either way, I had no urge to tell anyone else, including Noah. As long as the idea stayed in my head, nobody could judge me for it.

"I don't know," I said, deciding to play it confused. "Right now, I just want to make it through the next two years of high school and then move out of the house." That part was true. All I could think of was getting out from under my mother's thumb.

He sighed. "Yeah, I know what you mean."

"Your mom seems so cool, though."

"It's not my mom." He frowned, his eyes on his cup. Okay, now I knew for sure something was up with his dad. I wanted to know, but no way was I going to ask. He looked up at me, his blue eyes startlingly intense. "Can we change the subject?"

"Sure."

I couldn't think of anything else to say. We sipped on our cups, our eyes moving around the little café—the barista, the tables, the samples of coffee—looking at everything but each other.

"So you have no idea what you're going to major in?" he asked finally. I had a feeling it was an attempt to continue a safe conversation rather than really trying to pressure me to come up with something.

"Maybe foreign languages." It wasn't true, but it was the only subject that came to my mind.

"Which language?"

"French." It was the first thing I thought of, which was strange, considering I'd taken a year of Spanish in school already. But I'd always wanted to learn French, too.

"My mom can help you if you need," he offered. "The dialect might be a little different than the French they teach in school, though."

"Thanks."

We stood up to head back to the shop, not saying much. It was a comfortable silence, though—not the kind where you don't know what to say because there's nothing to talk about. I noticed that his hand tapped against his leg as he walked, almost like he was keeping time with a tune in his head. I wondered what kind of music Noah Grayson listened to. He didn't strike me as a Top 40 kind of guy, more an alternative rock fan like me.

The walk back seemed a lot faster than the time it had taken to get to the café. When we walked in, my mother was paying Ms. Frick. Noah called out to his mother, and she answered in French from the back of the shop. I suppressed the urge to ask Noah to speak in French, because then he'd probably try to have a conversation with me and find out just how non-fluent I was.

"Where have you been?" my mother asked. "We're ready to go and you don't even answer your phone."

"I left my purse here, and my cell's inside," I said, picking my purse up off the credenza.

"Here, help me with these." Mom thrust one of the bags at me and paraded out of the shop, Rory on her heels.

Noah and I stared at each other. "So I guess I'll see you at work on Monday," he said.

"Okay. I'll pay you back then, too."

"You never give up, do you?" he asked, his voice exasperated.

I grinned as I backed away. "Nope. But would you really want me to?" I waved to Belle and her tired-looking mother and skipped out the door. When I glanced over my shoulder, I could see Noah still watching me through the glass. Why had I said that? I'm sure my voice had sounded flirty.

My heart fluttered as I recalled his dreamy expression in the café. Of course I'd be excited about him actually having career goals. So many of my friends didn't see past Friday night baseball games and Saturdays at the beach. It was good to have a friend who looked forward to college. That was all.

Friend zone—that's where you need to stay, Noah. For my sanity and yours.

CHAPTER
9

Week three of SmartMart—the dreadful days of training were over, and I was officially a SmartMart employee.

Many of the employees gathered in the break room to congratulate me on my "graduation." I even received a Bessie-original certificate to celebrate it, complete with what she called "pixie dust" that was really a bunch of colorful glitter she tossed over the certificate. You would've thought actual fairies had stopped by to shower me in magic dust by the way Ruthie jumped up and down. Her enthusiasm was contagious, making me and everyone else laugh along with her. Bessie tossed some glitter at Ruthie, to her delight.

"Congratulations on making it through," Noah said as everyone dispersed back into the store.

"What, the Ninth Circle of Hell? I'm kidding," I said quickly when he frowned.

His face relaxed into a smile. "I know."

I picked up the little jar of glitter and shook it at him as he laughed, getting a rainbow of sparkles all over his red tie. He took the tie and shook it over my head. "Here, you need it more. I think Bessie missed a spot."

"Very funny." I shook my hair out and glitter sailed to the floor. "By the way, I have your dollar-fifty in my purse."

"My dollar-fifty?"

"Yeah, for the tea."

He threw his head back and groaned. "You're obsessed with that, aren't you? Keep it. You can just buy me a coffee sometime," he said. "Remember?"

This was the second time he'd suggested I buy him a coffee next time. Which would kind of be a just-hanging-out-as-friends kind of date. Which might be cool, actually. "Okay," I said.

"Good." He smiled and brushed glitter from my shoulder. "I'd better get back out there. See you later?"

"I'll be here."

The rest of the day was uneventful, but boring was better than chaos as far as I was concerned. I had to do the Dreadful Greeter Position by myself, which meant I didn't even have Ruthie's play-by-play to entertain me. I certainly got an eyeful of butt cracks, though. By the time the fourth beltless guy bent over to tie his shoe or try to pick up that stupid quarter, I seriously considered filing harassment charges. I was almost grateful for the never-ending chaos of a display that kept getting knocked around by shoppers.

With an hour left in my day and very few customers

coming through the door thanks to the downpour outside, I started to get delirious and built pyramids of green bean cans on the display shelf. At one point, Jake stopped to watch me. I set the can in my hand down, but the old man chuckled, reaching over to grab several nearby boxes of macaroni and cheese. He nodded for me to pick up the can I'd set down.

"Come on," he said gruffly, turning to walk toward the produce aisle. I followed, glancing behind me, but no one was around. "Days like this I'd rather be bowling," he said, stopping to build a pyramid out of the boxes on the floor.

"Excuse me?" The guy had obviously lost his mind.

"Bowling. Ever done that?"

"At a bowling alley, yes."

"Well, this is even better." He reached the third tier of boxes and stopped. "Go for it," he told me.

I stared at the pyramid, knowing I probably should just turn around and head back to my position and let the crazy old man play his game, but at the same time…

I backed up, hefted the can in my hand, and rolled it toward the "pins." Jake and I both laughed as boxes flew everywhere.

"Your turn to set up," he said.

I couldn't help myself. I crouched down to pick up the boxes and built a macaroni box pyramid—proud that I made four tiers instead of Jake's three.

"Okay, your turn," I said, facing Jake, but Noah was standing in his place, frowning, his arms crossed. Jake was nowhere to be seen—probably ran as soon as he caught sight of the manager.

"What are you doing?" Noah asked.

"Oh, um, I was just—"

"You can't stack boxes of food like that. What are you thinking?"

Crap. "I'm sorry. I'll pick it up." My face burning, I turned back to the pyramid of boxes. It sucked being called out by Noah like that. I'd hoped he'd have a better sense of humor. Or at least not make me feel like such a slacker.

A can rolled past me, knocking into the pyramid and scattering boxes everywhere.

I whipped around to see him smirking. "Told you," he said. "You didn't build it with enough support at the bottom. Way too easy."

I picked up the can of green beans and hefted it in my hand, walking toward him slowly. His eyes widened as if he thought I was going to throw it at him, though the shit-eating grin still lingered on his face. "Your turn to set it up," I said when I reached him. "Let's see if an architect can build a better pyramid."

A few rounds of macaroni bowling later and I was convinced this was the best greeter shift ever. It wasn't until I was clocking out that I finally caught sight of Jake, who winked knowingly at me. I laughed to myself. First Bessie, now Jake—was there anyone who wasn't trying to set me up with Noah?

And for some reason, I didn't mind at all.

The next day, Bessie set me up on the register. She stood with me as the first few customers came through, but the transactions were simple and the people were friendly. She soon gave me the thumbs-up and retreated to her own register a couple rows over.

Things were going pretty well for the first couple hours. Everyone smiled at me. Some even recognized that I was new and welcomed me to SmartMart. Another cashier named Kitty came by to relieve me for my first break, which I took in the break room by myself. Nice and quiet.

Then, like that day on the floor, all hell broke loose. This time, though, I was determined not to lose it.

"My daughter only drinks *organic* one percent milk," a woman said, stroking her daughter's fine blond hair like she was a china doll. She frowned at me like I had just offered her water from the sewer. "Only *organic*. You have every other percent in organic. Why not one percent?"

"I think we have the one percent in regular milk," I said. I didn't have any clue, but I'd say anything to get her to leave my line and go find it.

She clicked her tongue at me. "Only organic. Only one percent. How hard is that? Where's the manager?"

I wanted to ask her if she knew exactly how many kids who participated in the Let's Have a Ball camp would be happy with any kind of milk, but I didn't. Instead, I motioned to Damon, one of the managers who happened to be walking nearby, and congratulated myself on keeping my cool as he pulled her from the line to assist her.

"This package was already open. I don't want it." This

from a guy who tossed a half-empty package of chips on the conveyor. I smiled as I was taught and took it back, despite the fact that the kid directly behind him had chip particles sprinkled all over his shirt and was licking his greasy fingers. My instinct was to sling the rest of the chips over him, but I refrained like a good little SmartMart cashier and offered to replace it. Of course, the guy didn't want another. His kid already had enough grease in his belly to light a fire.

Lex 1, SmartMart customer 0. Hells yeah.

A couple customers later was a woman in a bikini top who should *not* have been in a bikini anything. I tried not to look at her boobs as I ran the groceries through, but here's how that went:

Cereal *(don't look at the boobs),* bananas, orange juice *(don't look at the boobs),* gelato, strawberries *(eyes up, eyes up),* milk, carrots *(don't look, don't look),* French bread, wine…

Yeah. I ended up looking.

I mean, who couldn't stare at those things? It was like she was trying to hold basketballs with two triangles of tissue and some dental floss. It fascinated and horrified me at the same time. I thought she saw me looking at them when she cleared her throat, but she seemed pleased. I noticed that the bagger Larry couldn't take his eyes off them, either. I snickered when he offered "Paper or plastic."

My guess was plastic.

The next couple people were okay, but then came *her*.

I could feel her presence even before sliding the first box of crackers across the scanner. She rose at least a foot over me, with hair that stretched even higher. She had authority here, and I was nothing but a flea to be squashed if I got in her way.

She was the customer. She was superior.

That was how she made me feel when she and her tired-looking husband pushed three overflowing carts into my aisle and a huge black binder was dropped on the counter. My jaw followed suit. I tried to pull myself together and started scanning the boxes of saltines. As I scanned the sixth box—was she saving up for the apocalypse?—the woman opened the binder, and light shone from within. I flinched before realizing that the light wasn't divine intervention but a result of fluorescents reflecting off the metal binder tabs. Inside were coupons. Hundreds upon hundreds of coupons, each in its own little plastic slot.

If there were a coupon hell, she would be queen.

I scanned the contents of her cart—boxes of Advil, bottles of deodorant, roll after roll of toilet paper. About twenty packages of toilet paper later, I decided she either had major bowel issues or she felt the need to TP someone's house. I really hoped for the latter.

Then came the Windex. Bottle after bright blue bottle of liquid flowed across the scanner, sloshing against the plastic like contained oceans. My tired eyes started seeing little fish swimming inside, but maybe it was just the lettering on the inside label.

After I finally made it past stacks of candy bars, count-less cans of beans, and several bottles of salad dressing, I eyed that big black binder. Did she seriously think she had enough coupons to cover this stuff? Fingers sore and stomach growling for my lunch break, I scanned the last items and cringed when I offered up the total: $525.32. Who spent five hundred bucks on groceries?

Unfazed by the total, the lady nodded and opened up the binder. Her fingers were quick as they flipped through the pages, pulling out stacks of coupons from different plastic card slots and stacking them across the counter. She was so fast that I was reminded of the poker competitions on TV that my dad liked to watch. She dealt me the first stack.

I'd processed a few coupons before, of course, but not this many. I scanned the first one for a bottle of Windex under the woman's steely gaze, and the deductions commenced. No problem. The second, the third, the… Good Lord, how many coupons did she have for Windex, anyway?

I was handed the next stack for juice boxes and started scanning. I couldn't help it—maybe it was because of the sheer number of coupons or maybe I was just getting loopy, but I got the giggles.

"Something funny?" she asked, arching an eyebrow.

"No, ma'am." I tried to fix my face in a serious expression as I continued scanning the coupons and held out my hand for the next stack. The coupons for crackers scanned until they stopped beeping midway through, so I took a look at the display.

"Oh, these were buy-one, get-one, so I don't think you can use more than one coupon on these."

"Yes, I can."

I stared at her. "Um, no ma'am, I don't think you can."

Without blinking and almost without looking, the woman reached into the back of her binder and slid stapled pages toward me.

"What's this?" I asked.

"The store's coupon policy. Read it."

I couldn't help it. I blurted out, "You carry around the *coupon policy* for this place?"

The woman glared at me. "Look, honey, why don't you call your manager for help. I don't have time for childishness." Her tone couldn't be any snippier.

Don't say anything. Don't say anything. I had to repeat it over and over in my head as I jabbed the number for the manager's office.

"Can I help you?" Noah's voice sounded behind me.

I slammed the phone down and whipped around. His eyes were amused. "How long have you been standing here?"

"A while." His smile grew. He was enjoying this way too much. He leaned in so only I could hear him say, "Actually, you did pretty well. I thought you'd have given up long before now."

I fought an urge to mash the coupons into his grinning face. "She wants to use coupons on all the buy-one, get-one things."

"Oh, that's fine," he said, smiling warmly at the woman. He pressed some keys and tried to show me how to process the additional coupons, but I was fuming too much to pay attention. It was only picturing how many ways one could murder someone with a stack of coupons that kept me from flinging them at him. At one point, he stepped back to let me continue, but now he was standing over my shoulder, watching me.

It was unsettling, to say the least. And my stupid hands were shaking, though whether from irritation or nerves I wasn't sure.

After a couple more screw-ups that Noah had to step in and assist with, much to the coupon diva's obvious annoyance, I finally finished. "Your total is $37.40," I said, so annoyed at this point that I couldn't muster up the proper enthusiasm at her ridiculous savings.

She thrust a fifty at me and I returned her change.

"What are you, stupid? You gave me a five. You're supposed to give me a ten," Coupon Cow snapped at me, waving the bill in front of my face.

I snatched it and jammed my fist on the button to open the cashbox. "Here."

She ripped the bill from me and frowned at Noah, shaking her head and clicking her tongue. He didn't respond. Larry and Jake, who had been helping bag the groceries, each grabbed a cart and helped her husband wheel them out. The woman grabbed her binder and followed, pausing as she passed us.

"You need to reconsider hiring teenagers," she said to Noah, jerking her head toward me. Clearly she missed that he was also a member of the Horrible Teenagers Club. "No manners whatsoever."

I shouldn't have let her get to me, but my body was shaking with anger. I was about to snap back when I felt warm fingers slide around my wrist, stopping me. Noah was still facing the woman, but his hand was behind his back, holding me still. The shock of his touch dissolved my retort and sent an unexpected ripple of pleasure down my spine.

"She's new, yes," Noah said politely. "And she is still learning. But she's also used to dealing with customers who aren't quite so high maintenance."

The woman's jaw opened and shut as her eyes dropped to his nametag. She didn't say anything, though. My jaw also dropped. I never would've expected calm, professional Noah to be rude to a customer.

We watched the woman follow her caravan of carts toward the exit. Noah still had a gentle hold of my wrist, but I didn't pull away. Just a slight forward tilt of my head and I'd be resting against his back. It was a weird moment that seemed to go on forever. When the caravan disappeared out the doors and there was no longer a reason to stare at the exit, Noah let go of my wrist, turning to face me. "You okay?"

I nodded, still shaky inside. I wasn't even sure if it was from residual anger at Coupon Cow, surprise at Noah's response to her, or a nervous reaction from his warm touch. Or the fact that standing so close to him, I caught the clean smell of whatever soap he used, which made me surprisingly uncomfortable. Noah, as my manager and general pain in the ass, shouldn't smell that good.

"Thanks for helping," I told him lamely.

"Sure."

We stood for a moment in awkward silence.

"Isn't it time for your lunch break?" he asked.

I glanced at the store's clock. "Yeah, I think you're right."

"We're on the same schedule today."

"Oh."

Was I supposed to ask him if he wanted to sit with me? Now that I thought about it, I realized I wanted to. Why not? We were friends. This wasn't middle school or anything. I opened my mouth, but he got there first.

"Want to have lunch together?" he asked, his words rushed together. "I mean, just in the break room. I brought mine."

I bit back a smile at the look on his flushed face, as if he was convinced I'd say no. Or maybe he was wondering if a manager was allowed to have lunch with a drone like me. "Sure," I told him. We headed to the lockers to get our lunches.

In the break room, Bessie was just finishing washing her empty container. She brightened at the sight of us sitting down together. Maybe it was just that he seemed so manager-like instead of the normal-looking guy who'd hung out with me at the coffee shop, but sitting across from Noah felt really weird.

We spent the first few minutes eating and not saying much. But the awkwardness fizzled as we started talking about the crazy coupon lady. Soon, we were both laughing hysterically.

"So she actually had a store policy in her binder. I mean, who does that? Get a life!"

"I know," he said. "The first time I saw it I was like, what the hell?"

"You know that show about extreme couponers—I thought there's no way people could be like that in real life."

He snorted. "My mom uses coupons, but not like that."

"I bet you see a lot of crazy."

"Pretty much, yeah. Not as much as when I first came here."

It was worse? That was hard to imagine. "You're probably just used to it by now."

"Maybe." He shrugged. "But the people who work here are really nice."

"If you say so. By the way, what's up with Ruthie?"

"What do you mean?" His eyebrows pinched in confusion.

"Every time I see her, she's yelling at me about her daddy's Lexus. Like I should know her dad or something."

A corner of his mouth lifted in a lopsided grin. "Yeah, I've heard her say that to you. It *is* a funny coincidence, you know. Your name being Alexis."

I resisted the urge to smack his arm. "What coincidence? Stop talking in circles, Noah."

His smile dropped. "Oh, sorry. I thought Bessie would've told you. Ruthie's dad left her when she was little. Bessie figured it out after talking to Ruthie's mom. Her dad's Lexus was the last thing Ruthie saw when he drove away from her and her mom. It was the last she ever saw of him."

CHAPTER
10

The bite I just took of my Twix lodged itself in my throat. It never occurred to me there was any meaning to Ruthie's ramblings.

"You okay?" Noah asked.

I swallowed and nodded, but I couldn't say anything. How could I? Ruthie's dad had abandoned her. This whole time I had cringed whenever she appeared, knowing she'd be yelling on and on about her daddy's Lexus. "I didn't know," was all I could say. *Lame.*

"She's different, I know. She can't help it. But she's nice, and she wants to help everyone."

"Yeah, I get it," I mumbled, grumpy now and irritated that he was talking to me like I was five. But mostly, I was mad at myself. And that pissed me off even more.

We sat there, nibbling and sipping, not saying anything.

My irritation lessened as I watched the guy sitting across from me, his eyes fixed on the soda can that he twirled in his hands. Sometimes, Noah talked like he was ten years older than me, not one, and it both intrigued and irritated me. But most of the time he was cool. The butterflies that fluttered in my stomach whenever he was around meant I liked him more than just a little. Like at the coffee shop—conversation with him was easy, so that was a plus.

Still, sometimes he acted nervous, and I wasn't sure why. If we were at school, I'd understand. I was involved in several clubs and always had a group of friends around. Loner guys like Noah didn't talk to any of us. We didn't go out of our way to talk to them, either. Didn't even notice them most of the time. But this was SmartMart, where the usual rules didn't apply. He was my boss and I was a clerk, barely out of training. And those eyes! If I stared long enough into those sexy blues, I'd lose myself. Girls would be all over him if he looked like this at school.

Although probably not—Noah's look may have changed, but I bet he'd still be a loner. And I'm sure few people would have forgotten what he did to Bryce. How would they feel about me becoming friends with this guy? Not that I even had to ask myself that question—I knew better than to think they'd be happy about it. Guilt nipped at my conscience as I recalled the ridicule Bryce went through when he was kicked off the team. For his sake, I shouldn't want anything to do with Noah, either. But I couldn't help myself.

Noah looked up to catch me staring at him. "What?" he

asked.

"Nothing," I said, fighting the blush I could feel spreading across my cheeks. "I was just wondering if you speak French?" *Now why did I ask that?* But it had been on my mind since that day at the shop.

He tilted his head slightly. "Yes, of course. My mom speaks to us in French all the time."

"Say something."

"Didn't you say you were going to major in French?"

I shrugged. "I didn't say I knew it, just that I was thinking about it for college."

"Ah." He pursed his lips for a moment, hopefully not thinking about how bogus my claim had been. "Okay. *J'adore avoir le déjeuner avec vous.*" His tone matched the seriousness of his eyes, which made my breath catch even as I recognized the *J'adore* as something to do with love. But didn't *vous* mean *you*? I swallowed hard. I wasn't exactly ready to hear *love* and *you* in the same breath from Noah.

"What does that mean?" I asked hesitantly, cringing inside that this whole conversation might go from easy to awkward in seconds.

He grinned. "It means, 'I love having lunch with you.'"

I crumpled up my napkin and threw it at him as he laughed. "You're horrible."

"I know what you thought I said," he said, still laughing and making my cheeks blaze.

I crossed my arms. "Whatever." But his adorably impish expression made me laugh too, despite myself. "Hey, what time is it?"

He glanced at his watch. "We have about a minute left. Guess we should get back."

I nodded and stood to throw away my trash, wishing that break was just a little longer.

"Got plans for the weekend?" he asked as he opened the door for me.

"This weekend?" It was only Tuesday. "Um, I have softball practice. Oh, and camp."

"You go to camp?"

"No. Well, there's one at the end of summer for softball I'm planning to go to. But I volunteer at a baseball camp for kids a couple days a week. Let's Have a Ball over at Hibiscus Park."

"Volunteer with kids? That's really cool." He stopped walking to stare at me, a direct but nervous look—a total switch from the goofiness earlier. "What about Saturday night?"

His voice shook slightly as he spoke, but the deliberate question made my breath catch as if he had trailed an invisible finger slowly up my arm, leaving a trail of goose bumps in its wake. I swallowed hard. "I'm going to a baseball tournament."

"Really? The Rays?"

The guy clearly didn't know baseball. Pros didn't play in tournaments. "No, it's for a local traveling team. My friend Bryce is playing."

His smile creased into a grimace. I didn't like the disappointed look he gave me. The idea of me going to a tournament—or doing anything at all—with his archenemy bugged him. I had wondered when this would come up.

But he didn't say anything else about it. Would he have asked me out if I had said I wasn't doing anything? Would I have gone? According to the silly butterflies in my stomach, there was a possibility I might've said yes.

"Guess I'll see you later," he said, backing away.

"Guess so." I turned to head to the cash register I had been working at previously. Maybe I should've told him I wasn't busy on Friday night. That would've been awkward, though. I wasn't the shy type, for sure, but did I really want to come off as desperate?

I was completely caught up in my thoughts and unaware of who was working the cash register until I almost ran into Roxanne.

"Oh, sorry. Am I supposed to relieve you?" I asked in the nicest voice I could manage. She looked at me, then over my shoulder at Noah. "Um, are you supposed to take a break or something?" I prompted.

"No." Her mouth tightened. "Go ask Bessie about your shift."

I looked around, but Bessie was not at the registers. "Do you know where she is?" I asked Roxanne.

"Do I look like a directory?" she snapped. "Go find her yourself." She mumbled something about idiot cheerleaders and turned her back to me.

Whoa—beyotch alert. I did a quick scan of the floor, then the stockroom, before heading back toward the office. Maybe today's rotation was posted somewhere. Bessie probably should've shown me that before leaving me on my own.

In the employee hallway, I scanned the various fliers that reminded people about safety and health, but no schedules were posted. One bright green flier caught my eye: *Employees must wash hands before each shift.* It was signed *Linda Munson* and had a clipart image of hands under a running faucet. Wash hands before starting each shift? Was Linda afraid we'd bring cooties to the customers or something? I laughed as I saw a similar sign posted next to it with the same clipart: *Customers must wash hands before shopping.* Now that would be nice.

"Somebody posted that sign as a joke," Jake wheezed as he walked up. "I guess someone thinks he's funny."

"I'd say that person is definitely funny."

Jake shrugged and shuffled off.

I went to Mr. Hanson's office and raised my hand to knock but lowered it when I recognized Noah's voice. I leaned in a little closer to listen.

"She's a valued customer, Noah," Mr. Hanson was saying. "She's very angry."

"I know, sir."

"Did you overhear the cashier saying something rude, too?"

Noah didn't hesitate in his response. "No, sir."

"The cashier didn't provoke her?"

"No, sir."

"Hmm. This isn't like you. What made you say such a thing to her?"

There was a long pause, at the end of which was Hanson's voice, not Noah's. "I'll let it go because your performance record has been stellar up to now. But if you want to keep your job in management, you have to suck it up and smile, okay?"

"Yes, sir."

"That's all." Hanson sounded so stern, so unlike his normal jolly self that it made me wonder how Noah was feeling. I knew how much he valued Mr. Hanson's opinion, so to be reamed out for something he wasn't even responsible for made my stomach churn.

I backed away as Noah yanked open the door, then stopped short at the sight of me. For a long, uncomfortable moment, we just stared at each other. I wondered if he knew I overheard the conversation. Why didn't he stand up for himself? It wasn't his fault the coupon woman was so bitchy. And it wasn't his fault I bitched back at her. But he never even mentioned me.

"Noah…" What could I say? *Thanks for taking one for the team?* Lame.

He nodded shortly and moved past me into the store. Mr. Hanson cleared his throat. "Can I help you, Miss Dubois?"

It wasn't Noah's fault, it was mine. That was what I should've said, but all that came out of my mouth was, "Um, I was just wondering where I'm supposed to go next. I mean, my rotation schedule."

He pointed toward a bulletin board I hadn't noticed. I searched the schedule with a finger, found my name next to women's apparel, and headed out to the floor.

I kept my eyes peeled for Noah. I had to know why he felt the need to cover for me. He didn't have to do that. I was perfectly happy to admit being rude to her—she deserved it. And *he* didn't deserve to get in trouble for it. I felt like telling Mr. Hanson, but that would make Noah look like a liar.

I found Noah in the electronics section, chatting with a couple other employees I didn't know. He stopped to look at me, eyebrows raised.

"Hey, can I talk with you for a sec?" I asked, ignoring the scrutiny from the other two guys.

He nodded to the others and followed me to the next aisle of DVDs. He crossed his arms, face impassive. Gone was quiet Noah or even the fun Noah from earlier—this one was all business, and for some reason, that intimidated the hell out of me.

"Yes?" Noah prompted.

Everything I was going to say flew out of my mind and left me with one word: "Why?"

"You're new," Noah said. "Hanson could've fired you for that. He hates his employees to be rude to a customer."

I wanted to tell him that it was fine, let him fire me. But I didn't. Though it was a crappy job, Noah was trying to give me a chance to keep it. He put his own neck on the line so I wouldn't get fired. I couldn't blow him off.

"But how did you know *you* wouldn't get fired?" I countered.

"I've been his top employee for the past year. I've never done anything wrong, so I figured I was safe." His eyes shifted away from mine as his expression softened. "Being perfect gets old, anyway."

"Well, thanks," I said. "That was nice of you."

He nodded. I added, "Guess I better get to work. I'll see you later."

He nodded again, fidgeting with a DVD on the shelf. I wondered what in our conversation made him switch from all-business manager back to shy teenager. As I walked toward women's apparel, I couldn't come up with any reason that Noah would put his job at risk for me. I mean, this was his *job*. He cared about it.

I didn't get it. I didn't get him.

But his sudden rebellion—that I could relate to. Since Rory was born I'd been constantly pitted against her. I heard it at family gatherings every year—how beautiful Aurora was, how she inherited my mother's grace, Aunt Peggy's talent, blah blah blah. Oh, of course I'd heard the same things when I was her age, but as I grew out of the pretty princess look, I'd hear much different things from my aunts: "Alexis, you sure have grown taller this year, which I guess is good for you if you want to play a boy's game like baseball."

Or, "Alexis, you'd be so much prettier if you didn't wear your hair in that unflattering ponytail."

Or even my favorite, "So, Alexis, are you doing anything this year? Oh, softball? How about anything feminine, like dance or cheerleading?"

Followed by my mother whispering something to her sisters that I couldn't hear but that was trailed by tongue clicks and commiserating smiles. Yes, I was pretty, but apparently that didn't matter because I played a sport.

Here I was worried about owing Noah a stupid dollar-fifty for the tea when I really owed him my job. And knowing Noah, he would never expect anything in return for either.

Maybe it wouldn't be such a bad thing to go out with him.

Working in apparel wasn't exciting, and I spent most of the time trying to figure out how to get out of a conversation with Merrill, one of the most boring people I'd ever come across. *Conversation* was a loose term—actually, she talked at me while I cleared clothes out of the changing room. Her voice was level—never rising above or below one tone. All I could think was that if I looked up the word *monotone* online, most likely it would be a recording of Merrill's voice.

I did discover while walking through the men's section that someone had pantsed two of the mannequins. The pairs of khakis were down around their ankles, and I could've sworn they were blushing. The prankster strikes again. Yes, I should've pulled the pants back up, but I started laughing and couldn't stop. A couple of customers stopped to stare at me—neither of whom noticed the half-naked figures. I turned to see Noah leaning against a shelf, watching me with a grin. I gestured toward the mannequins, and he laughed.

I wondered if Noah was the prankster. No, I decided. He didn't seem to have that kind of goofy sense of humor. Even the macaroni bowling was started by someone else. I really couldn't picture him yanking down the pants of dummies, though the mental image made me giggle.

I didn't see him again until I was clocking out.

"Shift over?" he asked, leaning against the wall next to

me. The butterflies started their flight again, but I was used to them now.

"No, I'm clocking in for the second time today, just for fun. Can't get enough of this place." I smirked at him. "Right?"

"I don't mind it. Not when you're here."

My mouth fell open at that, before I had the sense to clamp it shut again.

"I just meant that you're fun and all," he said quickly. "It's...different when you're around. I don't laugh half as much when you're not here."

"Me neither," I told him. "I like when we're on the same shift."

A long, awkward pause followed, like we were both waiting to see what the other was going to say. I wondered if he'd have an easier time asking me out if he wasn't technically my boss. If he wanted to ask me out, that is.

"Hey, maybe we should exchange numbers," I said before I could think about it and chicken out. "I mean, just in case I can't make it in to work or something. I don't have the call-in number." Yes, I got how dumb that sounded. The call-in number I'm sure was posted in a hundred places around here, and at the very least I could've asked for that number.

Noah's face grew serious. I could almost see his wheels turning, trying to figure out if it was appropriate to give me his number while we were working. Of course, I was now officially off the clock. I smiled brightly, and that seemed to do the trick. "Sure." He recited the number as I touched the buttons on my phone.

"Thanks," I said, waiting for his phone to register my call. I laughed when his ringtone went off. "*Sesame Street* theme? Really?"

He pulled his phone from his pocket and jabbed at the end button. "Damn it, Steve."

"Steve...sure..." I dragged out the words as he adjusted the settings on his phone, his face pink.

"He thinks it's funny. A couple weeks ago it was *Barney*. Trust me, *Sesame Street*'s nothing."

"You're cute when you're embarrassed."

"Well, you're cute when you're laughing at me."

Both of us stood there, frozen. Did we really just have that exchange? My face must be turning a gazillion shades of red. Just like his right now.

Roxanne walked up at that moment and pushed me aside with her hips to type her number in the clock. "Excuse me," she said, giving me the most fake smile ever. "Hi, Noah."

I gritted my teeth and resisted the urge to smack her platinum head.

"Hi, Roxanne," he said, his lips twitching at my obvious irritation toward her.

Roxanne stepped between us and deliberately turned her back on me. "Something smells," she said, her eyes moving over me. "If you're going to do that, Cheerleader, try taking it in the bathroom."

I gaped at her. Did she just insinuate that I farted? I clamped my mouth shut and shook my head as Noah pressed his lips together in an obvious effort to not laugh.

"Interesting," Noah said, his lips still twitching as he walked me to the front. "Somebody has it out for you."

"Yeah. I think she overheard you telling me my mom had to get me this job, and she hasn't let me live it down."

He frowned. "Crap, I'm sorry about that."

I waved a hand at him. "Trust me, it doesn't bother me. She just needs to get a life. And stop calling me a cheerleader."

"Yeah. She went to our high school, you know. I don't remember her—she was a senior when I was a freshman—but I guess she had some big problems there. She always says how much she hated school."

I thought about her comment about cheerleaders. My guess was she either got bullied by them or was one of the Haters—kids who talked smack about those of us in organized teams because they felt they could. I hoped it wasn't a bully thing, but either way, it wasn't my fault. I didn't even know her in high school.

Before I realized it, we were outside. I looked around for my mother's car but I guess she was running late. "My mom should be here soon," I said. "You don't have to wait with me."

"It's okay, I don't mind."

I smiled to myself. As we stood in the heat, I mentally ran through our conversation. It was nice. Friendly. I tried not to think about the fact that this guy, who knew nothing about softball, knew that I was on a traveling team, or that his smile lingered in my mind far longer than it should have.

Or that he told me I was cute. Now he had my number and I had his. I just wished I knew what to do with it.

An old woman walked out of SmartMart, struggling to carry an armful of bags. Noah shrugged apologetically at me as he offered to help her. I smiled as I watched him take the bags from her. Total gentleman. I leaned against the wall to wait for my mother, but the familiar red Mustang that swung into the pick-up lane wasn't her. Bryce stepped out of the car and waved to me. "Hey Lex! Let's go!"

Instinctively, I looked around, but Noah was busy loading groceries in the lady's car. "Thanks!" I slid into the front seat as he got in. "How'd you know I was getting off now?"

Bryce snorted, but before he could make his usual "that's what she said" joke, I smacked his arm. "From my shift. Get your mind out of the gutter."

"I went by your house to pick you up for practice and your mom said she was on her way to get you. I offered to come instead."

"Practice?" Crap, I'd forgotten it was Tuesday.

He stared at me. "Um, yeah, pitching practice like we do almost every Tuesday night. What's wrong with you?"

"Nothing's wrong with me."

He shook his head as he maneuvered the car to the road. "Sorry. Court said you'd been distracted lately, and when she gets pissed I hear all about it." He grimaced.

"What do you mean, distracted?"

"She says you don't talk to her as much as you used to."

I groaned. "I have a new job. Tell Court I can't exactly

talk while I'm working."

"Believe it or not, I did tell her that." He laughed. "Court is Court. So how is SmartFart anyway?"

"Meh. Boring most of the time." *Except for Noah.*

"My mom said she'd hire you at her store for the summer if you can get out of it."

"No, it's okay." He raised an eyebrow at me as I realized how quickly I'd said that. Not that working at his mom's store, Clique, would be a bad idea—in fact, I knew that Bryce and sometimes Court helped out there, so it could be fun. But I was finally getting the hang of SmartMart. It'd be stupid to leave now.

That's what I told myself, at least.

CHAPTER 11

Let's Have a Ball was easily my favorite part of summer. It was conducted at our community baseball fields on Saturdays, just before my regular practice, and the attendees were kids who couldn't afford summer camp. We had gotten to know them pretty well, since many of them had been with us from the beginning three years ago.

Funny enough, it was my mother who had suggested the camp as a volunteer activity when I was going into high school. The school had a fast-track program that offered college credits if you qualified, and that included having a certain amount of volunteer hours. Mom thought I could use my interest in softball to help out little kids, one of the few times I ever agreed with her choice for me.

She seemed to forget that it was her idea I got involved with it in the first place, though. I think she didn't expect

me to put that many hours into the camp and got annoyed
when she had to drive me there so much. Hello, did she
ever think of just getting me a car? But I knew the thought
of me driving myself around terrified her. She'd rattle off
statistics about how many teen accidents took place that
month whenever I bugged her about it. And even my dad
wouldn't budge. I think he read the same reports. But a
promise was a promise. If I could stick it out at SmartMart
for the summer—which I would—she'd have no choice but
to help me out with the car.

My mother dropped me off at the start of practice. Syd
was already jogging around the field with our group to warm
up, her brown ponytail wagging behind her. She used to be
catcher on the softball team but was switching with Emily
Grace for first base position next season. I liked Emily
Grace—she had a strong arm and was quick—but I was going
to miss Syd behind home plate. This would be my first season
pitching to someone else.

Syd waved as they completed their lap and headed
toward me, kids in tow. "It's about time you got here."

"Hey, Lex!" Andrew ran over to me from Bryce's group.
He was only seven—one of the smallest kids there with one
of the biggest personalities. He was also one of my favorites.
"Bryce said you'd help us catch."

"Catch what?"

"Duh, fish."

I smacked his cap lightly. "Have you been practicing?"

"Yep! My mom's been working with me."

I hugged him. "That's awesome." Andrew's dad wasn't

around much since the divorce, according to his mother. So for her to spend time playing ball with her son, even though she had two jobs, was a huge deal, and more than what many kids got. It was the best feeling knowing that the camp was actually bringing families together.

While Bryce practiced with some of the kids on their swing, I set teams up to toss the ball back and forth with each other, stopping every now and then to correct the positioning of their gloves. Occasionally, I'd look over at Bryce to admire his perfect stance as he swung the bat. I wish I had the powerful swing that he did, but no matter how much I practiced, I couldn't knock them out of the park like he did.

I did notice that he did this thing where he pointed the bat to the sky right between pitches. The other kids tried to mimic him. It never occurred to me that it was kind of a stupid thing to do. What was he doing, anyway? Praying to the gods for a hit?

My mother once told me that daydreaming was danger-ous. I always thought she meant it figuratively...until Andrew's ball smacked me in the forehead while I was watching Bryce.

The force stunned me, knocking me to the ground in shock. I thought when things hit you in the head, you blacked out or went dizzy or something. But the only thought that crossed my mind when the ball smacked me was my mother and her daydream warning.

"Oh my God, are you okay?" Syd's face appeared over me just as a searing pain shot through my head.

"I'm sorry! I'm sorry! It was an accident," I could hear

Andrew crying in the background.

"It's okay," I mumbled, pushing myself to my elbows. I touched the spot gingerly as Bryce came running over. "Shit, Lex, you okay?"

"Yeah. Just... Ouch."

Coach Marcus peered at my forehead. "You've got a pretty nasty bump there. We need to get you to urgent care."

"No, I'll be all right."

Syd pulled out her phone and poked at it with her finger. "I'm calling your mom."

"Don't worry, Lex. I'll take over your group," Emily Grace said, smiling though her eyes were fixed on my forehead. Everyone was staring at my forehead—crap, what did it look like?

With nothing else left to say, I had no choice but to let Coach Marcus's wife drive me to the clinic. Bryce followed in his truck with Syd right behind him. They were making way too big a deal of this.

The clinic was empty when we arrived, so the doctor was able to see me right away. They didn't bother to do a scan or anything, saying I was lucky the ball hit me where it did. Or, as the doctor said about the lump, "Better out than in." He gave me an ice pack and instructions for watching the lump in case it got worse. I was headed back to the lobby when my mother burst through the doors, her eyes wide.

"Oh, God, Alexis!" she cried, running to me.

I held my hands up. "I'm okay, Mom. Really."

"Let me see." She gently swiped my hair back and peered at my bump. "Oh my God, it's huge!" Of course, the rising level of her voice grabbed the attention of the doctor—and everyone else in the vicinity. He walked over and introduced himself.

"Don't worry about her, she's a lucky one." He winked at me.

"Lucky?" My mother's voice was piercing. "You call getting hit by a baseball lucky?" She pulled me to her, stroking the back of my hair like I was three. "It's not going to leave a permanent mark, is it?" she asked the doctor.

"Mom, I'm fine. Really."

"Honey," she said, touching the bump gently with a finger. I flinched. "I don't know that you should keep volunteering at that camp. Too dangerous."

"Dangerous? Give me a break, Mom, this was just a weird accident. I'm not quitting, and I need to get back."

"You're definitely not going back today."

"Yes, I am."

"No, you're not, and that's final."

I took a deep breath. "It's not just camp. I have practice today, and if I don't show…" *Coach will have Maggie replace me.*

Mom put her arm around me, and for one stupid moment, I thought she'd let me go. "Honey, I know softball is very important to you. But your health is very important to me. The doctor says you need rest, so rest you get."

I glared at the lab-coated prison warden, who was smiling and nodding in agreement.

While my mother talked to the nurse, I walked back out to the lobby. Bryce and Syd stood up, the concern in their eyes warming me.

I waved at them. "It's just a bump, no big deal. I need to get back to the fields—can I ride with one of you?"

"Um, are you sure?" Syd asked, staring at my bruised forehead. "You look like you need to hang low for today."

I laughed, wincing slightly as my head splintered. "I'm fine." My smile dropped as I tried for the desperate plea tactic. "Guys, you know Coach Santiago might replace me with Maggie permanently if I don't show up to practice. I've already missed too many."

"No big deal," Syd said. "I'll make sure he knows what happened."

Bryce nodded. "I'll tell him, too. He's not an ass—he'll get it." But underneath the reassuring words was a nervous tone that told me Bryce wasn't so sure. He played, too. He knew.

"She's going home," my mother said as she walked up. She wrapped an arm around my shoulders. "Alexis needs rest. I'd appreciate it if you told her coach."

Syd and Bryce nodded and offered reassurances as my mother steered me to the car. I knew better than to argue with her. It didn't matter, anyway. I was already forming Plan B in my mind.

As soon as we got home, I took two ibuprofen and told her I was going up to my room and to please leave me alone until dinnertime. She agreed, touching my cheek fondly. Her sincere concern made me almost feel bad about lying to her.

As soon as I got to my room, I looked at my phone. Noah's number was still in my recent calls folder. Most of my friends were already at the field. Bryce would be getting ready for his tournament, so he'd have left.

I pressed Noah's number.

A couple rings later, he answered. "Hello?"

"Hey, it's Lex. I need to ask a huge favor."

CHAPTER
12

A half hour later, we were on the way to the field in
Noah's beat-up SUV. It took a bit of tiptoeing to get
out through the back door, around the pool, and back to
the front of the house, but thankfully my mother was in the
kitchen and totally oblivious. I didn't even want Grandma
to see me. I figured on the question of my health, she'd be
right there with my mother.

I arranged my hair across my forehead to cover the
bruised egg so Noah wouldn't freak out and tell me to stay
home, too. Once I got to the field, I'd be good to go.

"Thanks for picking me up," I told him. "I hope I didn't
bug you in the middle of something."

"Oh, yeah, no. I mean, sure. No, you didn't bother me. I
was just sketching and stuff."

"Cool."

"Yeah. I was kind of surprised you called. Not that it's a bad thing," he said quickly. "But I didn't think I'd be first on your list."

"Most people are already out at the field." I smiled at him. "Lucky for me that you didn't have to work today."

His responding smile was genuine, sweet, heart-melting, and I *really* wished he'd cut it out. It was so hard to concentrate on anything when he turned on the Smile to Kill All Rational Thought.

When we got to the field, I climbed out of the SUV and grabbed my bag with my mitt and bat. Leaving the car running, Noah got out and walked around to my side. "Thanks again," I told him, setting down the bag to pull a hair tie from my pocket. "I really appreciate it."

"You're welcome. Well, I guess I'll see you..." He stopped, staring at my forehead as I pulled my hair back. *Oh crap.* I let it fall back around my face, but it was too late.

Noah raised his hand to gently brush my hair back. "What happened to you?" he asked, his voice low.

I pushed his hand away and smiled widely. "Got hit with a ball at camp today. It's no big deal."

"No big deal?" He raised an eyebrow. "Is that what really happened?" His gaze was direct. What did he *think* happened?

"Trust me, I remember. One of the little kids accidentally clocked me with a ball when I wasn't paying attention. My mom didn't want to take me to practice because she was worried. Which is nuts—I'm totally fine. Not even a little headache."

He didn't look convinced. "If you got hurt that badly, maybe you shouldn't—"

"Noah, stop. I said I'm fine." I picked up my bag again and walked away, pausing to say, "Thanks for the ride. I'll catch you later."

I hurried to the field without looking back, reassuring people as I passed them that I was okay.

Syd was warming up when I approached her. She clicked her tongue and shook her head. My mother incarnate. "I'm surprised your mom changed her mind," she said.

"She didn't."

"Who got you here, then?"

"Just…someone. Are you ready to practice or are you going to give me a hard time, too?"

She tisked again but backed away and tossed the ball to me. A few minutes later, Maggie walked over to ask if I could throw with her. Regardless of what Holly said before, I couldn't just ignore her. So I said, "Sure," and moved over to practice a few pitches with her. Coach Santiago said he was glad to see me "finally" and didn't say anything about my forehead. He complimented Maggie on her pitches and didn't say anything about mine. Which was unnerving, to say the least, but there wasn't anything I could do but pitch the hell out of my arm. Hopefully he'd notice anyway. The man was hard-core, but he was a good coach.

At one point, I glanced over at the short metal bleachers and noticed Noah sitting there, watching. Probably waiting to see if I'd keel over or something. Still, the fact that he cared enough to stay was sweet and totally in line with everything I knew about him.

After practice ended, I wandered over to the bleachers, well aware that Syd hadn't left yet. She was in deep conversation with Emily Grace, probably discussing their upcoming switch of positions. Oh, well. If Syd saw me talking to him, so be it. I kind of hoped she did notice. I needed to be able to confide in *someone*.

"Hey," I said to Noah as he jumped down from the top metal bench.

"Hey," he said.

"You stayed for the whole thing?"

"Yep." He smiled. "You have a good arm."

I knew I was blushing—I could feel the burn in my cheeks. "Thanks. I like to play." *I like to play? What am I, five?*

"So you said you have a game next Saturday?"

"Yeah, Saturday night after work. We scrimmage with another local team. It's not a real game—just a practice game that doesn't count."

His deep blue eyes transfixed me to the point where I couldn't remember what I was saying anymore. I cleared my voice and continued. "It's not like people come to scrimmage games or anything." And Bryce would be there. *Don't say you'll be there…don't say you'll come…*

"I'll come."

My heart soared—damn it. I didn't want to get him into a fight with Bryce. I didn't want them anywhere near each other. But at the same time, I was glad he'd offered. "Thanks."

"Lex?" a voice said behind me.

Here we go. I turned to see Syd approaching, her fingers tugging at her ponytail as she stared at us. Or more specifically—stared at Noah. "Hey, Syd. You remember Noah Grayson from school?"

"Um, yeah." Her direct look at me clearly said, *Do you?*

"He works with me at SmartMart."

"Oh." She smiled politely as she shook Noah's extended hand. "Nice to meet you." She turned to me. "I was just going to see if you needed a ride home." Her eyes flickered to Noah uncertainly.

"I can give you a ride," he spoke up quickly. "I really don't mind."

Every fiber of my inner being said *yes* to Noah. But that would leave Syd open to calling Court, and Court and Bryce were absolutely the last people I wanted to know about Noah. It might've been better if they had seen him at SmartMart that first day and commiserated about how awful it was that I had to work with him than know that we were friends.

"I'd better go home with Syd," I told Noah. If he was disappointed, he didn't show it.

"Okay," he said. "See you Monday?"

"I'll be there."

He headed back to his beat-up SUV. I walked with Syd to her car, but as soon as Noah drove away, she grabbed my arm. "Spill. Now."

I sighed and shook my arm loose. "He's a friend. Well, really, he's my boss."

"Wait, *that's* the hot manager you talked about?" She snorted.

"What?" I asked, annoyed, though I'd known this was going to happen.

"Oh Lex, you're going out with your boss, who happens to go to our school, who happens to be that slimy kid who told on Bryce and got him suspended and turned the whole school against him. Yeah, I think you can guess what's *what.*"

I crossed my arms. "I'm *not* going out with him. And he's not slimy—he's a really nice guy. So what if he happened to tell on Bryce for spray-painting private property? Nobody seems to remember that Bryce was being an idiot for doing that in the first place. No, all they remember is that Noah told on him."

"And that's all they're ever going to remember," Syd said, her tone dead serious. She tilted her head a little. "You like this guy?"

"I...I don't know. He's a friend. That's all. And barely that—he's my manager."

She sighed. "You know this is a hard one to take sides on, don't you? I don't care how long ago it was, it was still pretty sucky for him to tell on Bryce. And you know Bryce is going to be pissed."

"I know. And I'm not asking you to take sides. Just please, *please* don't say anything to Bryce or to Court. Just pretend like it didn't happen, that's all I ask."

"Mistake."

"Maybe. Still—please trust me."

She sighed heavily. "Okay. You like him. I know you do. I

mean, look at him—he's tall, dark, and hot. What happened to him, anyway? I remember him being this scrawny guy who couldn't put two words together, not even when Bryce was cussing him out."

I brushed away the memory of Bryce screaming at Noah. Even if we were only in ninth grade, and even if getting kicked off the team meant he lost his position for a while, Bryce had acted like a jerk toward him. I didn't want to admit it then, or really even now, but it was true. And it made me wonder, if Maggie ended up in my position as starting pitcher, would I hate her as much? I had to hope not.

"You really think Noah's hot?" I asked as we got into Syd's blisteringly hot car. She cranked on the air so high it almost swallowed her words.

"Oh yeah. Great eyes. Too bad he kept them hidden for so long."

And just like that, everything was okay again. Bryce and Court would be a different story, of that I was sure. But maybe they didn't have to know. Not for a while, at least. Having Syd know about Noah was enough, and it was such a relief, like someone popped a couple of the overfilled balloons in my chest. I could breathe again.

At least until I got home.

As soon as I tried to sneak back in the house, my mother was waiting for me, arms crossed. Grandma sat in her chair, her face unusually grim. *Uh-oh.*

"What is wrong with you?" my mother yelled. "You were supposed to be upstairs resting."

"I know, I'm sorry. I just couldn't miss practice."

"I was so worried. I took a cup of tea to your room and you weren't even in there."

Tea? Oh, man...

"Do you know how scared I was?"

"I know, I'm really sorry. I left a note on my bed."

"Yes, a note that told me you were going back to that practice where you got hurt in the first place. That was supposed to make me feel better?"

And the award for World's Worst Daughter...

She crossed her arms tightly, as if doing so would press down all the anger and hurt inside. "Sorry isn't good enough. I'm going to have to pull you from softball during the summer."

The grief inside me at hurting my mother turned into a bitter knot in my chest. "Mom, you can't do that." I fought to keep my voice level.

"I can and I am. You need to understand—"

"The only thing I understand is that my coach will replace me as pitcher if you do this. Permanently."

"You're overreacting."

"No, I'm not. I already know they've been talking about it because I've missed too many practices for my stupid job."

"You'll just have to deal with it."

I stared first at her, then at my grandma, who was wearing a sympathetic expression but didn't say anything. What could she say? When my mother made up her mind, nothing could change it. I turned and stomped up the stairs to my room, slamming the door behind me. Unbelievable. Yes, I got that it was wrong not to tell my mother where I was going. I didn't blame her for being mad. But canceling my entire summer's softball practice?

I peeled off my clothes and slipped a T-shirt over my head. Now what? I could text Syd—she'd be mad as hell on my behalf. I opened up my text messages and started scrolling, hesitating at the sight of Noah's name. I opened the conversation and typed.

I'm grounded from softball the rest of the summer. Thanks a lot Mom.

Another minute later before his response came. *The entire summer? Why?*

Because I sneaked out today.

Oh. That sucks.

Tell me about it.

A tap on the door sounded. It didn't take long—it never did. My grandma was always good for a hug. I walked to the door and opened it.

My mother. Great.

I crossed my arms. "What? Screwing up my life not enough now?"

"Well, I'd like to talk to you if you can put your attitude on hold for a few minutes."

She pushed past me to walk over to my bed, crossing her legs elegantly as she sat. "I don't know what's gotten into you lately," she said, and her voice had lost its edge. More tired than anything. Her eyes were pink-tinged—had she cried?

"Nothing's gotten into me."

"Then why the rebellious act?"

I groaned and sank down next to her on the bed. "Look, Mom, you of all people should know how important softball is to me."

I threw the "of all people" without really meaning it. She never did understand, and I didn't expect her to. But she nodded anyway.

"I know. And I've been supportive of it."

I decided to ignore that. If she was feeling supportive now, I didn't want to ruin it. "Look, I'm already missing some practices because of my job, and with our tournament coming up in a few weeks, I can't afford to miss more. Holly showed up at work the other day with Maggie Martin and said Coach is going to replace me with Maggie if I keep missing practices. Permanently. And I believe it. She's already gotten better this summer, and Coach doesn't accept excuses for being late. If I don't show, I'm going to lose my spot as primary pitcher or even get kicked off the team completely. All the work I did for nothing. And then forget about being team captain next year."

My voice cracked. It was like I could see my dreams dissolving into a cloud of dust. Coach Santiago was probably a nice guy off the fields, but understanding was not in his nature.

Mom stared at the floor for a couple minutes, not speaking. "If I were to let you go back to practice," she said slowly, "would you stop acting like the world's against you and try being a part of this family again? Actually help out with Aurora's pageant needs and stop complaining about them?"

My heart fluttered to hear her say "back to practice." I barely registered what she was saying about being part of the family again, but I nodded earnestly.

She sighed and put an arm around my shoulders. I leaned into her, trying not to inhale too much of her strong flowery perfume. The hug felt good. Not as comfortable or familiar as Grandma's, but still nice.

"And I'm taking you shopping this weekend whether you like it or not. Your underwear is fraying at the edges."

She lifted the hem of my T-shirt slightly and clicked her tongue. I tugged it down to cover myself, but she was already standing to leave. She hesitated. "I hope you know that I love you," she said quickly. "I may not always say it, but I do."

She closed the door softly and left me alone. My phone buzzed. I picked it up to see a text from Noah.

Are you okay?

I inhaled deeply and texted him back. *Yep. Softball is still on. =)*

I set the phone down and stared at the closed door. My mother's words were unusually kind and sincere. Not in the form of a backhanded compliment, not followed up with snark or even a comparison to Rory. For the moment, I could pretend I was just as important in my mother's life as my perfect sister. For the moment, I could believe she accepted me for exactly who I was. And though I knew it would only last until the next time I disappointed her, I relished the tenderness.

I n the morning, I found Grandma sitting in her chair downstairs, toothbrush in her hand as she watched TV. I gently removed it from her grip, startling her. "I think you forgot to leave this in the bathroom."

She glanced at the brush. "Odd," she mumbled, turning her gaze back to the screen. I shook my head and ran the toothbrush upstairs to her bathroom, then headed back down to the kitchen, past Rory at the counter where she was eating pancakes. My mother was arguing with my dad, which was becoming the norm around here.

She turned to me as I sat at the table. "By the way, Alexis, I need you at Rory's pageant in a couple weeks."

"I can't—I'm working. SmartMart, remember?" I smiled inwardly—*thank you, O Scheduling Gods of SmartMart, for making sure I work every Saturday.* "Hey Dad, is Grandma taking the medicine when she's supposed to?"

He nodded. "Yes, but honey, remember, the medicine is part of a clinical trial. It's not supposed to cure her."

I ignored him. He always told me not to get my hopes up, but the doctors thought it would help, so I believed them. That's why they were doctors, for heaven's sake.

Mom snapped her fingers between us. "Still talking here. You'll just have to call off work. Rory needs you."

"I can't just call off. It doesn't work that way."

She took a deep breath and closed her eyes. "It's a job, Alexis. Call in sick or something."

"This isn't kindergarten, Mom. If I'm scheduled, I need to show up. I have responsibilities." I wasn't opposed to calling in if I really needed or wanted to, but definitely not for some stupid pageant. No way.

She didn't say anything for a minute. Then her lips pulled slowly upward. I was in shock—was that an *approving* kind of smile? She tilted her chin slightly toward my dad, who was nodding at me. "See?" she said triumphantly to him. "I told you, this has been the best possible thing for Alexis. She's finally learning responsibility."

My momentary elation at their pride in me faded as the curves of her mouth slipped into a straight line across her face. "Honey, I'm glad you're taking your job seriously, really I am. But I'm afraid I don't have any choice. I need you at the pageant. Remember your promise to support your sister when I allowed you to continue with softball. Find someone to cover your shift."

I glanced at my dad—the guy who always preached the importance of a strong work ethic should have my back, right? But my mother also turned to him, her face tense with expectation. *Come on, Dad, don't give in.*

Dad shook his head. "Lexie, go with your mother and sister to the pageant. And Meredith," he said, turning to my mother, "hire another coach or get your sister to help or something, but next pageant leave Lexie out of it if she doesn't want to go."

"But my job—" I started, until he held up his hand.

"You have plenty of notice to give your shift away. You need to be there to support Rory. Do it for your sister."

I dug my fingernails into my fists so hard that I was sure the skin would break. "First you guys stick me at SmartMart where I didn't want to be in the first place, then you try to keep me from working my shift. Talk about setting me up for success."

I turned and stomped out the door. My mother I understood—she was always like that—but now Dad? And how was I supposed to get out of work? I never even asked for my softball practices. I didn't know what the protocol was for getting someone to cover a shift. It's not like I'd been there long enough to ask.

The next day, I dutifully asked a couple of my coworkers if they were off that next Saturday, but they were working already. I happily called my mother with the news that I couldn't get out of my shift.

I tried.

I couldn't.

End of story.

Except…

I knew my mother really wanted me to join her at the pageant, but I didn't realize to what extent she'd go to arrange it. I never thought she'd go that far. Not even her.

CHAPTER
14

I wasn't the first person to find out what my mother had done. Or even the second. By the time the scheduling manager, Damon, called me into the office after lunch, I was noticing smirks and hearing snickers from other employees. Most of them hid their grins behind their hands, but their eyes were fixed on me. I stopped by the mirror in the hall, but everything seemed okay—hair pulled back into a ponytail as usual, no lip gloss on my teeth, nothing weird. I went into the office and sat down as Damon pulled out the schedule.

"So we've covered your shift on Saturday," he said, showing me the spreadsheet where my name was marked through with a red *X*. "Roxanne agreed to pick it up. I suggest you thank her."

"Covered my shift?" I asked, the words coming out slowly. "But I didn't ask Roxanne." Or Damon. Truthfully,

I had only asked about three or four people, and I never would've asked Roxanne even if there was a game I was dying to go to and she was the last person at SmartMart. "Cold day in hell" didn't even begin to cover it.

"I asked her for you," he said. "When your mom called Mr. Hanson, he asked me to find someone to cover your shift." He ran his hands over his bald head, his face growing stern as my mind tried to process what he just said. "Listen, Alexis, I know you're new here and you're still in high school, but in the future, if you need to change your schedule, please handle it by finding someone yourself or asking me. I'm the scheduling manager and that's my job, okay?"

Damon stood, but I didn't move. My *mother* called Mr. Hanson? Of all the things she could've done…

"Are you okay?" he asked as I stared at his desk, unmoving.

Okay? No, I was mortified. I stood slowly and walked out of the office. Judging by people's reactions to me this morning, Damon hadn't exactly kept it a secret.

I zombie-walked toward my register, barely nodding at Carmen as I relieved her. I did notice the sympathetic look she threw me. Another tally mark in my head for someone else who was in on it.

I was going to let my mother have it when I got home.

Ruthie was bagging for me today. She didn't laugh behind her hand or even give me a compassionate smile. She wasn't that subtle. But she knew about what happened—oh yes, she did.

"Your mom called Mr. Hanson," she told me matter-of-factly. Loudly, too, causing another associate to giggle as she walked by.

I wanted to crawl into one of Ruthie's bags. "Yeah, I know. I wish Damon hadn't told everyone."

"Damon didn't tell everybody," she said. "Roxanne did."

I stared at her. This shouldn't surprise me at all, as much as Roxanne seemed to hate me. "What exactly did she say, Ruthie?"

Ruthie straightened. "She said it like this: 'Lexus's mommy called Mr. Hanson because Lexus wanted to get out of her shift. Lexus couldn't do it herself because she's a stinking spoiled brat.'" She grinned, proud of her perfect imitation of Roxanne's whiny voice.

"Stinking spoiled brat, huh?" I set my jaw.

"I'm sorry," she said, her smile fading. "That wasn't very nice of her to say, was it?"

I shook my head. "No, it wasn't, but it's not your fault." I smiled at her, and she appeared relieved, but inside I was seething. Leave it to Roxanne to tell everyone. I didn't know what she had against me, but I was going to find out.

Ten minutes later, I saw Roxanne heading toward the employee door. I flicked off my register light. Thankfully there was nobody in line right now.

"I'll be back, Ruthie," I told her. "Go bag for Bessie or someone."

I walked through the break room and into the bathroom after Roxanne had gone inside. I leaned against the sink to wait, but at the last minute grabbed some paper towels and shoved them into the sink's faucet. A childish thing

I wouldn't have even done as a child, but it seemed to fit the situation here. *Take that, Roxanne.* Soon, I heard the toilet flush and Roxanne appeared, her eyes narrowing when she saw me. "What do you want?" she asked harshly, sidestepping me to wash her hands.

As soon as she turned on the water, it sputtered and sprayed sideways, right into her shirt. She jumped, cursing, as the paper towels fell into the sink. Shaking her arms out, she glared daggers at me. "You dumb bitch!" It was a total overreaction—she wasn't even that wet.

I shrugged. "You think I'm a stinking spoiled brat, so I may as well act like one."

She grabbed the wet paper towels and threw them at my head, which I easily ducked to avoid. "Your aim sucks," I said calmly. Probably better if I'd have yelled back at her, because my coolness seemed to anger her more. She picked up the bathroom soap dispenser and threw it at me, grazing my shoulder hard. It clattered against the tile.

"What is your problem, anyway?" I asked, kicking the soap dispenser back at her. The bottle hit her in the shin.

Her lips flattened. I was sure steam was going to roll out of her ears. "You're my problem. You and people like you." She looked at me with her face pinched. "Thinking you're so much better than everyone else because you have Daddy's money. Just another dumb blond cheerleader. I had enough of your type in high school. I don't need your shit at work."

Nothing against cheerleaders, but I was really getting sick of her calling me that. "I'm not a cheerleader. And just because you were bullied in high school or whatever doesn't mean you can bully me here."

She shook her head. "You are just like the rest of them. You and your precious golden locks and your precious BMWs." I opened my mouth to say I didn't own a BMW, until I remembered that my dad did.

"Jealousy doesn't look good on you," was all I could think of to say.

She snorted. "Jealous? Yeah, bitches like you would—"

A sound at the door made us both turn. Carolyn, the manager, was staring at us, her eyes shocked. "What the..." Carolyn's eyes traveled over the wet paper towels and soap dispenser leaking pink fluid on the tile. Her face screwed up in anger. "Clean up this mess. Now!" she barked as she rotated on a heel and left us.

I picked up the wet paper towels and tossed them in the trash, then turned and walked out, letting her deal with the soap on the floor. No way was I staying in the bathroom with Batshit Cheerleader-Hater from Hell.

I went back to my register, but it wasn't long before Mr. Hanson appeared, beckoning to me. Roxanne was behind him, her face sour. We followed him to his office, past Noah, who had a mixture of confusion and amusement on his face. I rolled my eyes at him as we went into Hanson's office.

CHAPTER
15

The good news: I wasn't fired.

The absolutely-horrible-almost-rather-be-fired news: Mr. Hanson felt that since Roxanne and I trashed the employee bathroom and used "potty words," as Carolyn told him, and because we obviously needed to "hone our teamwork skills," our punishment should fit the crime. It was just a couple of paper towels and some soap, but the way Carolyn described it, we were in the middle of a war zone.

So, for the next three weeks, we were put on employee bathroom duty together. Mr. Hanson gave us a list of our chores, making me feel ten years old again, and put Linda Munson, the Cleanliness Queen of SmartMart, in charge of showing us what to do. From the sign she had posted on the bulletin board about washing our hands before working to the time she freaked out over someone in the break room using the same knife in both the peanut butter and jelly jars, Linda seemed like such a germaphobe that I had a feeling HAZMAT suits would be needed as part of our uniform.

I hated cleaning bathrooms. Rory was a pig, and my mother gave me the honor of cleaning both of our bathrooms, since I was older and supposedly able to use chemicals that she was not. So those bathrooms were bad enough, but the employee restrooms—I wondered if anyone ever cleaned them.

And Roxanne—oh, Roxanne was pissed off, to say the least.

"I hate bathrooms," she muttered under her breath as we followed Linda to the break room. Of course, her single statement was punctuated with the F-bomb and other "potty" words, as Mr. Hanson called them. "This is your <insert parental insult> <insert curse word> <insert threat of death> fault."

I ignored her.

Linda opened the little closet in the bathroom. "Put these on," she said, tossing each of us a pair of latex gloves. She took out a pair of cotton ones, slipped them on her own hands, and pointed to the toilet paper dispenser. "Replace the toilet paper when low, keeping a spare just above it. Soap dispenser refill is in the closet—it always must be full. Use the sponge on the top shelf for the sink. Scrub the tile every day with the sponge on the bottom shelf. Use the bowl brush for the toilet. I want to see my face in the reflection of the bowl."

I started snickering at that, and I could see Roxanne

biting her lip to prevent a grin, though her look turned evil when she caught my eye. So much for "we're in this together" camaraderie.

The nasty bathroom duty made me dread going to work every day. As soon as I got home each night, I stripped my clothes off and took the hottest shower I could stand. And since Mr. Hanson made sure we had shifts together, which were labeled *Bathroom Duty* on the posted schedule, that meant having to listen to Roxanne's constant bitching and snide comments. In my mind, I pictured a big red IGNORE button that I'd push every time she'd say something.

"Your hair is so thick and coarse, you must have to use a lot of grease on it."

IGNORE

"I never realized how big your nose is. I could drive a car up that thing."

IGNORE

"Here, you do the floor." She tossed the scrub sponge at me. "You don't have to worry about breaking your nails, since they're so short and scraggly in the first place."

IGNORE

"I bet you have a hard time finding a two-piece bathing suit, seeing as how your top half is twice the size of your bottom."

"At least I *have* a top half." The words slipped out before I could pull them back. Roxanne's eyes narrowed, and she kicked the bucket of water toward me, smirking as it sloshed all over my uniform. My shift was almost over anyway, so I didn't care.

By the time Friday got here, I couldn't wait to go hang out

with my friends and not give SmartMart a second thought. Syd and I managed to pry Court away from Bryce for the evening so we could go walk around the city of Tampa for a girls' night. Tampa wasn't big like Miami-big, but it was huge for those of us from a neighboring town with a population under fifteen thousand. We piled into Court's convertible, put the top down, and cranked the music up.

We ate pizza, strolled around the district of Ybor City for a bit and got some ice cream, but it was late so most of the shops were closed. Court then drove us downtown where most of the nightclubs were located, but considering we weren't old enough to get in, it wasn't as fun as I thought it would be. We were about to give up and go home when I saw a black sign hanging over a doorway across the street with "Cooper's" printed on it in familiar white block letters. It looked like a bar.

"Hang on, guys." I threaded my way through the cars to the other side. The smaller print under the name on the sign announced, "A Bitchin' Good Time."

I stepped up to the doorway and peered into the smoke-filled, crowded room, then stepped all the way in. Leather-clad men and women were crowded around small tables, drinking their beers and laughing. I could hear Court and Syd calling me, but I ignored them.

"Hey, honey, you lost?" A woman wearing a short leather skirt and black Cooper's shirt with tattoos snaking down her arms walked over to me. She had a nametag that said "Yvette."

"Sorry, I'm leaving." I started to head back out into the

fresh air when I noticed the tall dark-haired bartender with the friendly grin. He was talking to another bartender and pouring something amber-colored into shot glasses.

What the hell?

Keeping my eyes fixed on him, I pushed my way forward, past Yvette and the customers, until I squeezed into an open spot at the bar. Noah's face froze when he saw me. For a moment we stared at each other, then his eyes dropped to the glass in front of him. His hands seemed to shake as he poured something from a blue bottle into the glass and mixed it with something from a soda gun.

He handed the drink to a customer, then turned to me, his face stone-cold.

"Well?" I asked, refusing to be intimidated. This was Noah Grayson, a seventeen-year-old boy, who was definitely not old enough to be doing this job. Syd told me the only work she could get at Chili's was hostess because she was too young to serve alcohol.

"What are you doing here?" he asked in a hard voice.

"What am *I* doing here? Are you serious? What are *you* doing here? Aren't you supposed to be twen—"

He held up his hand to stop me, scowling. "Go outside."

"No."

His mouth dropped open. "No?"

"Not until you talk."

He closed his eyes. "Fine. Outside, though. I'll be there in five."

I nodded and turned to see Court and Syd staring at me. Court waved toward me as if to call me outside, and Syd's eyes were roving around the bar, her face almost frightened. It was then that I noticed that all the people looked...well, scary, honestly. All tattoos and beards and leather—and many of them had stopped to look at me. *Not one of us* was written clearly on their faces.

"Can I help you?" a woman with a spiky collar asked me. I realized I was staring at her.

"Sorry," I mumbled, backing away.

"A little young, aren't you?" a man's voice behind me thundered. I kept my eyes glued to the floor and pushed my way back through the smoke out to the street. Immediately, hands pulled me aside.

"Are you crazy? What were you doing in there?" Syd shouted in my ear. Court yelled pretty much the same thing. They were giving me a headache. I pushed away from them when I saw Noah appear from the alley around the corner. Court would see him now, but how long was I going to keep this up, anyway?

"Give me a second, please, guys," I said over my shoulder as I walked to meet him. "Hey," I said, as if I were just checking in for a shift at SmartMart. He looked so different in his jeans and black shirt, his arms crossed, wearing a scowl instead of his usual pleasant expression. His hair was gelled slightly to give the front an interesting lift. Not bad, just...different. Which made me wonder which was the real Noah—this badass-looking bartender or the sweet manager at SmartMart.

"Hey." His eyes were focused on Syd and Court. I turned to see them staring at us, Syd shaking her head and Court with her mouth wide open. I knew they thought I'd lost my mind, but I didn't care.

"They won't say anything," I told him. His eyes moved back to meet mine. He looked so worried that I felt myself soften. "I won't say anything, either."

"What are you doing here?"

"Just walking around. We were about to leave, actually, and I saw the sign. It matched your shirt from the other day, so I figured something was up."

"Detective Lex. Nice." His face relaxed into the usual shy smile, but he didn't say anything else.

"Don't you have to be twenty-one to bartend?" I prompted him.

"Eighteen," he corrected. "And I turn eighteen in November."

"Yeah, but how…"

He rubbed at his arm, looking around nervously. "They think I'm eighteen already. I might've put the wrong year on the application by accident."

The idea of smart, straight-acting Noah Grayson lying on his job application was shocking to me. I couldn't help but laugh.

"What?" he asked.

"You don't seem like the lying type."

"What type am I?"

"I don't know," I said. I waved my arm toward the wall behind me. "Not the work-in-a-bar-full-of-motorcycle-guys-and-tattooed-people type. Do you have one? A tattoo, I mean?"

"Maybe."

My heart thudded harder. I had said it as a joke, but the possibility of him having a tattoo hiding somewhere was definitely...interesting. "You're kidding," I said, not liking how my voice cracked.

"Maybe," he said again. "Just because we work together doesn't mean you know everything about me."

True. But I was ready to rectify that little problem. "What if I wanted to know more about you?" I challenged.

He tilted his head slightly to study me, his eyes suddenly wary. Not even the tiniest hint of a smile. Did he not trust me? Crap, and here I thought he wanted to ask me out before. Maybe I was wrong.

At that moment, the side door to the bar opened. A bearded guy wearing a black Cooper's shirt emerged carrying a bag of trash, which he threw into the bin next to us. "Getting busy in there, Grayson," he said gruffly. He looked at me, then turned back to the bar.

"I've got to get inside," Noah said as the guy disappeared. "You promised you wouldn't say anything, right? Not even to your friends?" he asked. "Other than them." He nodded at Syd and Court, who were still watching us from afar like we were part of some reality show. "I'm guessing they figured it out."

My heart sank. All he cared about was me not telling anyone that he worked at this bar. He didn't have any response to what I said about getting to know him better. He didn't even look interested, just cautious. "Of course I won't say anything," I said, trying to keep my voice light.

"Neither will they. But you better give me the full scoop later, okay?" His eyebrows pinched at that. I quickly added, "About the job, I mean."

His face relaxed. "Oh. Yeah, sure. You got it. I'll see you tomorrow?"

I nodded. "My shift starts at ten."

I watched him head toward the bar's side door, and when he turned back to wave at me, I dropped my gaze quickly like I'd been caught staring at his butt. Okay, so maybe I was staring. "Get a grip, it's Noah Grayson," I muttered to myself. "Just a good buddy who apparently wants to remain that way." I turned back to my friends.

"What was *that* all about?" Court asked, her face awed.

I rubbed my eyes, suddenly very tired. This was the longest day ever. "Nothing. Can we just go home?"

"No, I want to know. Who is that guy?"

I stared at her. We weren't standing that far away—couldn't she tell that was Noah?

Then I remembered that I had spoken with the guy a few times my first day at SmartMart and hadn't even recognized him. Talk about clueless.

"I already told you," Syd said to Court. "That guy just works with Lex at SmartMart. I guess he bartends here part-time, too." She raised an eyebrow at me and I nodded. "Anyway, let's go. I'm so freaking tired. Are we going shopping tomorrow, by the way?"

That caught Court's attention. "Yeah, I need some new jeans and a phone case—mine's beat up."

Syd winked at me conspiratorially as Court went on

about things she needed to buy. I smiled halfheartedly at her. I knew Syd still had reservations about the whole thing, though what that "whole thing" was, I had no idea. Noah's only reaction to me saying I wanted to get to know him was suspicion and a total lack of enthusiasm. I guess Syd thought that telling Court about Noah and risking her running to Bryce with the news would threaten what Noah and I had.

Which was absolutely nothing at all.

CHAPTER 16

At SmartMart the next day, the display on the time clock showed that I was ten minutes early for my shift. Mr. Hanson didn't like us clocking in more than a couple minutes before our scheduled shift, since he said it added up to too much overtime. I went to the bulletin board to check out my rotation. Today I would be on the floor with Carolyn as the manager. And, of course, my hour in the stupid bathroom was penciled in. Lovely.

"Lexus!" Ruthie's voice sang out. She went into her usual chatter about her father's Lexus. Remembering Noah's story about her father, I turned and smiled as big as I could.

"Hi, Ruthie!"

Her eyes lit up, and it occurred to me to wonder if Ruthie knew I had been less than enthusiastic about seeing her before. I hoped not.

"Where are you working today?" she asked. "Are you with me at the door?"

"No, I'm in the grocery section." Her face fell. I added, "I'd much rather work with you at the door." That made her grin again. It was so easy to make her happy. But it was true, too. I'd take the Cart Game over working the sales floor under Carolyn's supervision. I walked with her back to the time clock.

"Me, too! Okay, I'm going on break. See you later," she sang, typing in her code and walking to the break room.

Bessie appeared from around the corner. "That was sweet of you, Alexis," she said quietly. She reminded me of the Blue Fairy from Pinocchio who granted wishes when you did something right.

"What was sweet?"

"You and Ruthie. You've really taken to her, just like everyone else."

"Yeah, I guess I have."

"You've got a good heart. I know Noah thinks so."

My heart fluttered at that. "Noah?"

"Yes. I can tell about you two, and just so you know, I give you my full stamp of approval." She winked at me.

"We're just friends," I said. The worst part was that it sounded like an excuse, and it really wasn't.

"I'm sure." She smiled, then glanced at the clock. "What time does your shift start?"

I looked down—I was now three minutes late. "Crud." I punched in my numbers quickly.

"Don't worry about it. You're already on bathroom detail—I don't think they'll punish you further." Bessie walked off, whistling happily. I had to admit, there was something about Bessie's wit and kindness that did remind me of my grandma. It made me want to hug her and throw things at the same time. How unfair was life to take someone as wonderful and loved as my grandma and destroy her mind? Life could really suck.

On the floor, I found Carolyn sorting out cans of tuna. "You've been trained in Grocery," she said in her scratchy voice. "You should know what to do. Come bother me if you have real issues."

I moved to the back of the store, as far from her as I could get, and started organizing the soda bottles.

"Hey, there," Noah said next to me. I jumped at the sound of his voice and dropped a two-liter bottle of soda on my foot.

"Owww! Shit!" I cried out, ignoring the look of disgust from a passing shopper.

"Oh, jeez, I'm sorry," he said, picking up the bottle and setting it on the shelf. "Are you okay?"

I wiggled my toes in my shoe. Not broken. "I think so. Warn me if you're coming up behind me like that."

"Okay. I'm sorry."

His lips pursed nervously as his hand moved to fiddle with something on the shelf. I couldn't help but remember how he looked last night—so confident. It was strange now—like talking to Clark Kent after finding out he's actually Superman.

A customer walked up to him to ask about yogurt, so I moved over one aisle to the paper products section. A few minutes later, Noah appeared, taking care to warn me in a loud, exaggerated whisper before he got too close. I whipped around with a couple packages of toilet paper in my arms and tossed them at him. "Think fast!" He smiled and put the packages on the shelf. I thought about setting up the packages for bowling, but I had a feeling Noah wouldn't be up for it. There was a tightness around his eyes that wasn't there before I saw him at the bar.

For a few minutes, he helped me organize the shelves, which weren't that disorganized in the first place. I couldn't get that strange look of his last night out of my head when I suggested I'd like to get to know him. Why was he hanging around me? Unless he was trying to be BFFs or something. I had Bryce and Syd—I wasn't really looking for another BFF. But I'd take friends over nothing.

I finally turned to him. "I clearly remember Carolyn being scheduled as the manager on duty for this section."

He smiled slightly, but his eyes were serious. "I wanted to talk about last night," he said, his voice not exactly quiet. A guy walking nearby snickered at that. Noah's face reddened. "Sorry, I mean, um…"

"I get it, okay?" I looked around, but the guy had already turned out of the aisle. "You have my number. You can call me later." *Because that's what BFFs do, right?*

"You have your game still, right?"

"Yeah. Are you coming?"

He nodded. "Yeah. If that's still okay."

I bit my lip. If he came to the game, Bryce would see him. Visions of Bryce chasing Noah around the field with a baseball bat were already haunting me. Did I really want to tempt fate? Although it might be easier to explain being "just friends" to Bryce than if Noah and I were actually more.

"I don't have to if you don't want me to," he said quickly.

"No, I want you to. It's just...the games are kind of boring."

"Boring?" He frowned. "That's not it, is it?"

Bryce will be there and will want to kick your ass. Every-one you hate will probably be there. I don't want to cause open season on you.

Nothing I could say would fix this, so I put on my brightest smile and said, "I want you to be there. Definitely."

He nodded, though he didn't look convinced. "Okay. Seven o'clock, right?"

"Yes."

"Do you need a ride?"

I shook my head. "I have one, but thanks."

Noah nodded again and walked away. It was almost funny that my initial worries about working at SmartMart were about being considered a freak, like the oily-haired lady who just ripped open the toilet paper package to rub her face on the tissue. Gross. I turned my back on her and went to the next aisle. Now I had to worry about this, too. But then, as Grandma said, it was everyone else's problem with Noah, not mine.

CHAPTER
17

I didn't see Noah at my game, though I did think I spotted his old SUV at one point, but I couldn't find him in the stands. I did get a text from him that evening: *Great game.*

Great game? So he *was* there. *I didn't see you in the stands.*

I was on the other side.

Oh. Thanks. Knowing he was there, watching me play, made my heartbeat skip a little faster, even if it was just a friend thing. Maybe by sitting on the other side he was avoiding trouble with Bryce, who *was* sitting in the stands. I didn't know.

Sunday was the Fourth of July. I spent the morning hanging at the house with my grandma, who seemed fine except for when she forgot where she put something, and once it looked like she was going to make tea but changed her mind and left the stove on. I found out and quickly shut it off before my parents realized it.

In the afternoon, I went to the beach with a bunch of friends. We played volleyball in the sand and grilled hot dogs and went swimming, and the entire time I tried not to notice the feeling that something was missing. I wanted Noah here with me. I wanted to lie next to him on the sand and talk about life and freaky SmartMart shoppers and anything that made us laugh. And maybe he'd see that I wasn't just an employee or a friend, because the longer I thought about it, the more I let my thoughts entertain what it'd be like to be more.

I wasn't scheduled at SmartMart until Tuesday, so Bryce and I spent Monday morning practicing at the field. Coach had asked him if he could help Maggie pitch, too, but Bryce told him he didn't have time. I knew he only said that for my sake.

"Don't worry about Maggie," he said as he slipped the glove over his hand. "She's nowhere near as good as you, and Coach Santiago knows it. Seriously, she can't even throw a fast pitch."

I smiled at him. I didn't think Maggie was as bad as that, but I appreciated his support anyway. "Thanks, Bryce."

"How's SmartFart going now? Any better?"

"A little better, yeah."

"So my mom and I were there last night and guess who I saw?"

"Who?"

"That douchebag, Noah Grayson."

My throat went dry as Bryce frowned at me. "Why didn't you tell me he was working there?"

I shrugged. "Not a big deal. He's one of the managers. Did you, um, talk to him?" I knew my voice shook a little, but Bryce didn't seem to notice. He tossed the ball into the air and hit it with his bat.

"Hell no. I was tempted to knock over that display of cereal he was working on, though." He chuckled.

Seriously? I loved Bryce, but really? The mental image of Noah scrambling to pick up cereal boxes while Bryce laughed on the side was too much. "Real mature, Bryce. Yeah, and before you open your mouth, I know he ratted you out in ninth grade. But oh my God, that was two years ago. When are you going to get over it?"

Bryce's arms dropped to his sides, the bat hitting the ground with a thud. "Are you serious? You think I should forgive this guy for screwing up my life? Did you know Coach didn't even know about the spray-painting until he went and told? It wasn't like they were torturing him or giving him an ultimatum. He didn't have to do it. He just did."

Bryce's face was red now—jeez, any mention of Noah really set him off. I didn't want to argue with him—especially considering he was using his own time to help me pitch. "Okay, okay. Forget I said anything."

His eyes narrowed as he stared at me. "You don't talk to him, do you?"

I tossed the ball I was holding into the air. Catch, toss, repeat. "He's a manager. I have to talk to him sometimes."

"But you don't hang out with him at work?"

I laughed nervously. "No."

Technically, I hung out with Noah on break, not during working hours. It was crappy justification, but I couldn't bring myself to tell Bryce we were friends. Not with the way he was acting—all tense and annoyed. Why make things harder for all three of us?

But the better, decent part of me felt like I just ran Noah over with a semi. I completely played off our friendship like it meant nothing. Maybe Noah had good reason not to want to be more than friends with me.

The rest of the week at work was okay. Noah and I even joked here or there about some of the weird SmartMart customers who came into the store, but the guilt ate at me for not telling Bryce we were friends. I tried to avoid being around him whenever I could. It just hurt too much. The whole thing sucked, honestly, because the one thing SmartMart had going for it before was that I was able to talk and flirt with Noah. But since he had no interest in going out with me, and since I made it clear to Bryce that I barely talked to the guy, we were doomed to remain in the Friend Zone. It wasn't that long ago that I actually hoped he'd stay there.

Talk about irony.

Grandma shook her head when I told her about the whole situation. "You're playing with fire by keeping all this secret, my girl. Sooner or later it'll blow up in your face. The trick now is to figure out how to balance your relationships going forward."

"There is no relationship with Noah, Grandma. Not like that. I mean, we're friends—just friends."

"Really?" she asked, looking directly into my eyes and making me blush. "Exactly. Honey, you ain't fooling me. You can't just close yourself off to someone because of what other people think. Hearts don't work that way."

"Hearts?"

"Yes, hearts. Our hearts connect with others all the time, the electricity zipping and zapping all over the place. We can't even sense it most of the time, but then we meet The One, and the beat changes ever so slightly to match theirs. That's what they call a match—when the music inside your chest beats in synchronization with the one you're meant to be with. You'll know when it happens."

I waited, but she didn't say anything else. "When what happens?" I finally asked.

"True love." She winked and chucked me under the chin gently. "You'll see."

True love? I smiled and pretended to get it, but honestly, Grandma had such a hippie view of things that I wasn't always sure what she was talking about. No way was I in love with Noah—definitely not. Probably not, anyway.

Friday morning, I woke up almost wishing I were scheduled at SmartMart. It was the only way I could've gotten out of the next two days at the Coastal Princess Pageant. It was six a.m., way too early to be awake, in my opinion.

My dad was already downstairs making coffee for himself and my mother, who was running around the house like a bat out of hell. I raised an eyebrow at the pancakes on the griddle. He smiled. "I feel kind of bad that I'm not going with you, so I thought I'd make you girls some breakfast," he said.

"You feel bad?" I asked skeptically. "Really?"

He winked. "Chocolate chips?"

I nodded and watched as he poured a liberal amount of chocolate pieces into the batter. Rory walked in and squealed when she saw the pancakes.

"Thank you, Daddy," she said, hugging him around the waist. I stifled a giggle at her pre-pageant "look," complete with hair rolled in thick foam curlers and pink fluffy bathrobe. She looked like a tiny version of the crazy cat lady who visited SmartMart every Sunday morning to load her shopping cart with cat food.

Grandma was in the kitchen, too, sitting at the breakfast table with a newspaper in front of her. She wasn't reading it, though, just staring out of the window, her mouth parted slightly. She was wearing her heavy robe, too, which wasn't like her in the summertime. My heart leaped into my throat.

"Good morning, Grandma," I choked out. She didn't turn her gaze from the window. I slipped into the seat next to her, wondering what I could say or do to bring her back.

I sifted through various memories to find something to trigger her mind. Dad had told me it might help.

"How long do you think he's going to keep that up?" she said finally.

I followed her gaze. Mr. McCarthy across the street was watering the sidewalk as he gaped at the fancy red car that was parked on the street.

"I mean, it's a car. Move on already."

I laughed, my entire body relaxing in relief. She was still here. "It's a pretty slick car, though, Grandma." I poured syrup over the pancakes in front of me. "Are you staying home while we're gone?" I asked Dad. Medicine or not, I knew he didn't want Grandma to be alone.

"I can't. I have a meeting this morning. Patty will be here in about an hour, though. She'll stay with Grandma until I come home this afternoon."

Grandma looked at me. "Where are you going?"

"Pageant, Grandma. Rory's in it, remember?"

She waved a hand at me. "Oh yes. Yes, I remember. Are you ready?"

"As ready as I'll ever be." I tucked my hands under my chin with an exaggerated grin.

She laughed, which turned into a hacking cough. She took a drink of water and smiled at me. "Well, have fun." She patted her hair. "I was quite the looker in my day, you know. I bet I could still win a crown or two."

"I bet you could, too," I said, kissing her cheek and noticing that she looked older this morning. Not that she had more wrinkles or gray hair, but there was something that seemed "gray" about her, like her skin had cooled from its usual peachy warmth. "You okay, Grandma?" I asked as she coughed again.

"Oh, sure. Just feeling a little under the weather, but I'm fine."

My mother appeared then, carrying a big plastic bin through the kitchen on the way to the garage. "Alexis, help me carry Rory's stuff to the car."

I rolled my eyes at Grandma, who rolled them right back at me.

The rest of the morning was a whirlwind of preparation, with my mother at the center of it all. Grandma went up to her room during the worst of it. Even my dad, who'd been so happy earlier, looked stressed as my mother ran around the house like a maniac, packing up huge hairpieces, yelling at Rory to get her sparkly earrings, calling me to grab things for her. I threw a T-shirt and jeans into my overnight bag along with a toothbrush and hairbrush, and I was done.

"Break a leg," Dad said to Rory as she moved through the kitchen with several stuffed animals crammed under her arms.

"Don't say that," my mother screeched at him. "This isn't a theater production!"

His eyes widened comically and he held up his hands. "Sorry. What am I supposed to say?"

"Just wish her luck, Jackson. We're in a hurry." She pecked him on the cheek as she passed.

He gave Rory a big hug. "Knock 'em dead, kitten," he whispered to her. Then he turned to me, his Cheshire Cat grin saying it all.

"Yeah, no kidding," I responded.

He laughed and hugged me, too. "Good luck. I'm sure you'll survive. Call me if you have any good stories to tell."

I went upstairs to see Grandma before we left. She was sitting in her chair by the window, gazing out at the street. I leaned over to give her a kiss on the cheek.

"Wish me luck," I said.

She tilted her head, her eyebrows pinched in confusion. "For what?"

I sighed and wrapped my arms around her shoulders. "Nothing. I love you."

"I love you, too," she said.

It was enough for me. I went outside to join my mother and sister in the Tahoe. We were Coastal Princess Pageant-bound, on the road for the five-hour trip to Tallahassee.

We made it to the Marriott in Tallahassee by late afternoon, unloading all the bags and suitcases from the car onto one of the rolling carts. The lobby was big, with a chandelier hanging over the center like a crown. Strangely appropriate.

I recognized my mother's all-important air as she checked in at the front desk. She was hard enough to deal with on a regular day. She was going to be impossible tomorrow. I found myself wishing that Noah were here to be annoyed with. I should've asked him if he was coming, though I had a feeling he was working. Working was a much better choice than listening to little girls and their mothers whine all weekend.

Our room was large enough, but by the time all Rory's

crap was unloaded—mostly by me under orders from Mom to move this box and that suitcase—I'd be lucky to find a spot to sleep. I felt like Cinderella without the fireplace or the promise of a fabulous ball. My mom started unraveling Rory's curlers for some welcome reception that was to take place after dinner. The idea of hanging out in the room with Rory's whining and my mother's demands was unthinkable. I escaped to go for a walk.

Even though it was only five o'clock, the hallways were full of heavily perfumed women with daughters who looked like normal kids now but by tomorrow would be decked out in full pageant regalia. Bellmen ran back and forth with carts loaded down with luggage, boxes, and bags of dresses, wigs, and makeup.

I leaned over the railing on the second floor to stare down into the lobby.

"Hey, Lex."

I whipped around to see Noah and his sister walking toward me. Belle was wearing the cutest little sunflower dress and holding Noah's hand. Noah was wearing jeans and a plain gray T-shirt, looking probably the most relaxed I'd ever seen him. My heart skipped a tiny beat to see him. Okay, so maybe it was more than a tiny beat.

"Hey," I said. I crouched down to smile at Belle. "Hi, Belle!" Her sweet curls were as adorable as the last time I saw her. I hoped they weren't going to stick some ugly wig on her head. "Remember me?"

She nodded and put her arms around my neck. I lifted her up and held her close, noticing that she smelled like sunshine.

Noah watched us. "She doesn't usually go to people like that."

I tilted my head forward and Belle did the same, resting her forehead against mine, her little nose touching mine. Had Rory been this adorable when she was three? I doubted it. "She probably remembers me from that dress store. When did you guys get here?"

"About fifteen minutes ago. My mom is in the room unpacking."

"Yeah, mine, too. My dad was lucky enough to be able to stay home. Is your dad here?"

He frowned. "No."

I rubbed my nose against Belle's, making her giggle. "My mother and sister are sorting through wigs and stuff right now. I had to get out of there."

I set Belle down, and she immediately ran off to peek into a big pot of yellow flowers.

Noah leaned against the balcony railing next to me. "Are we okay?"

"What do you mean?"

"You've been kind of, I don't know, quiet."

"I'm fine," I said, though in my head all I could think was how I lied to Bryce about him. Why did I have to be such a chicken, anyway?

He cleared his voice. "I'm sorry I haven't been totally up-front with you about stuff. Like Cooper's, and...well, other stuff."

I finally looked at him. "Other stuff?"

His gaze cut over to me, but he didn't offer anything more. What other stuff was he talking about? Of course, like he said, I didn't know everything there was to know about him. He had seemed worried about me getting to know him, and at the time, I thought it was because he wasn't interested in me that way. Now I wondered if it was for another reason altogether.

I turned to face him squarely, and though his eyes were on me, he kept his grip on the balcony railing. Not completely closed off to me, but almost. "Noah," I said gently. "Why can't you trust me? Talk to me."

He stared at me for a long time, then finally released his grip to face me. He opened his mouth to speak.

And in the grand clichéd style of the worst movies ever made, my mother and sister showed up to completely annihilate the moment. *Damn it.*

"Alexis Jasmine, what are you doing out here?" my mother asked. "Come on, let's go eat." She turned back to the elevator and jabbed the button, her eyebrows raised at me expectantly.

I groaned as Noah smiled widely. "It's not my fault she named me that, okay?"

He held up his hands, still smiling as I walked past to join my mother and Rory in the elevator.

"Hey, Lex," Noah called. I turned around. "You going to be around after dinner?"

"Yeah. Meet you back here at eight o'clock?" I said the words as the elevator doors closed, so I didn't even know if he heard me or agreed to it. My mother surprisingly didn't say anything about Noah, though she arched her eyebrow at me. Grateful not to have to answer any questions, I stared out the glass of the elevator until we stopped on the first floor.

If my mother hadn't barged in, I would still be there, talking to Noah. He was about to confide in me, I knew it. There was something up with that guy that had nothing to do with me. But then again, he did have Belle, so it's not like we could really have a heart-to-heart while she was exploring all the flowerpots on the second-floor balcony.

Dinner was a buffet in the hotel's restaurant that offered discount coupons to pageant participants. This translated into more than fifty obnoxious women and girls standing in line, each with an "I'm so above this" look on their faces. The look would only last until they reached the food, then they'd dig in like it was their last meal on earth. My favorite was the woman behind me who kept complaining that as the pageant coach for some kid named Shelby, she should be given priority access to the buffet. I pictured her dropping down from the ceiling *Mission: Impossible* style to scoop up the food before everyone else could get some.

"That's Shelby's coach," Rory whispered excitedly. "I wonder if Shelby's eating dinner here tonight."

My mother turned a derisive look on the woman, who I hoped wasn't looking back. "She's probably getting her food for her, like a servant," she whispered to me. She shook her head. "Divas."

I snickered. My mother calling anyone else a diva was what I'd call ironic. But to her credit, she'd never ask to be given priority at a buffet. Some of these women made her look like a saint.

As soon as we were finished with dinner, I wandered aimlessly through the hotel, flicking at plant leaves and checking out the fish in the big lobby tank until eight o'clock finally arrived. I made my way up to the second floor and leaned over the railing.

It was only a couple minutes later when Noah leaned next to me, his arm almost brushing mine. "Hey."

Friend zone or not, my heart still fluttered at his proximity. "Hey." His hair was slightly damp and untidy, like he'd taken a shower and not bothered to brush it. Definitely a good look for him. "Where's Belle?"

"She's with my mom, getting ready for tomorrow."

"Yeah, same with Rory. I didn't see you in the restaurant."

He shrugged. "My mom brought a cooler with cold chicken and fruit from home."

"I bet it was a lot better than the food at the buffet."

The lobby was still busy with people checking in, so we walked through the conference center, stopping to check out the ridiculously tall crowns and sparkly tiaras proudly displayed on a long table.

"Tomorrow's going to suck," I said.

"It's going to be crazy here, that's for sure."

"I wonder if we stacked up all the tiaras and crowns, how long it'd take to knock them down with a bowling ball," I mused.

Noah snorted. "I could knock them over with a baseball."

"I could with a Wiffle Ball."

We went back and forth until Noah won with a single

piece of the worn conference hall carpet. It was a ridiculous game, but strangely hilarious at the same time. We were laughing so hard that the lady watching the table clicked her tongue at us in disapproval.

I grabbed his arm, enjoying the look of surprise on his face. "Come on, let's see if they have anything in the store."

The "store" was nothing more than a tiny gift shop. We idly sorted through shells, postcards, petrified alligator heads, and other "unique" Florida gifts that pretty much every store and gas station in the state carried. We each bought a soda and headed out to the pool. It wasn't a very big area, but there were chairs around and only a couple people actually in the pool. The lounge chairs we chose were near the hot tub, the steam of the tub mixing with the damp in the humid summer evening. The silence between us became awkward, like Noah was trying to think of something to say that would explain his weird distance. Maybe I just needed to start somewhere less intense.

"So," I said cheerfully, "how long have you worked at that creepy-ass Cooper's?"

He laughed and threaded his hands behind his head to stare up at the darkening sky. "Cooper's isn't that bad of a place, actually. I applied there a few months ago after a customer at SmartMart told me about the job. He was a regular at Cooper's and said the bartenders make really good money. He referred me to the bar owner."

"Didn't they check to see how old you are?"

"Um, yeah. I might've had one of my friends make me a fake ID. The manager barely looked at it, just scanned it in with my application."

Ha! A fake ID—Noah wasn't so perfect after all. "But why? I mean, you already have a job at SmartMart. And you could've gotten a job at a restaurant or store or something."

His eyebrows dipped slightly. "Those places don't pay anywhere near what Cooper's does. We need the money. My dad…"

He didn't finish. I didn't ask, though now I was really curious. Was his dad laid off? Or maybe he didn't make much money at all. And why would they do pageants if they didn't have much money? Pageants were expensive—I knew because my dad was always complaining about it. But no way was I going to ask about that.

We sat for a moment without talking, watching a mother dry off her daughter and scoot her toward the exit gate as a man and woman stepped into the pool, holding hands. The woman squealed as the guy pulled her into the water.

"Anyway," Noah said, swinging his legs around so he could sit facing me, "I don't want anyone to know about Cooper's. Mr. Hanson doesn't even know."

"Yeah, but you were wearing the T-shirt in plain sight."

"Trust me, no one would think twice if they saw it. And no one I know would actually go there."

"Does your mom know?"

"Yes. She doesn't like it, but she doesn't have much of a choice. We need the money. Thanks for not telling your friends, by the way. Especially Bryce."

"What do you mean, especially Bryce?"

"Oh, please. Bryce would do anything to turn me in for

something illegal. You know it's true."

Well, that one shut me up. He was probably right, though I still didn't like him making that assumption. It wasn't for him to call my friends out to me. "Look, I get why you don't like Bryce, and I get why he doesn't like you. But you make all these assumptions about everyone else, when you don't even make an effort to get to know them. You sit in the library, hidden behind your stack of books, not talking or even looking at anyone. You think I haven't seen you at school, but I have."

"You think I want to be alone? You think that's my choice?" He shook his head. "You don't know anything about me."

"Then *tell* me," I pleaded, sitting up to face him. We were so close that our knees bumped against each other. "You keep shutting me out, and I don't know why, except maybe because I'm friends with Bryce."

"That's not why." Noah sighed and stared at the pool. "But since we're on the subject, tell me so I understand. What is so great about that guy?"

"Why should I tell you that? You'll always look at him as your enemy, so why should I even bother?"

He didn't answer, just stared at the pool. I cursed silently. I hated justifying my friendships to Noah—I didn't owe him anything. But at the same time, I wasn't doing Bryce any favors by staying quiet.

"Ever since middle school," I started, my voice low, "Bryce has been there to help me with my pitch. I wouldn't have made All-Stars without him. I wouldn't have the chance at the Fastpitch tournament. He's practiced with me almost every week since forever. Without complaining. Not only that, Bryce was the only person who listened to my Olympic dreams and didn't make fun of me." As soon as the words were out, I wanted to pull them back. I didn't talk about that anymore, to anyone.

Noah's eyes widened. "Olympic dreams? You didn't tell me about that."

"Forget it." I shook my head and stared out at the couple who were now starting to make out. Like that was what I wanted to see right now.

"Wait, hang on. What Olympic dreams? For softball?"

I peered over at him, but he didn't look like he was on the verge of laughing or even feeling dumbfounded. He looked more awed than anything, which could've been a trick of the dim lights.

"Yes, for softball. And yes, I get that it's not an Olympic event right now and there's no guarantee that it'll come back and that if anything I'll probably end up coaching girls' softball as best case scenario and I better have a back-up plan." I rushed through the words as Noah slowly smiled. "So go ahead, it's okay—everyone laughs about it." Now that I thought about it, I didn't really want to stay around for him to laugh about it. I was tired.

I got up to walk away, aware by the scraping of the pool chair that Noah was getting up as well. I kept walking, but Noah was faster. He slipped his hand around my wrist to stop me.

"Lex, I think it's the coolest thing I've ever heard."

I stared up at him. Maybe he thought humoring me was the best way to get back on my good side. Damn it, if that was the case, it was working. His eyes were sincere, though, and the sincerity so intense that it sent a shiver through me. Noah of course would know nothing about softball or probably even how hard it would be to make Olympic trials if they did bring it back. But did that even matter?

Noah's hand slid slowly down from my wrist to my hand, his fingers tucking gently through mine. "I think you're amazing."

His hand was warm, which I expected, and comfortable, which I didn't. I guess I thought holding Noah's hand would be like one of those awkward moments in church when you have to hold hands with the stranger next to you during the Lord's Prayer and all you can focus on is not squirming.

And he wasn't laughing at me. Not even a little. I smiled then, and Noah's face lit up. It occurred to me how infrequently I'd seen his smile lately. I'd missed it, and not only that, I'd missed the immediate reaction my body had to it.

Several kids came out to the pool, shouting and laughing and splashing into the water. It turned into a kid free-for-all, so we walked hand in hand back through the pool area into the hotel. I found myself wishing there was somewhere else to go, but the industrial area and nearby construction didn't exactly offer great opportunities for a walk. Noah didn't drop my hand, even when we got into the elevator.

"Floor?" he asked.

"Four."

"Me, too." He punched the button. As the doors closed and the elevator started humming its way up, our proximity to each other in the small space became much more apparent. I gazed up at him; his eyes were already on me. In the gentle whirr of the elevator, we stared at each other.

It was right then, as the space between heartbeats decreased just enough for me to notice, that I realized something about Noah Grayson. It wasn't just a good friend vibe or even a simple attraction. It was a tickle that began in my stomach and slowly spread throughout my body. Whatever this was, it left no doubt in my mind that I felt much more than "just friends" with him. Regardless of the trouble it'd surely cause for me with Bryce, and of the Friend Zone that Noah kept trying to shove me in, I was falling hard for this guy. Although from the way his eyes stayed on me, I had a feeling he was right there with me.

We got out of the elevator and walked down the hallway together, stopping at my door. "Mine's back there," he said, nodding the way we came.

Then came the inevitable awkward moment of standing there, not knowing what to say or do. I had this really strong desire to kiss him. His eyes slid down to my mouth. I stepped forward—just a tiny step, but it was enough. His head bowed as his hand moved to my waist, his touch setting my skin on fire. My eyes closed…

The slam of a nearby door snapped them open again. We jumped apart as a woman walked past us, chuckling softly. Another door down the hall opened and some kids ran past, yelling. What the hell—*now* this floor would be busy?

"All the kids who aren't in the pool must be in this hallway," he muttered as another couple of girls ran out of the elevator, followed by their tired-looking mothers.

"Apparently." I pulled out my room key as the noise level around us increased. It was almost like we were the players in some sadistic game—How Many Potentially Mind-Blowing Moments Can Be Destroyed By Pageant People. "Guess I'll see you in the morning?"

"I'll be here."

The three words were simple, but they shot a thrill of promise through me. He still hadn't confided in me, but I knew it was just a matter of time now. And a matter of time before he'd kiss me. I couldn't handle many more of these near-misses.

I opened the door, closing it behind me softly. The room was dark except for the soft light in the corner where my mother was reading. She lifted a finger to her lips and nodded toward the bed, where Rory was sleeping. I nodded, hoping my madly beating heart wasn't audible to anyone else but me, and moved into the bathroom to splash water on my face.

Noah Grayson. He was my boss. An outsider. Bryce's archenemy. Always so closed off to me. How could I possibly like this guy, much less fall for him?

But underneath all my excuses and questions and worries was one simple truth.

I liked him…

…and more than that.

Much more.

CHAPTER
18

My favorite part of pageants was…well, nothing. From the time the sun came up, my mother became Queen Bee of Pageantry, and Rory was her little princess. Poor Rory had to stand in the tub while my mother sprayed fake tan all over her body. Or maybe *poor* wasn't the word for her, considering she kept telling my mother to spray more, more, and more. I finally took the bottle away and called enough.

After applications of blue eye shadow, fake eyelashes, sparkly body glitter, pink frou-frou dress, and a huge poofy wig, not to mention episodes of "You're not doing this right—you're not doing that right," we were ready to go downstairs. Rory had mentally changed into *Princess Aurora* and was enjoying ordering us around, whereas I, her lowly servant, was ready to throw a chair out the window.

"She looks gorgeous," my mother gushed as Rory twirled around.

I lifted an eyebrow. "She looks like a birthday cake."

She ignored that comment. "Grab those bags and hurry up. We're supposed to be down in a few minutes, and they'll deduct points if we're late."

We shuffled out the door with arms loaded with bags of makeup, costumes, and other crap as Princess Aurora stepped in front of us like she owned the hallway. *Get in line,* I wanted to tell her as other little girls paraded out into the hallway with the same air. We passed Noah's closed door, but I was sure they were already downstairs for the three-year-old competition.

We registered at a table set up in the hallway outside the conference rooms. My mother announced Rory's name importantly, accepted her credentials, then migrated over to another table that had a banner of a national television network.

"Look at this," she said, tisking at a flier that announced casting calls for an extreme couponing show. "Like anyone really wants to put themselves on TV for that?"

I thought of my experience with the savage coupon lady at SmartMart. She would probably jump at the chance to show everyone how to save an obscene amount of money with an obscene amount of coupons.

"Oh, look, Alexis," she said, moving to the next flier. Her voice was lighter and much more enthusiastic. "*Pageant Moms* is looking for people to participate in their show."

Pageant Moms was a reality show about pageant girls

and their families. My grandma used to love watching it, mostly so she could point out what horrible parents the mothers were. I could practically see the wheels churning in Mom's head, so I pulled her away quickly.

"No, Mom. No." *More like hell no.*

The conference room for the pageant was large, which was good because it needed a huge amount of space to be able to fit all the massive wigs. Every little girl seemed to be sporting them, even the two-year-olds. Like a toddler would have that much hair in the first place.

There was another room adjacent to the room that actually held the pageant where the girls could get prepared for the next step. There was a table of fruit and pastries laid out, too, and I noticed some plates piled high. I shook my head as one woman smacked her daughter's hand for trying to add a pastry to her plate. When her daughter turned around, her mother took the pastry instead.

The camera crews were set up in the corner. Several women were hovering around them with their kids, obviously hoping to get noticed. Rory would probably migrate to the cameras, too. She loved being on video. I couldn't imagine anything worse than being filmed at one of these things— or anywhere, actually. Even when parents showed up to softball games with video cameras, I had to block them out or I'd end up walking the batter.

I spotted Belle and was really glad to see her soft, natural curls cascading down to her shoulders. At least she wasn't sporting a wig. Noah was on his knees next to her, smiling as he tickled his sister. I walked over to them.

"Belle's group starts in a few minutes," he said. "Want to come or do you have to hang out here?"

"Sure, I'll watch."

I tried telling my mother I was going to watch some of Belle's age group, but she waved me away. Her eyes were on the cameras in the corner, and she was encouraging Rory to finish eating her fruit so they could go have a look. Good for me for me—the less questions the better.

I went with Noah to watch Belle line up with the other three-year-old girls. She was by far the most beautiful with her dark hair twirled in yellow bows and her large blue eyes. Noah clapped and cheered proudly as she stepped up the stairs and turned slowly so the judges could see her bright yellow cupcake dress. The dress that looked ridiculous on the older girls looked sweet on her. She smiled widely and received loud cheers from the audience as she skipped off the stage to her mother.

Rory's age group went up next. A flurry of blue, pink, and green dresses twirled around the stage, all looking the same to me. Rory was in her favorite pink cupcake dress, her wig of curls massive on her head. But she smiled sweetly at the judges and did her walk the way my mother had her rehearse a hundred times. Everyone clapped as she curtsied. She glanced coyly over her shoulder as she walked off—a little too staged, I thought, but everyone seemed to eat it up. I had to admit, compared to the others in her age group, Rory was easily the most comfortable with all this. As much as she loved pageants, I could totally see her realizing my mother's dream in the Miss America pageant someday.

While the five-to-seven-year-olds finished their turn to a round of applause, a little girl next to me screamed at her mother that she wanted to go to the pool and not do any more "pageant stuff," and her mother was yelling back that she'd better, since she paid all the money. That set off another little girl's screaming.

"I can't take any more of this," I grumbled to Noah as they announced the eight-to-ten division. He nodded and we left. I stopped in the "green" room next door, but my mother already had Rory talking to someone with a camera. I started toward them until I heard my mother say, "Yes, Aurora does have a sister…" I pivoted on my heel and darted out of the room as quickly as I could.

Noah and I walked as far as we could to the other side of the conference center to get away from the craziness. Unfortunately, the other side wasn't far enough, so even in the quietest corner we found we could still hear the high-pitched giggles from the girls and yelling from their mothers. This hotel was way too small.

I lay down on the carpet and Noah stretched out next to me. He was close, though we weren't touching. Just a few inches and we would be. I wondered what would happen if I accidentally stretched too far and let my hand brush against his. Would he take it? It was weird—last night we'd held hands and almost kissed. Why was this so difficult?

As if in response to my question, a couple of kids chased each other down to our side of the conference center, laughing and yelling. They touched the wall and then ran back. With the pageant hammering at us from all sides, the memory of last night seemed almost surreal.

"These things really suck," I said, looking over at him. His profile was strong, his nose longer than most, but not in a bad way.

"Agreed."

"I mean, even the name is stupid—Coastal Princess Pageant. Tallahassee's nowhere near the coast. And I have to put up with a batshit-crazy mother while Rory turns into Princess Aurora and lords her royal self all over."

"The only reason I tolerate it is because of Belle." He smiled. "But those other monsters…ugh. And I don't mean the kids, either. Not that I'm talking about your family or anything," he said quickly.

I laughed. "It's okay—my sister and mom get crazy, but nowhere near some of those people. Those women are so, like, 'I don't care if I'm pulling your hair. You better smile and like it!'"

Noah raised his voice up to a shrill pitch, "Oh, yes, you will get spray-tanned so you can look unnaturally natural!"

"I forgot your blush in the room. Pinch your cheeks until they bleed!"

"Stick these spiders on your eyes so you can have nice, long eyelashes."

"Get yourself on camera ASAP. I want to make sure they know how horrible I am."

"You lost your front teeth? Put these fake teeth in so you can look like Great-Grandma."

I reached over to pucker his mouth with my hand. "Oh, but you'd look sooo cute with those pretty fake teeth. Sooo cute."

"Oh yeah? Well…" He turned on his elbow and pinched my cheek. "You need some color in those cheeks."

Our laughter died as we realized we were facing each other, arms entwined. The proper reaction might be to pull away quickly, but I didn't.

Noah's eyes widened. *Oh, boy.* My heart hammering, I drew my arm back slowly, brushing against his. His hand caught mine as it passed. "Lex…"

Without hesitating—without thinking, even—I leaned forward and pressed my lips against his. He tensed in surprise but immediately relaxed into the kiss. His lips were warm and soft on mine, a sweet kiss that lasted only a few seconds. I pulled back, knowing I was blushing and not giving two flying flips about it. Noah's face sported this sexy smile as he studied me. I was the one who kissed *him*, and he was the one acting all confident about it. What the hell was up with that?

Then I noticed he didn't look worried anymore. Not even a trace of the reserved concern in his expression. He slid his fingers slowly down my arm, wrapping his hand over my wrist to pull me back to him. He jerked away when my phone started clanging.

"Oh, shit," I said, scrambling to pull it out of my pocket. "Sorry, it's my mother's ringtone. What?" I asked into the phone as I sat up, not bothering to hide my annoyance.

"Where are you?" Her voice was high and screechy. I held the phone a few inches away as she continued to yell. "Rory needs her cowgirl costume for the talent competition, so get down here now." I could hear Rory screeching in the background for Mom to call her Aurora.

I pressed the end button. "Guess I better get back before she has a conniption." I scrambled to my feet and Noah did the same. "Is there anything worse than a mother who's into pageants? Seriously."

"Agreed."

By the time I made it back to the prep room, my mother was in what could only be described as a full-on tizzy. She yelled at me for taking my time. "Open the small red box and pull out a couple hair clips. And get the pink polish— she chipped her nail."

I was so ready to take all the bags of crap to the second floor of the hotel and toss them over the railing. But I followed my frantic mother into the crowded pageant room, the hodge-podge potpourri of perfume giving me a nasty headache.

"I need to lie down," I said to my mother. And by lie down, I meant escape this nut house completely. "I'm not feeling a hundred percent."

"But Aurora is about to go on. You don't want to miss her cowgirl act, do you." It wasn't a question. But she did give me a Tylenol from her purse and rubbed the back of my neck.

I sank into a chair as Rory lined up with the other kids and pressed my fingers to my temples while the girls pranced around the stage in various versions of sexy costumes. One girl was dressed in a glorified bikini and danced to a hip-hop song. I wondered if her mother realized what the lyrics were about. The woman stood just behind the judges, shaking her hips and waving her arms in front of her like a moron, trying to get her daughter to mimic the moves, while the music went on about the joys of stripping. The mom was about ten times more enthusiastic than her daughter.

Finally, it was my sister's turn, and my mother jumped up and waved at her. I watched as she did her lasso trick—consisting of her throwing the loop around a wooden "cow"—and, of course, shaking her hips to country music. She pointed her finger out to the crowd and nodded her head quickly in the typical pageant move that I never understood, my mother pantomiming her moves. Then her act was finished, and the crowd clapped enthusiastically.

"Please, Mom, can't I go up to the room for a bit? My head is killing me," I said as Rory danced off the stage. Thankfully my mother was in a better mood now that this part was over.

"Fine, fine," she said, waving her hand. "Go lie down. Be back as soon as you can."

I walked away, nodding as I passed Belle and her mother. Noah wasn't with them.

As soon as I got out of the room, I literally ran all the way back to the elevator. It felt like escaping Alcatraz. One of the bellmen gave me a sympathetic look as he punched the fourth floor for me.

"Pageant?" he asked. I nodded and rolled my eyes, to which he laughed.

I walked down the hallway, rubbing at my temples. A few doors from my room, I heard yelling. It sounded like it was coming from Noah's room, but the voice wasn't Noah's.

CHAPTER
19

"I KNOW YOU'RE HOLDING OUT ON ME, NOAH. WHERE'S THE MONEY?"

Someone spoke in a lower voice. I couldn't make out what he was saying. I backed against the wall, my heart racing. Was this Noah's dad? Noah said he wasn't here, so did he come here just to yell at him?

"DON'T YOU TELL ME I'M NOT DOING ANYTHING FOR THIS FAMILY, YOU LITTLE SHIT! DON'T YOU CALL ME DRUNK."

There was a scrambling from inside and what sounded like something hitting the wall. I reached into my pocket to pull out my cell, not sure who I was going to call, but I couldn't let this go on. Then the door opened and Noah appeared. He yanked the door shut behind him and took a deep breath, and only then did he see me, my phone in hand. He froze, his eyes wide.

Neither one of us said anything for a long moment. His hair was a little on the wild side, like he'd shuffled his hands through it a few times. I stepped toward him but he stiffened, holding a hand up to stop me. I stopped. "Noah…"

"Don't. Go away," he said roughly.

"But—"

He stepped forward. "Go away, Lex. Leave me alone." His voice was sharp.

He stalked toward the elevators. I went to my room and sat on my bed in the darkness, my headache forgotten. *Noah has an abusive father?* I hugged my knees to my chest. How could he be so calm all the time? Was his dad like that with his mom and Belle, too? Just the thought of anyone screaming at that sweet little girl made me sick to my stomach. And poor Noah…

I gazed at my cell phone. Should I text him? Or maybe I should give him some space. Now it made sense why he had two jobs. He must be supporting his whole family. Did his father even work?

Oh God. The last thing I told him was all about how having a pageant mom was the worst thing in the world. Maybe this was what he had been afraid to tell me and why he kept himself shut off most of the time.

My thumb moved over another phone number in my contacts list. I pressed it and waited.

My dad's voice was cheery as ever. "Hey sweetie! How's the pageant going? Are you surviving?"

His voice was like a warm hug—he was exactly the kind

of dad Noah deserved. Tears pricked at my eyes. "Yes. It's great."

"Great? That doesn't sound right. Everything okay?"

I didn't say anything. The fact was that my dad always knew when something was wrong, while Noah's dad screamed obscenities at him. "I'm good, Dad. I just missed your voice is all."

"Ah." He was silent for a moment. "You sure? Are Rory and your mom okay?"

"Yes, everything's good. I'm just tired. Pageant stuff, you know. How's Grandma doing?"

"She's just fine. And hang in there, the pageant's almost over." He asked me a few more questions, mostly about how Rory was doing in the competition and stuff.

All this time, I was worrying about stupid SmartMart, about having to attend my sister's pageant, and how to make my mother happy with me. And the whole time, Noah had *real* problems. He said I didn't know everything about him. He was right.

I had no idea.

After hanging up with my dad, I went into the bathroom to splash cold water on my face. But Noah—where was he? I finally texted him, even called him, but he didn't respond. I had to find him.

I walked around the lobby, the conference center, even the pool, but I couldn't find him or his family. My mother, however, did spot me. "Where have you been?" she asked, grabbing my arm too hard. "They're going to be doing awards soon. You okay?" She peered into my eyes. "You haven't been crying, have you?"

I forced a laugh. "No, of course not." I reached out to tug on Rory's curly wig. "Can't you take this stupid thing off her?"

"No, no, no!" Rory yelled, holding it with two hands. "Momma said I could wear this home tonight."

I glanced around the room as the judges started announcing prizes for the babies and toddlers. Against the other wall, I saw Noah talking to his mother. Their heads were close together, foreheads almost touching. His mother was frowning. Belle was spinning, watching her skirt flare around her. Her happiness was a relief. I was glad she wasn't in the room earlier. It made me wonder, though, how often she was there.

"Now the awards for the three-to-four-year-olds," the judge announced. Rory complained about how long it was taking to get to hers, but I moved a few seats over to tune her out. Belle's mother was walking her to the stage, corners of her mouth lifted high, though the smile didn't reach her eyes. I glanced over at Noah, but his face was expressionless. He caught me staring at him but turned his attention back to his sister.

Awards for ridiculous things like Most Beautiful and Most Talented were announced. Most Beautiful was always handed out to the girl who least looked like a child, most like a Barbie doll. The girl who won this year was four but looked more like twenty. I recognized the one for Most Talented. From what I remembered, she went onstage and proceeded to strut her stuff in an outfit that would've made

Lady Gaga blush.

Belle won Best Personality, which I thought was true in her case. The runner-up titles were granted, as well as the award for Queen. Belle didn't win any of those awards, and she looked sad about it, but her grinning mother was whispering to her. I knew what she was saying. It was dumb, I always thought—if you didn't win Queen, you won a bigger title. But little kids didn't get that. I didn't even get it.

Rory did, though. When her name wasn't called for one of the lesser awards, she beamed from ear to ear and curtsied like someone had given her the Miss America crown. My mother jumped up and down. "She's going to get something bigger!" she said in a giggly voice, grabbing my arm.

I shrugged her off and made my way over to Belle. Noah's eyes narrowed as I approached, but I ignored him, dropping on a knee to congratulate his sister. She was tired, yawning and looking slightly grumpy. I didn't blame her. I stood up and smiled at Noah's mother, but she, too, looked warily at me. Her attention was diverted when the pageant director called the names of those contestants who won a higher title. I noticed Rory running up to the stage. Belle was also called—her mother immediately picked her up and carried her toward the other finalists.

That left me and Noah, who was still ignoring me. Embarrassed, maybe. I thought about going back to my seat but changed my mind and walked up to him. He stiffened visibly when I touched his wrist, but I continued, sliding my hand down to thread my fingers through his.

Slowly, Noah's slender fingers relaxed and wrapped

around mine. The gesture was gentle and sweet, though heat flooded my veins. I wanted to wrap my arms around him as tight as I could.

Noah shifted slightly and I gazed up at him. His blue eyes had softened and were focused on mine, his face serious in a heart-stopping way. With our hands entwined, we were no longer just two semi-normal teenagers in a room full of crazy. We simply existed in this moment, quickening heartbeats made obvious by the rising and falling of our chests. Everything outside of us was a blur. Everything else be damned, I wanted this to happen.

Someone bumped into me as she moved past, and just like that all the surrounding noise of pageant mothers and their kids came back.

Moment ruined. Again.

I could hear my mother's voice calling to me from the other side of the room. I untangled my fingers from Noah's, shaking my head at his amused look.

"Not funny," I whispered.

He grinned widely. "Go ahead. I'll catch up with you later."

"I'll catch up with you later" was becoming the tag line for this stupid pageant.

I moved toward my mother, who also looked amused. "So he's your boyfriend now?" she asked.

"No, he's just a friend," I grumbled. I hated that I could feel my face burning. Noah was still watching me, his thoughtful expression making my heartbeat trip over itself.

"Uh-huh," Mom said, winking, but her attention quickly

moved back to the stage to watch the announcements for the higher titles.

The Mini Supreme turned out to be little Belle, who looked confused and sleepy as they put the crown on her head. I caught Noah's big grin as he watched his sister try to pull the crown off. The prize was five hundred dollars. I hoped that would be enough to keep his father from screaming at him.

Next up was the Grand Supreme title, which went to an older girl in a long purple ball gown who looked twelve or thirteen. She looked weird up there with the little kids, but she grinned proudly.

The final award was for Ultimate Grand Supreme, which always sounded to me like the title for a pizza. I glanced at my mother, who was biting her nails and looking like she was going to spontaneously combust with nerves. Rory, on the other hand, seemed calm and confident. She knew she had it in the bag. A small, terrible part of me almost wanted her to lose, just so it would knock her down off her pedestal. She was always so cocky after winning a pageant.

But, of course, that wasn't going to happen today. Rory assumed the appropriate look of surprise on her face when the announcer called out "Aurora Grace" as the winner of Ultimate Grand Supreme. I clapped as my mother jumped up and down ungracefully, yelling out "Woo-hoo, Aurora!" She threw me a look as if I should be jumping up and down, too.

Then it was over. Rory had her huge trophy, her massive crown that slipped over her forehead, and her two thousand dollar prize check that I knew Mom would put in her college account. I guess Rory was onto something. It was certainly easier than working a bazillion hours at SmartMart. I responded to texts from Syd and Court, telling them the result, and slipped my phone back into my pocket.

As the pageant people started taking pictures of the winners, Noah came up beside me. "Hey," he said.

"Hey."

"Long day."

"Yeah."

That was it for conversation, but the electricity bouncing between us startled me. Had it always been there and I just was too clueless to notice? It reminded me of what my grandma had said about electricity and beating hearts. If there was ever an example of that, it was Noah and me.

After pictures, the woman from the *Pageant Moms* show interviewed the winners, starting with Rory. They asked to interview Belle, too, but her mother declined, claiming Belle was too tired. As the woman set up Rory on padded blocks, Noah turned to me.

"Guess we have to go pack," he said as his mom motioned at him to follow her. "Maybe I'll see you before we leave."

I nodded as my mother pulled me over to the cameras. I yanked my arm away. "Mom, you are crazy if you think I'm going to let them interview me for that stupid show."

"I wasn't going to ask you to," she whispered. "Keep your voice down." But as she let my arm go and didn't pay any more attention to me, I knew that's exactly what she was planning. I wondered when she would stop trying to get me involved in the whole pageant thing. Probably never.

On the way upstairs to the room, I called Syd, who I knew would listen to me and not judge.

"So now what?" she asked when I told her I was falling for Noah. I didn't say anything about his father—that wasn't my secret to tell.

"I don't know. I've got to say something to Bryce about us, I guess."

"I wouldn't," she replied. "You said Bryce freaked when he found out Noah is working at SmartMart with you. If you tell him you're dating now, he'll go ballistic."

"So? What's he going to do, beat him up? Bryce isn't like that."

"Maybe not, but he could make life back at school pretty bad for the guy. Even worse than now. And you might lose Bryce as a friend."

"I honestly don't care anymore," I told her, even though that wasn't completely true. "Jeez, why can't he just get over it already? It was two years ago."

"I know."

I could see my mother waving at me.

"Gotta go. I'll talk to you later," I told Syd and pressed end.

After packing up all Rory's crap into a bell cart, we headed downstairs. I looked toward Noah's door, but no one appeared. I really, really hoped his dad wasn't still there.

We were cramming our stuff in the car when I heard Noah call my name. My heart jumped into my throat at the sight of him jogging toward me. We walked a little ways from the car, and I could feel my mother's eyes on me.

"Everything okay?" I asked him.

His friendly eyes became guarded, but he nodded. "So you're back to work on Monday?"

"Yeah. You?"

"Yeah." He reached out and twirled my long blond strands around his fingers, a half smile forming on his face. It was such a familiar yet sexy gesture. It made me want to throw my arms around him and kiss him, and screw what my mom would think.

"Come on, Alexis, time to go," Mom called from the car. *Not helping here, Mom.*

I took a deep breath. "If my mom wasn't looking, I'd kiss you." The words were bold—maybe it was too much. I had to remind myself I made the first move earlier.

His smile deepened as he placed my hair back on my shoulder, his fingers grazing my collarbone as he pulled away. "Your mom won't always be looking."

Oh, sigh.

For most of the drive back, all I could think about was Noah. Were we a "thing" now? He didn't say as much, but I had to assume so. But on the other hand, he didn't ask me out. Of course, my mother had been watching. And there was the issue with his father—was he going to talk to me about that?

My phone buzzed when we were an hour from home. Already? I smiled and looked at it, but the text was from my dad. *Lexie tell mom to call me.*

Him calling me Lexie via text was all it took for my heart to leap into my throat. It meant one thing.

Grandma.

CHAPTER
20

I have no memory of the conversation my mother had with my dad on the way home except for two words: "Grandma's missing." The remaining hour in the car felt like an eternity, and as soon as we reached the house, I jumped out of the Escalade and ran inside the house calling for my dad. He came to me immediately, his face drawn and tired.

"Don't worry, sweetie," he said as he hugged me before I could say a word. "We'll find her."

I knew it was pointless, but I ran upstairs to her room, to my room, to Rory's, then to the back porch, calling for her the whole time. I could hear my mother talking with my dad, who was not sounding as composed with her as he had with me.

"I shouldn't have let her go for a walk. I should've known this would happen."

"You couldn't have known anything." My mother's voice was calm. "She's gone for walks before with no problem. Stop beating yourself up."

"How long has she been gone?" I asked, joining them.

"Two hours now," he said, his voice shaking slightly.

Mom placed a hand on his arm. "Max will find her." Max was Dad's friend who was a police officer. But I didn't want to wait for Max. I went out front, ignoring my father's call not to wander off looking for her. It was almost dark and she had to be scared to death. Dad seemed certain it was a memory issue. For the first time since Grandma was diagnosed with Alzheimer's, I hoped it was the memory. Otherwise it meant someone could've… I couldn't finish the thought.

I started down the street, calling out for her. I ended up at Syd's house at the end of the cul-de-sac. Her mom answered my knock and told me she hadn't seen my grandma. Syd offered to drive me around, so for the next hour we combed our neighborhood streets. Our community was large, and by this time she could've gone anywhere. I checked in with my parents now and then to see if she'd been found.

She hadn't.

I started crying as the rain began to fall. Every drop felt like a hammer as I thought about Grandma lost in the chilly rain. Syd reached across to take my hand. "She's probably made her way to a neighbor's house, Lex," she said softly. "She'll be okay, I promise."

Syd couldn't know that for sure, but I still clung to the words like they were lifelines. All my stupid mind was doing to help was playing images of Grandma passed out on the sidewalk or huddled under some gas station awning.

My phone buzzed as we drove slowly through the Falcon's Run subdivision, calling through the drizzle for her. I looked at my dad's text and sank back into the seat in relief: *Grandma's back!*

Five minutes later, I was running up the wet steps to my house, pushing past two officers to wrap my arms around my soaked grandma. She kept her hands at her sides, stiff as I hugged her. "I don't know what everyone's so fussed up about," she said, her voice crisp as I released her. "I was just walking."

"We caught her two neighborhoods over, yelling at someone for stealing her son's car," the policeman said. He looked at my dad's car. "His was a black Beemer like that one, so I'm guessing she got confused and thought she was at your house."

Dad nodded. "Mom gets confused easily."

Grandma crossed her arms. "I absolutely do not. There is nothing wrong with me."

"Do you want to go change?" I asked her, looking at her wet robe and hair under the towel that someone had thrown around her shoulders. She looked at me, then down at her dripping clothes.

"I suppose so. Got caught in a storm. You know it's storm season and all."

I glanced quickly at my dad. "She was just telling me the other day about it being a bad storm season," I said hopefully.

"It's like that every summer," he said. "It doesn't mean anything."

It meant something to *me*. I took Grandma's hand. "Come on, let's go upstairs and get dried off," I said. She nodded and walked with me, her body bending slightly at the waist. She looked so much older right now than she had this morning. My heart, which had been so full from my weekend with Noah, was now shriveling.

I filled the tub with warm water and got her a change of clothes, stood just outside the door as she took her bath, then tucked her into bed when she was done. I kissed her on the forehead as she closed her eyes. "I love you, Grandma," I whispered. She didn't respond, though her lips curved up slightly. She looked so shriveled all curled in the blankets, shivering. I grabbed one of her afghans from a chair and placed it over her, then turned out the lights and sat next to her on the bed, watching as her chest rose and fell. *Shallow breaths*, I thought. As she slept, I spoke my end of the conversation I'd wanted to have with her before I found out she was missing.

"We just got back from Rory's pageant, Grandma. I really wish you had been there. You would've been proud of her. She won. You would've been proud of me, too, for not actually going crazy..." I trailed off. But Grandma wasn't crazy, just forgetful. "Anyway, I hung out with this awesome guy. Noah, remember—my hot manager?" I smiled slightly. "I think he likes me, and I like him, too, in the way you talked about with electricity and matching heartbeats." I leaned closer to whisper, "I even kissed him."

Grandma didn't stir from her sleep. My heart hurt, having this one-sided conversation when all I wanted was for her to wake up laughing and chuck me under the chin to tell me "way to go." If that made me selfish, I didn't care. I wanted my grandma back.

I walked slowly back to my room, picking up my phone to send a quick text to Syd to thank her for driving me around tonight. A text that I hadn't noticed earlier was highlighted. It was from Noah.

Thanks for making today bearable.

Oh, Noah. He made me feel happy and confused and petrified and tingly—all the right feelings at the wrong time.

~~*Thanks for being there today*~~
~~*Thanks for being a good*~~
~~*My grandma was*~~
~~*Nobody can*~~
~~*I really want*~~

My dead brain couldn't even handle a simple text. I tossed my phone into my nightstand drawer and lay down on the bed, threw my arm over my tear-swollen eyes, and sobbed until I passed out.

On Monday, Grandma had a fever and could barely get out of bed. I decided to call in sick to work so I could go with Dad and Grandma to see Dr. Ahmed. My mother thought it would be too hard on me, but Dad encouraged it. He was worried, and I had a feeling my going along was more for him than for me. Grandma was so weak and shaky that it didn't take long for Dr. Ahmed to diagnose her with walking pneumonia, which apparently she'd had for a while without us even knowing, and tell us that with her running around in the rain last night, we were lucky it wasn't worse.

Dr. Ahmed prescribed medicines for her and ran some tests. He talked to us using words like brain plaque and advanced neurodegenerative process and cellular integrity that were just fancy ways of saying her Alzheimer's was progressing. He tried to be sympathetic about it, but I could tell he'd seen enough of these cases to make us just another family who didn't understand the disease and needed coddling.

He did recommend that since Grandma had started wandering outside of the house, for her safety we should get a home health care provider who could be with her during her waking hours—more than what Patty could do. Dad gave me a look that I knew all too well, but honestly I didn't care what Mom thought about having someone else in the house. Grandma needed help. Dr. Ahmed also suggested that we consider a nursing home. I almost let curses fly off my tongue at that one.

I looked at my phone to see a text from Noah that he'd sent earlier. *You okay?*

I knew he was worried, and I felt horrible about not responding to his text last night, but with the words "nursing home" still reverberating in my ears all I could do was text a simple *Yes.*

He responded with *Want to talk?*

The tears started pricking my eyes as I thought about talking to Noah. I typed *No thanks.* I didn't want to get into it. To tell him what was wrong meant I had to relive the past thirty-six hours, and I didn't have it in me to do that.

At least Bryce and Court knew about it because Syd told them, so there was no having to re-hash everything with them. They sent me texts to tell me they were thinking of me, but that was it. I appreciated the distance.

I called in to work again on Tuesday, choosing instead to sit around and watch episodes of *Bonanza* with Grandma. She slept most of the time, though when I tried talking to her about stuff, she'd smile and seem interested. I told her how much I liked Noah. She had an entire conversation with me about him, laughing as I told her how we both were practically gagging over the whole pageant thing. Then when I mentioned him twenty minutes later, she asked, "Noah who?"

So I stopped talking about him and watched the shows with her instead. My mom tried to get me to do something—anything—else, but I refused. Dad gave me these annoying sympathetic looks all the time, but at least he left me alone. A nurse who would be with Grandma five days a week showed up Tuesday afternoon to introduce herself to us. She kind of creeped me out, with her short, straight dark hair, round glasses, and purple jacket and pants. She reminded me of the Johnny Depp version of Willy Wonka.

I went to work on Wednesday. I was on the register the entire time, so even though I saw Noah walk by a few times (and once to check my cash), I didn't say much to him except for a generic "Hey."

He caught up with me on my break, literally right as my fifteen free minutes started. I had a feeling he'd been waiting for the break to start.

"Hey, Lex," he said, walking with me into the employee area. "You okay?"

"Yeah. Why?"

"You just don't seem like yourself today."

I shrugged, stopping at the time clock. "I'm just tired, I guess."

"Ah." He watched as I input my ID to clock out for break. I didn't meet his gaze as I punched the numbers. Just one look into those beautiful, serious blue eyes and I'd lose it. The only thing I could do was swallow over the lump in my throat and focus on not crying, because all I wanted to do was fall into his arms and sob. I could *not* do that. Not here.

"Do you want to talk about it?" he asked softly, his fingers lifting to brush my hair from my shoulder. The touch almost unraveled me.

"No, I'm okay." I smiled too brightly at him and backed toward the ladies' room. "I'll see you later."

I stayed in the bathroom for several minutes, breathing and trying to hold it together. Finally, I went to my locker to check my phone, terrified that there'd be a text telling me Grandma relapsed or something. But the only text was from Syd.

Still going to the game? It's ok if you aren't.

Yep

Whacking the crap out of the ball was exactly what I needed right now.

The scrimmage didn't start until six p.m. Syd picked me up from work and took me straight to the fields. Being the best friend that she was, she didn't say anything about my grandma. She squeezed my shoulder once, and that was all I needed to know that she understood everything.

For the first time in days, I poured my heart into something. I played the shit out of that softball game, and even the coach said it was my best game yet.

After I had pitched the last out, all my teammates cheered my name. Syd gave me a huge hug and whispered in my ear, "If your grandma was watching this game, she'd be so proud of you."

Bryce ran onto the field to give me a hug. "Lex, you were amazing," he said, lifting me off my feet and twirling me around, making me laugh.

"Thanks," I said as he set me back down. His arms felt good—not as good as Noah's, but still comforting. He leaned down to say softly in my ear, "I know it's been tough, but you played a good game out there."

"Thank you," I murmured. He turned to talk to Coach Santiago.

"Um, Lex," Syd said, nudging me. Noah was jumping down from the bleachers and walking toward his SUV.

I ran in his direction, but he was already at his SUV by the time I'd made it to the parking lot. At least he'd sat in the bleachers this time. Had he tried to skip out before Bryce had seen him? The fact that I'd ignored him all day gnawed at my heart. Here was a guy who had tried to conceal his own awful truths, who had just started to trust me, and I couldn't even return that trust. Now that my game was over and I felt a little better, my rudeness was apparent.

I owed him an apology. And the truth about how I felt.

CHAPTER
21

The next day at SmartMart, we were so busy that I didn't have the chance to talk with Noah. When we did interact, he was polite and friendly in a manager-to-employee kind of way, but he didn't go out of his way to joke around like he used to.

Syd invited me and Court to go to the beach after work, since my shift ended early. With the crappy week I'd had, I agreed, and soon we were relaxing on the smooth white sand of Clearwater Beach. Noah was still on my mind. I didn't text or call him, even though I wanted to. I didn't like the coldness that had somehow settled between us, but aside from an apology, I didn't know what else to say.

"So we can go to that Mexican restaurant you like," Syd said after Court left to go to the restroom. "Unless you want to go somewhere else."

"Doesn't matter. Mexican's fine."

She got up on her elbows. "Are you okay?"

"I'm okay. You don't have to worry about me."

She sighed. "I *am* worried about you. You haven't been yourself lately at all. I mean, I know things at home aren't so great with your grandma and all. I totally get that. But then there's Noah. What's going on with you guys right now, because you haven't said much at all lately."

I shrugged.

"You still like him, right?" she asked.

"Yeah."

"Great. Then when are you going to tell Bryce? Not to mention Court, who's going to be pissed that you didn't tell her first."

"Bryce would totally lose his shit over it, so the longer he doesn't know, the better, I think. And I'm not sure if I trust Court enough."

She thought about that for a moment. "You're right about Bryce, but you probably should go ahead and let Court in on it. She won't tell him. Not if you really don't want her to and specifically tell her not to say anything."

Syd clearly trusted Court a whole lot more than I did. And even though Court was my friend, I wasn't sure if I wanted to test that theory.

After dinner, Court drove us back over the causeway. "Do you want me to drop you guys off at home?"

"Sure," Syd said, flicking a worried look at me. I hadn't eaten much of my taco salad, something Syd commented on, since usually I ate the entire thing, shell and all. "Home is good."

Home? Home meant seeing Grandma in bed, frail, with a nurse by her side instead of me. Home meant my mother frantic about pageants or whatever had her going at the moment and my dad a nervous wreck about Grandma.

As we exited the causeway and were about to take the turnoff for our town, I put my hand on Court's shoulder.

"Keep going, Court."

"Why?"

"Just do it."

She sighed but did as I asked, her face kind of amused and annoyed at the same time. "Yeah? Now what?"

"I want to walk around the city."

"Oh. Okay, cool."

"No way," Syd piped up. "We're not going back to that Cooper's bar. That place is a dive. Besides, it's about to rain."

I ignored her. "Just do it, please."

Court drove us back into downtown, pulling into the metered parking space a couple blocks away from the bars. The streets were filled with people walking in and out of bars and clubs. I stayed a few steps ahead of my friends to avoid questions from Court. It wasn't long before the sign for Cooper's appeared.

I hesitated. "I don't even know if he's working tonight," I said to Syd when they caught up to me.

"Who?" Court asked. "Who are you talking about?"

I stepped up to the door, my friends right behind me, and peered inside. There were too many people to get a good glimpse of the bar, so I stepped in. I moved forward faster than my friends, who seemed too afraid to go past the entryway. *Chicken.* I was almost to the bar when a heavyset guy in leather stepped in front of me. Sidestepping him, my eyes moved over the bar. *Damn, no Noah.* Maybe he wasn't even working tonight. He said he usually worked Thursday nights, but he could've given away his shift. A heaviness pressed down on my chest, making it even harder to breathe in the crowded, smoky room. I had counted on him being here.

"Hey, baby!" the leather guy said, rubbing my shoulders. I smacked his hands away.

"Could you be a little more disgusting?" I yelled over the noise.

"I could, yeah," he said, moving around so that he blocked my view of the bar again. "We could go somewhere and I could show you how disgusting I can be."

Oh, crap. I swallowed hard and backed away, but there were too many people. Pervy Guy pressed himself closer to me and grinned. He smelled of cigarettes and beer. I was going to throw up.

Someone grabbed me by the arm and jerked me back. I turned to see Noah shaking his head at the guy. "She's jailbait, dude." Pervy Guy glared at him but moved away. I sagged in relief, but Noah didn't let me relax. "What the hell are you doing?" he yelled over the crowd. "You shouldn't be here."

His tone grated on me. "I felt like it," I said. Which wasn't true, of course. I *really* didn't like being in this bar.

He leaned in to peer at me. "What's going on with you? Are you drunk?"

"Are you serious?"

He rolled his eyes. "Come on."

Still holding me by the elbow, he pushed me out in front of him, past Court and Syd, until I was outside on the sidewalk, people shoving their way past us, some pulling out umbrellas even though it wasn't raining yet.

Noah glanced around, then pulled me into the alley next to the bar. The girls waited at the entrance to the alley, and I could see Court waving her arms furiously toward us as she talked to Syd. The cat was out of the bag now, and I couldn't care less.

"You came here a second time?" Noah asked, releasing me to run his hands through his hair. "How stupid can you get?"

"Stupid? You're stupid," I yelled, feeling ten years old.

"I have to go," he said, walking past me toward the alley entrance of the bar. I grabbed his arm.

"Wait. What the hell is your problem, Noah? Talk to me."

"Talk to you? I've tried talking to you but you keep tuning me out."

I sighed. "I know I've been ignoring you, and I'm really sorry."

"You seemed to have no problem paying attention to Bryce."

I opened my mouth, then closed it again. *Bryce?* "What does Bryce have to do with it?" I asked.

He crossed his arms as he glared at me. "What's between you guys, anyway?"

"We're friends. You know that."

He snorted. "Friends."

What the…? "This is ridiculous. Bryce is one of my best friends. I don't get why you guys can't just—you know—coexist."

He raised an eyebrow. "So does Bryce know that you and I are friends? Is he wanting to 'coexist' too?"

"*Really?* And they say girls create drama." I ignored his question. Bryce didn't know how I felt about Noah, but that wasn't the issue right now. "So hang on, why are you still acting like this about me being friends with Bryce, anyway? It doesn't affect you."

"Didn't look much like friends to me the other day." He looked away, his jaw set, and I could see his Adam's apple bobbing in his neck as he swallowed.

Oh.

Oh!

The pieces fell into place. Noah had seen Bryce hugging me—and I guess if you saw us from a distance, it'd look like we were *together* together. Was he jealous? All the butterflies in my body took flight as if I had just walked through a field of them.

"Noah, look at me," I said in a softer voice.

He did. Only now did I see the shadow of hurt in his eyes—how did I miss that before? Noah had been nothing but nice, and I did everything I could do to shut the guy out.

"Look, I don't know what's…" He hesitated, his scrunched forehead smoothing as his eyes moved to my trembling lip. "Hey, are you okay?"

The softening of his expression and his obvious concern was my undoing. The balloon of pressure in my chest that had been building for weeks—my grandma, my mother, my position as pitcher on the team, my anxiety about Noah—released. I started to cry. And not the pretty cry, either, but the full-on sob.

Noah immediately pulled me into his arms. He didn't ask me questions, just held me as wave after wave of tears shook me. I didn't even have the strength to feel embarrassed about it. I'd try to get myself together, then thoughts of my grandma stuck in bed while the Willy Wonka nurse attended her entered my mind and the waterworks started again.

Finally, I pulled away from him, wiping the tears with the back of my hand. Noah removed the bar rag from his belt and handed it to me. I blew into it, not caring that it stank like booze, then tossed it into the Dumpster next to us. A few wet drops skimmed my arm. Of course, now it would rain. How poetic.

"I'm sorry," I said, my chest still shuddering. "I shouldn't have called you stupid. I just wanted to come here to see you and tell you that I'm sorry. I'm just having kind of a tough time at home, and—" I stopped, swallowing hard to keep from sobbing again.

His hand cupped my jaw, his thumb sweeping rogue tears away. "It's okay," he said softly.

The gentle intensity of his blue eyes tugged at my heart. Like that moment in the hotel elevator, something shifted between us—magnetic poles struggling to find each other. Weeks of teasing and flirting and toying with each other building up to this one moment. Taking a deep breath, I slowly moved my hand up his arm, ignoring the misting rain and the calls from Court and Syd that they were going to get the car. I was fearful that he'd pull away, that I'd misread the clues from him. We'd only kissed once—very briefly—and I'd initiated it.

Noah didn't make a move—his eyes widened slightly as I closed the distance between us, my body pressing against his, but he didn't lean in or anything like I expected. If anything, he looked nervous. He closed his eyes, the knot in his throat rising and falling as my fingers traced the line of a silver chain peeking out from under his shirt. I'd never noticed it before. "You're kind of going through some stuff right now," he said hoarsely.

"I know." I touched his face with my fingers. "I'm an emotional basket case and it's raining and we're standing in this alley being all awkward together. But I know you feel the same way. Tell me that you don't."

Noah kept his eyes tightly shut. I sighed. "What are you so afraid of?"

"I'm not afraid," he said, opening his eyes so that they swallowed me whole. I could see some sort of internal struggle playing out on his face, almost like he was standing at a crossroad and wasn't sure which direction he should take: the lonely, safe road he was used to or the one heading toward the emotional train wreck that was me.

Pressing my hands on top of his shoulders, I lifted myself up on my toes and leaned until my lips were against his ear, his cheek rough against mine. "I know you feel the same as me," I whispered. "And I want to be with you."

It was like I lit a fire within him. Noah pulled me around until I was flat against the wall, his fingers in my hair, his lips against mine. I couldn't take in enough—breathing his air, sliding my hands down his arms, around his waist. The rain fell, but we kissed on as time stood graciously still. In the drizzling haze, we pulled in all the colors around us, leaving the world muddled and gray.

Noah Grayson consumed me.

He broke away first, resting his forehead against mine. We were soaked now, but I didn't care. I could hear someone catcalling from the opening of the alley. "I have to go back to work," Noah said, his voice hoarse. I nodded even as I pulled him back to me. I twined my fingers in his hair as we kissed. It wouldn't be easy to untangle myself from this guy—even if I wanted to.

Noah spoke something against my mouth. Whatever he was saying barely registered. Something about my friends.

"Hey! Lex!"

I looked over to see Syd hanging out Court's window, waving to me to come with them. I smiled slightly, raising my hand to wave back but otherwise not moving. I didn't ever want to move.

"You have to go, too," he whispered against my temple. He stepped back and smoothed a hand through his wet hair, his darkened eyes staying fixed on mine. "So we...we need to figure this...us...out."

I smiled. "Okay, so when?"

He glanced toward Court and Syd, who were calling for me again. "Tomorrow night. After work."

I nodded, backing away toward the car. "It's about time, Noah Grayson," I said softly.

"I could say the same for you," he called out, just as quietly.

Touché.

CHAPTER
22

Syd and I stopped at the park near our neighborhood on our way back home so I could talk to Court. We sat in the swings and I talked fast with the occasional helpful interjection from Syd. It took a *lot* of convincing to get Court to a place where I felt she wouldn't say anything to Bryce. Mostly, she was mad at me for making out with the same guy who got her boyfriend in trouble—something she remembered all too well.

"He's an asshole for what he did to Bryce," she said for the third time as she scuffed her sandal in the sand.

"He's not an asshole," I said wearily. "He's one of the nicest guys I've ever known." Didn't I just have this conversation about Bryce with Noah? How many times was I going to have to defend my friends from each other?

Syd threw her hands up. "Look, Court, obviously Lex

likes the guy. She knows what happened, but it was a long time ago. Can't we just drop it? For the sake of our friendship?"

Court thought about it. "Maybe," she conceded finally. Syd and I breathed a sigh of relief, glancing at each other and grinning. "But," she said, "Bryce and I are honest with each other. If he asks me a direct question, like if you guys are dating, I'm going to have to say yes."

"Not really," I said quickly. "We aren't dating. He hasn't officially asked me out except just to talk."

Court snorted. "Yeah, because making out with him in a dark alley certainly doesn't make you guys official or anything."

I laughed and reached over to give Court a hug. "Thanks. You're a good friend."

She grimaced. "I still don't like the idea of you dating that assho— I mean, that guy, and I totally think it's gonna blow up in your face eventually, but whatever. Hey, what time is it?"

I pulled out my phone. *Oh shit.* "It's one a.m. I was supposed to be home an hour ago." About ten texts and missed calls littered my notifications. My parents were pissed. "My phone was on silent. We've got to go."

Oh, yeah, they were mad. As soon as I walked in the door, my parents started in on me. Admittedly, I did kind of deserve it.

"Where were you?" my dad asked, finally stopping long enough for me to answer the question.

"I was with Syd and Court. We were at a playground."

"A playground?" my mother screeched. "Highly unlikely. Are you sneaking around with that guy from the pageant?"

"What? No, Mom, Syd and Court and I were talking about stuff and time got away and my phone was on silent. I'm sorry." I knew I was blushing, though, and I knew she could tell. Her eyes narrowed.

"Were you drinking?"

"We weren't drinking, doing drugs, or having sex. Does that cover everything?"

"That's enough," my dad said. "You're grounded for two weeks."

"Just two weeks?" my mother chimed in, but my dad held up his hand.

"Lexie hasn't done this before and she won't do it again, right?" He looked at me sternly.

I shook my head. "I won't. And I'm sorry I worried you."

I *was* sorry. The worry in their eyes reminded me of how I felt when Grandma went missing. I was surprised I only got two weeks.

I went upstairs, then stopped. *Crap.* Noah and I were supposed to go out after work tomorrow to talk about *us.* I couldn't help but smile, in spite of everything, about being able to say that.

I texted him. *Still at work?*

Just finished. You're up late.

Look who's talking.

Good to see you have your text humor back.

I grinned. He was so cute it made my heart hurt. I typed, *What r you doing right now?*

Thinking about you
Good things?
Yep. So tomorrow night?

I stared at that. I was grounded—I had to come straight home from work. But I still typed *Yes*. I'd figure it out tomorrow. I shivered. Kissing Noah was like striking out the last batter in the final inning. It was incredible, and I wanted more.

The next day, my dad took me to SmartMart. "What time do you get off work?" he asked.

My shift today was from one to six. I took a deep breath. I never lied to my dad. It wasn't something I'd ever even considered before. So I don't know why the words "Nine thirty" popped out of my mouth so easily. "And one of my coworkers will give me a lift—you don't have to pick me up." Okay, so that technically wasn't a lie. Noah was my coworker, after all.

"Okay," he said, clapping his hands together as if to emphasize his point. "Straight home after. Got it?"

I nodded and got out of the car, smiling at Roxanne as she walked into work. I caught the sneer she gave my dad's BMW, but I really didn't care about her issues with me right now.

I went into the hallway to clock in and check my rotation. As I was staring at the schedule—sales floor today, ugh—Noah came up behind me.

"Hey Lex," he said softly. He stood close—so close— but didn't touch me. It sent goose bumps popping up along my skin.

I turned around, tempted to let my hands cruise along his waist, but afraid he'd back away since we were at work. I wished he'd say something so we weren't just standing there. "How are you?" he finally asked.

"I am fine. How are you?" I said in a robotic monotone, which made him laugh.

"We're at work," he said, but his shoulders relaxed a bit.

"So?" I grinned wickedly at him.

He was blushing now. He opened his mouth to say something right as Mr. Hanson walked out of his office. Immediately, Noah straightened up and put his supervisorial look on. I bit back a grin.

"Everything okay?" Mr. Hanson asked. He nodded at the rotation schedule posted. "You're on the floor today, right, Alexis?"

I nodded. "Yes, sir."

He glanced at his watch. "Well, I believe your shift started five minutes ago." He smiled from Noah to me, and I wondered if he knew. But how could he? Noah and I just figured it out ourselves.

I moved past Noah and out the doors to start my shift on the floor. All the things I'd wanted to say to him, I didn't. Well, what was I expecting, for him to come up and kiss me?

It took about ten minutes for Noah to find me. I was dealing with a customer whose daughter had misplaced her stuffed toy. Her mom kept speaking in Spanish, I guess to calm her. The sobbing little girl had apparently been crawling through the paper towels and toilet paper, so I started pulling them all out to search for the toy.

Noah appeared then. My progress on the toy hunt slowed considerably with him next to me. "Can I help?" he asked.

"Sure. We're looking for what I think is a stuffed elephant. Rosa left it here." I smiled at the little girl, whose huge eyes were fixed on me as if I had her life in my hands. The little girl said something in Spanish to her mother, who responded.

"Ah," he said to Rosa. "*Sonría, por favor. Lo vamos encontrar.*" Oh, of *course* he spoke Spanish. I took a deep breath and continued the hunt. Was there anything about this guy that wasn't freaking amazing? The words *too good to be true* rang in my head, and I hoped this wouldn't be one of those *Lifetime* shows: "He was perfect in every way, and no one would've ever guessed that he wore his mother's dresses at night and buried bodies of his victims in the back-yard."

Halfway down the row, I came upon the soft pink elephant hidden on top of a package of Angel Soft. "Here you go, Rosa," I said, handing it to her. Her mother, who had been searching the top shelf for some reason—as if a little kid could reach that high—kept thanking me over and over in Spanish.

"No problemo," I kept repeating as I replaced the toilet paper package. I finally backed away and disappeared to the next aisle as fast as I could.

"You were great over there," Noah said behind me. I whipped around.

"Stalking me?" I teased.

"Possibly."

I reached out to slide my fingers around his waist. His breath intake was sharp, his eyes going wide. I touched his cheek with my fingers, turning his face down to me. "I want another kiss," I told him softly. "But I don't want to wait until later."

"Me neither." He leaned in, but a noise on the next aisle startled us both. He straightened and cleared his throat, but I noticed he didn't back away from me. Progress.

"So, you still want to go out tonight?" he asked.

"Of course. What do you want to do?"

"Unless you had other ideas, maybe we could go to dinner at Columbia."

I grinned. A real date. Columbia Restaurant was one of my favorite places to eat. My parents took me when they got the urge for good Cuban food. I was glad I packed nicer clothes. "Columbia sounds great."

"My shift ends at six thirty, could you wait until then?"

"Of course."

He nodded as he backed away, his eyes on mine. "I'll see you then."

My shift went pretty fast. I didn't have as much crap from customers as usual—maybe Fridays were slow in the world of crazy—and since Noah was the supervisor for the floor today, I had plenty of time to watch him. I noticed his customer service skills were amazing. He was all business with customers, but whenever I appeared in his vision, he stopped what he was doing to watch me. It started an exciting game of cat and mouse. Coincidentally, we seemed to be in the same aisles most of the time. Every once in a while I'd brush close by him, especially if he was with a customer, just to watch him get flustered.

I passed Jake after my break and noticed he was removing a brick of cheese and a plastic knife from his locker. I didn't pay much attention until an hour later, when I overheard one of the other employees talking to Mr. Hanson and Noah about cheese. They were all laughing.

"What happened?" I asked.

"Someone left a block of cheese in the guys' bathroom and a knife stuck in it with a sign that said 'Feel free to cut me,'" the guy said, still chuckling. "It was hilarious to me for some reason, maybe because I was having a pretty crappy day before that. So I guess the prankster is a guy." He walked off, still laughing to himself.

Jake? Weird old Jake was the prankster? The man who was always talking to himself was the one pulling all the pranks? Of course, now that I thought about it, I did see him talking to the vending machine not long before my quarter got stuck in the goo. And he was the one who had the idea for macaroni bowling. It should've been obvious, actually.

As the other guy walked off, I looked at Noah and Mr. Hanson. "I think I know who the prankster is."

Mr. Hanson put his finger over his lips and winked at me. He tapped Noah's arm. "I'll be in the office if you need anything."

"Yes, sir." Noah was smiling at me as Hanson walked away. Wait, was I the only one who wasn't in on it?

"You know?" I asked him.

"All the managers do. Mr. Hanson told us a while ago."

"But…" All I could think of were the mannequins with their pants down and the goo in the coin return slot. Hanson actually approved of that? "Why?"

"Mr. Hanson figured it out a long time ago, but he asked us not to say anything."

"I mean, why does Mr. Hanson allow him to keep doing it?"

"Because when Jake got hired, he put on his application that he just retired from years of performing as a clown. Mr. Hanson feels like it's sort of Jake's way of staying in touch with that part of his life. It makes him happy, you know? And keeps the other people who work here happy, too."

Wow. "Mr. Hanson is pretty cool."

Noah nodded. "Probably the nicest person I've ever known. He's like a father to me." His expression darkened as he looked away.

I bet. Mr. Hanson wouldn't scream and curse at Noah. And I wondered if Mr. Hanson knew about Noah working at Cooper's, too. At this point, it wouldn't surprise me. "So Jake doesn't know that you guys know?"

"Nope. Mr. Hanson wants to keep it that way. It's all part of the fun."

As I went back to my position on the sales floor, all I could think about was how Mr. Hanson not only allowed Jake to keep his job, he encouraged the pranks just to make his employees happy. Probably thrilled to hear the Cut The Cheese Guy laughing about it, especially since he'd said he'd had a rough day.

Not so long ago, I thought how awful it would be to work here. I'd look at people like Ruthie and Jake and think they probably couldn't get a job anywhere else. But now I realized they probably wouldn't want to work anywhere else. People like Noah, Jake, Bessie, and Ruthie—they were all offered opportunities here that they may not get at another job. My assumptions about working here were wrong.

I passed a man with a key fob pierced through his cheek. Okay, so maybe not all my assumptions were wrong. SmartMart attracted weirdos like nowhere else.

Toward the end of my shift, I was on my toes, trying to reach a box of cereal on top of the wrong shelf when an arm reached around me to pluck it down. Noah placed the box on the shelf behind me, his other hand reaching around me as if getting something else and effectively trapping me between his arms.

"Thanks," I told him, reaching up to twist his tie around my finger. God, he smelled good. I pressed my fingers against his collarbone. "You don't wear that chain at work?"

He shook his head. "It fits Cooper's better than Smart-Mart."

I tugged on the tie slightly as his eyes focused on my mouth. He leaned in, his lips just touching mine.

"Well, well, well." Roxanne sauntered toward us, hand on one hip. "Isn't this cozy?" Noah jumped back, but I just glared at her.

"Shut up, Roxanne," I told her. "This is none of your business."

"Uh-huh." She shook her head at Noah, tisking. "Shame, shame, manager boy. This will get you fired from the program for sure."

Noah didn't say anything, but I knew he needed this job and everything that went with it. For her to target Noah instead of me, the person she actually hated, didn't make sense. It did make me want to grab whatever was in arm's reach and chuck it at her as hard as I could.

"What do you want?" I asked Roxanne.

"Well, for starters, I don't much like cleaning that bathroom with you. I think you can handle it all on your own, don't you?"

I shrugged. "Fine."

"And, just because I can't stand you, how about telling Mr. Hanson that you volunteer to clean the bathroom for another month or two. Make it two."

I gritted my teeth. To be honest, I'd expected worse from her. Someone as vicious as Roxanne should have a better imagination. So I did the only thing I could do. I flattened my lips into a grimace and wrinkled my forehead as if I was in terrible pain.

"No, anything but that," I said, my voice cracking slightly. I could've worked up a tear or two, but it might be a little too over the top. "We were almost done with it!"

Roxanne smirked.

"You don't have to do that," Noah told me firmly. He looked at Roxanne. "Why are you acting like this? Lex hasn't done anything to you."

She grinned, her teeth showing large and white between her red lips. Even with her platinum hair, she reminded me of Maleficent from *Sleeping Beauty*. It wouldn't surprise me if she morphed into a dragon and engulfed us and the entire cereal aisle in flames.

"Alexis has you fooled, Noah. I know her type—she's only here for a summer job and you're nothing more than a fling to someone like her. Trust me, I'm doing you a favor by turning you in to Mr. Hanson."

Noah's face darkened. "You don't know her at all," he said, his voice low enough to almost be a growl.

Roxanne's eyes widened slightly at his anger. She opened her mouth to say something else, but I held up my hand. "Fine, Roxanne. Two more months of..." I sighed dramatically. "Bathroom duty. Alone. And you'll keep this to yourself, got it?"

She smiled then, a genuine-looking smile that could almost pass for friendliness if I didn't know better. "Absolutely. Of course, you realize this is only for *this* occasion. If I catch you at it again...well, there's so many more things you could do for me, cheerleader."

She winked at Noah. I sagged against the shelf as she walked away. "Two more months of bathroom duty," I said loudly. "I can't imagine anything worse." Okay, that was definitely too over the top, but Roxanne seemed to have a skip in her step as she turned the corner out of sight.

Noah stepped quickly toward me. "You don't have to do that," he said earnestly. "I'll tell Mr. Hanson about us myself. He's a reasonable guy."

I straightened and smiled at him. I loved hearing him say the word "us." "No, Noah. You don't want to lose your job. Trust me, it's not that big of a deal."

"Really?" He narrowed his eyes at me. "Why do you suddenly seem okay with it?"

I shrugged. "Bathroom duty sucks, but it won't be two months. Remember, I go back to school in a month. Then I'll be done with this place for good."

He grinned, then his face fell. "A month? That's it?"

I took his hand. "That's it for SmartMart, not for us. You're going to be at school, too, remember?"

His fingers curved around mine, but he was still frowning. "Yeah, I remember."

"Noah, we'll still be together there. If you want to be, I mean."

"Of course I do. It's just…we're in different, um, circles."

"Yeah, well, I don't care. Neither should you. Now you better let me get back to work before the all-powerful Roxanne comes looking to see if we've broken her commandment."

He laughed and lightly kissed my lips. "I'll see you after work." Then he disappeared.

My shift couldn't end fast enough.

A t five o'clock, I finished my bathroom shift alone. It actually wasn't as bad without Roxanne—no one to torture me with backhanded comments about my clothes, my hair, my life. I even grabbed my cell from my locker, plugged in my earbuds, and listened to music as I cleaned. My imagination wandered, and I pictured Noah walking in and closing the door so we could make out. Maybe if I figured how to get this done in less than my scheduled hour, we could put the rest of that time to good use. Employees were allowed to use the regular customer bathroom when I was cleaning this one, so it's not like we'd be interrupted. Or maybe I could forego cleaning the toilet just the one day.

Nice, Lex. Fantasizing about making out with Noah while you're scrubbing a toilet. Gross.

At six, I clocked out and went back to the bathroom to change into a sundress—unusual for me, but we were going out, and I wanted to look nice for once without my mother here to see me. I brushed my hair out, applied some lip gloss, and went into the break room to wait for Noah. He showed at exactly six thirty, his eyes focused on his cell. He had a frown on his face. His eyes lit up when he saw me, though. "Wow! You look fantastic."

I smiled. "Thanks."

"Man, this really sucks. My mom needs to go out, so I have to stay with Belle at the house. I'm sorry, Lex. I can drop you off at home, though. Maybe this weekend?"

"Sure," I said halfheartedly. But then again, we didn't really have to go to dinner. And my parents thought I was getting off work late, anyway. "You know, I don't have to be home until nine thirty. How about I go to your house with you?"

He frowned. "My house?"

"Yeah. I can help you watch Belle. Why are you looking at me like that?" It was like I had offered to cut off his head or something. Did I overestimate how he felt about me? Or did Roxanne finally get to him? I cocked my head. "You didn't really get a message from your mom, did you?"

"What? Yes, I did."

"Look, if you're having second thoughts about this, just say so."

He held out his phone to show me the text. "Trust me. I'm not being weird on you right now. I really do have to watch Belle."

"Well, does your mom have a problem with you bringing a girl over or something?"

"No." The pink tinge in his cheeks flushed into red.

"Is, um, your dad home?"

"No. I guess it'd be okay. I don't live in the same, um, neighborhood as you do, though."

"Oh, jeez, I don't care about that, Noah. If you live in a trailer with no electricity I don't care." I hoped he didn't really think I was that shallow. "I just want to hang out with you."

His lips pursed, then he nodded. I followed him out of the store, taking his hand as he helped me into his SUV. I watched as he made his way to the driver's side, pumping the clutch a couple times to get it to start.

Noah's house was definitely not in my neighborhood,

nor in the next or the next. It was what could be considered "across the tracks" in a movie—a small, old stucco home with faded yellow paint on a street where lanky, barky dogs ran free. The roof looked like it was missing some shingles, and the driveway was cracked in several places. The yard was mowed, though, and a cute little elf statue was sitting beneath one of the shrubs. A little girl's pink bike was sitting on the front porch, streamers cascading from the handlebars.

"Belle rides a bike already?" I asked as Noah took my hand to help me out of the SUV.

He nodded. "With the training wheels. She could probably ride without, but she's afraid, so we leave them on."

I snorted and tried to cover it with a cough. Trying to get a three-year-old to ride a bike without training wheels? Rory couldn't ride until she was six. Noah was adorably clueless.

As soon as we walked into the house, Belle threw herself at Noah. He lifted her up and swung her around, kissing both her cheeks as she giggled. Her attachment to him—and the light in his face as he held her—was sweet. Adjusting Belle to his hip, he led me into the living room where his mom was waiting to take the keys to the SUV. Mrs. Grayson remembered me from the pageant and was very kind, asking me in her lovely French accent to make myself at home. She kissed her son on the cheek and Belle on the top of her head, promising to be back in a couple hours.

The living room was small, the furniture worn, but it was clean and organized. I sat down on the carpet to play puzzles with Belle, at her insistence, while Noah changed into shorts and a T-shirt. We colored princesses and read Dr. Seuss and played in her little plastic kitchen until Noah called us for pizza. The three of us sat down together at her little table and ate on little toy plates, sipping pretend tea from toy cups. At one point, my imagination ran away and pictured this as my family, with Noah as my husband and Belle as our daughter. But then I realized how weird and embarrassing that thought was and pushed it out of my mind quickly.

At seven thirty, Noah announced bedtime for Belle. I was impressed that she didn't fuss about it, which was more than I could say for Rory at that age. Now, too, in fact. Rory got away with doing whatever she wanted, ending up going to bed past nine o'clock after "one more glass of water, one more hug, one more TV show."

I helped Belle brush her teeth and tucked her into her big girl bed, which was actually a cute little plastic-framed bed close to the floor. I pulled the pink comforter covered with Disney princesses up under her chin as Noah turned out the light. He closed the door behind us.

We were alone.

He looked at me. "Want to hang out in my room? We could watch TV in there, I mean." He blushed. Shy Noah was back.

I nodded and followed him a couple doors down to his room. It was a typical guy's room, I guess—painted in dark gray with silver blinds to cover the window instead of curtains. The room smelled like Noah, a faint, intoxicating mix of soap and the beach. Missing were the gold and silver trophies and medals that littered Bryce's room; instead, several large framed black and white photographs of tall buildings adorned the walls. I recognized the Hearst Tower in New York and Chicago's Willis Tower, but the others were strange to me.

"That's the Gherkin in London," Noah said when he caught me staring at a weird rocket-shaped building. "It was built to be environmentally friendly, using the building's own natural ventilation to use half the energy of a normal structure that size. Look, see?" He ran his finger along the arc at the top of the Gherkin. "There's a curved lens on top in the observation deck that allows a 360-degree view of London."

"What's that one?" I pointed to a squatty circular structure that looked like it was made from a honeycomb.

"The Kreod. It's in London, too. It's a perfect example of how you can make cutting-edge buildings with sustainable, eco-friendly materials." He smiled at me. "I admire structures that are architecturally creative but have less of an impact on the environment. I want to be able to design them someday, too." He turned his gaze back to the Kreod, his smile as tender as when he watched his sister twirl around the living room.

"Have you ever been there?" I asked. "London, I mean?"

"No. But I will someday."

I had no doubt that he would. Noah was determined to make the most of his life. Those qualities that had made no sense to me a few short weeks ago fell into place. He didn't want to be a store manager—had no desire to remain at SmartMart the rest of his life. He just wanted to do his best, learn as much as he could, and get those jobs that would help him afford a college education for the job he wanted most. I knew if anyone could do it, Noah could. And if he could, I certainly should be able to do what made me happy, too, without worrying about what my mother thought. She used to say I should be an optometrist or therapist or anything that made sense to her. The thought of going into medicine was as exciting to me as getting my braces in middle school.

I moved over to Noah's dresser, peering at each of the pictures—one of Noah and his sister with Mickey Mouse, another with his friends around a table playing some card game. I recognized two of the three guys as his friends Miller and Steve. They went to our school, but I didn't really know them.

Noah watched me as I walked around his room. I sat on his bed, but he didn't move. "Why are you so nervous?"

He gave me a brief "are you serious" kind of look. "I don't know. Um, because you're in my room, sitting on my bed?"

"Really? This is your bed? I had no idea."

"Funny."

"Have you ever had a girl in your room?" I asked, running my finger around the geometric circles on the bedspread.

"No."

He perched on the edge of the bed. I scooted next to him. "Noah, relax. We've already kissed, remember?"

"I know."

"Did it suck that bad?" Maybe I wasn't a good kisser. Nobody ever told me if I was or wasn't.

"Are you kidding?" he asked, half laughing.

I leaned closer to him. "So, then, what are you worried about?"

"I just… Look, we're going back to school in a few weeks. What happens then? Do you know what school is like for me?" I didn't answer. "Exactly," he said. "You don't remember much because I disappear at school. The few friends I have aren't treated well at all. They're called loser and dork and geek to their faces. But at least they're being noticed. No one notices me anymore, Lex. Ever since ninth grade I've worked hard to blend in with the background, and trust me, that's how I want to keep it. You don't. You're popular, beautiful, friendly, everyone loves you. And now you're dating the guy everyone thinks told on Bryce. So don't tell me it's going to be easy for us."

His eyes were pinched slightly at the corners as he stared at me. How long had this been bugging him? It's nothing I wasn't aware of, and I'd thought about it plenty when I started to realize I was interested in Noah.

I sighed. "Noah, for such a smart guy, you just don't get it. You're an amazing person, and I love hanging out with you. You're funny, generous, kind, hot"—*oops, that one slipped out*—"smart, everything that you don't even see. I'm not the only one who sees that in you. There's Mr. Hanson, Bessie, Ruthie, even Roxanne. You're a good big brother to Belle and so much more responsible than most guys in high school. And who cares what happened years ago with

Bryce? Really, I don't. Not anymore."

He stared at me for a moment. The corners of his mouth tugged up slightly. "You think I'm hot?"

I felt my cheeks heat. "Did you hear anything else I said?"

He reached for my hand and pulled me closer so that I stood in front of him. I ran my fingers through his soft, dark hair, smiling at the way he closed his eyes. Had we really only kissed twice? It seemed like we'd been together forever, though not in a boring, "old comfortable shoes" way. It was more like a slow shiver that started in my shoulders and worked its way down an invisible line throughout my body, stimulating every single one of my senses so I became more aware of *me* around him.

"If we're together," I told him softly, "why do we care what other people think?"

He wrapped his arms around my waist, his blue eyes finally fixing on mine. I sensed the shift in him—from nervously awkward Clark Kent to confident Superman— and a sense of satisfaction filled me.

"You are awesome, you know that?" he said.

"All those adjectives I came up with for you and that's all you've got? Awesome?"

He tilted his head. "Awesomely awesome?"

He reached up to caress my cheek with his hand, then slipped it around my neck to pull me to him.

The spark created when our lips touched turned into a full-on blazing inferno as our mouths melded together. My body went limp in Noah's arms. I couldn't get enough of him, the taste of his lips, his air. He pulled me closer until I was straddling his lap, his hands sliding down to fit around my hips as we kissed. I was lost in him.

Of all the moments in my life, of all the kisses from whatever guys I thought were important at the time, Noah's kiss made my skin tingle as if my body was just now coming alive. He'd never be able to convince me that I was his first kiss, but I didn't even care.

It was only a couple minutes later when we heard the sound of the screen on the front door slamming. Noah's head jerked to the side, listening. We could hear the water running in the kitchen and glasses being clinked around.

Noah smiled at me and leaned back, resting on his hands as I scrambled off his lap. Oh, sure, *now* he was calm and confident. "Your mom is home? I thought she was going to be out a couple hours?"

"Don't worry. She'll be okay with you being in my room, trust me. She'll probably just be happy I have a girlfriend." He stood up and held out a hand to me.

Girlfriend? I had to stifle a juvenile urge to giggle. He hadn't officially asked me, but who cared? I was Noah's girlfriend. Hell yeah. I took his hand and followed behind him.

As we entered the living room, Noah jerked to a halt, allowing me to bump into him. He didn't say anything, but his hand squeezed mine harder. I peeked around his shoulder, and my heart almost stopped.

It wasn't his mother who stared back at us.

CHAPTER
23

A tall, dark-haired man stood in front of us. Didn't he say his father wasn't home? And were Noah's parents still together? We never did get around to talking about his father. He made it clear it was a subject he didn't want to discuss.

"Noah." The man nodded shortly, then his eyes moved to appraise me. I was surprised at how young he was, definitely younger than my parents. He smiled and raised an eyebrow at Noah. "I hope I'm not interrupting something."

Noah had my hand in a steel grip, and it was starting to ache. "No, sir. Lex just got here. I'm taking her home as soon as Mom gets back with the truck."

His dad pursed his lips as he looked out the small kitchen window. "Where did she go, anyway?"

"She had errands to run. She'll be back soon."

The man moved over to us and Noah stepped to the side, pulling me with him. "Hi, you're Lex? I'm Noah's father, Tom."

He smiled and held out a hand. I pulled my hand from Noah's and shook it. His demeanor was nice, his smile and soft voice not at all matching the scary shouting that I'd heard at Rory's pageant. I wondered how it could be the same guy, but it had to be, with the way Noah was reacting.

This was one of the most uncomfortable moments ever. I glanced at Noah, who was still staring stonily at his father.

"Well...?" Tom asked Noah, an eyebrow raised.

"Well what?" Noah asked. I thought I could detect a note of sarcasm in his voice, and I could tell his dad did, too.

Tom glanced at me and laughed, but his voice wasn't light. "Funny, Noah. Don't you have something for me?"

"No."

Tom's eyebrows dipped slightly and the corners of his mouth twitched. "Well, now...we need to talk about that."

"I have nothing to say," Noah said.

His father was getting angry, I could tell. Why couldn't Noah just give him whatever he wanted or at least pretend politeness? He wasn't being anywhere near as rude as Rory or even I could be to my mother, but I got the feeling this was a really bad choice here. The tension in the room escalated to the point where I wasn't sure if the air conditioner had gone out.

Tom's eyes narrowed. "Why don't you have your friend wait outside for you."

"No," I said quickly. Two sets of eyes fixed on me. My

voice sounded in a higher pitch. "I need Noah to take me home now. My mom wants me back." I took my cell phone out of my pocket with trembling hands and waved it. I remembered his mom had the SUV. "Noah, we can walk, right?" Obviously, we couldn't. I lived miles from here. But I couldn't leave him with his dad.

Noah blinked at me, then nodded. I grabbed his hand and we walked out the door. My entire body was shaking so hard that I missed my step from the doorway to the porch and dropped my cell phone. The cover flew off in two pieces.

Noah picked up the pieces and put them in his pocket, then wrapped his arms around me. "It's okay," he said, rubbing my back. "C'mon, let's go for a walk."

I nodded, taking a deep breath to calm down and relieve the shakes a bit. Noah kept an arm around my shoulders as we walked past old homes and overgrown yards that made the neighborhood look run-down.

One block over was an old playground with slides and teeter-totters that looked decades old and not exactly safe. We climbed up into a boxed-in fort at the top of the slides—the type of place I hadn't crawled in since I was probably six years old. I laid my head on Noah's shoulder, sighing as he rested his cheek on my hair. We didn't speak for a while, just listened to the sounds of summer twilight—the crickets chirping, birds calling, and somewhere far away someone mowing his lawn. Gentle, peaceful sounds that did nothing to calm me.

"I'm sorry," Noah said quietly.

I lifted my head to look at him. His eyes seemed sunken

in, and he looked so much older now. He and I were almost the same age but with completely different problems.

Most of mine were trivial; his were real.

"Why are you sorry?"

"You know. My dad and all…"

"Whatever's going on with you and your dad isn't something you should apologize for." I hesitated. "What *is* going on?"

He shook his head and stared out at the fading swirls of pink and peach in the sky. "I've never exactly lived up to his expectations. Overheard me once telling my mom that I wanted to go to school to get a degree in architecture and after laughing his ass off, he told me with a brain like mine, I'd be better off becoming a starving artist. Emphasis on the starving. He didn't even care that my grades were As and Bs. I wasn't good enough."

The words hurt. Even though my dad didn't really understand my goals, he always supported me. "Is he like that with Belle?"

"No. Not right now, at least. He loves Belle. Whatever she wants, she gets. But me…"

He trailed off, his jaw set. He looked like I did when I was trying to keep from crying. I slipped my fingers through his, stunned at how matter-of-factly he said everything. His mom obviously believed in him, but for his dad to make such hateful comments to his face like that, it was amazing that he had any goals at all.

"Anyway," he continued, "it's gotten worse over the last year, but at least I don't have to see him that much.

He works outside of Tallahassee and comes home maybe a couple times a month. The construction job was the only thing he could find after he got laid off about a year ago. That's why I had to take the second job at Cooper's. I think he comes home just so he can get the money I make, but Mom and I are the ones who pay the bills, so I don't give it to him anymore."

"Does he hit you?" I blurted out the words, then bit my lip. I wanted to know, but what would I do if it kept going on? Confront Noah's mother? She must know about it, so as nice as she was, it pissed me off that she'd allow that to happen to her son.

Noah shrugged. "Not really. Most of the time he just yells at me."

In other words, yes. "He might've hit you tonight."

"Nah. Mostly if he's had anything to drink. It's a lot harder now that I'm taller than him."

I wasn't sure about that. His dad looked angry enough to punch him if I hadn't been there.

"We don't have much money, as I'm sure you figured out," he continued. "I've been working extra at Cooper's to help pay for Belle's pageants and my college savings, and with my dad out of work, it's been really tough. I do it, though. That's why the management job is important to me. You know, it's not like I don't have dreams, too," he added, his eyes meeting mine almost accusingly.

"I never said you didn't have dreams."

"Not directly, but I remember once at school, you were talking to some freshmen about how students in extracurricular activities would be more successful than the ones who weren't motivated enough to get involved. But do you know how much time and money sports, band, or any of those other things cost?"

I stared outside at the darkening sky. That did sound like something I would've said, probably at Open House when I was recruiting for softball. "I'm sorry. I guess I didn't realize what I was saying."

Noah tilted my chin toward him. "No, *I'm* sorry. That was lame of me to say."

"It's okay." I scuffed my shoes against the top of the slide. "I'm surprised you actually remember something I said."

"I remember everything when it comes to you."

God, I loved the sentimentality of him. Every word that would never come out of a normal guy's mouth was gold from his. I stroked his palm with my fingers, noticing how shallow the lines were. I hoped there was nothing to the whole palm-reading thing. Noah deserved a long, happy life.

We stayed on top of the playground set, talking and kissing until it was completely dark. I finally pulled away to press the button on my phone. Nine o'clock.

"I'm going to have to start thinking about getting home," I whispered. It was so tempting just to make out all night. But that would be the last time my parents let me outside, I was sure.

"Okay," he murmured, but he didn't release me. We kissed for a little while longer, but I finally pushed away.

"Noah, I've got to get home."

We crawled out of the fort and slid down one of the slides. It made me smile that we were actually sliding on a playground for our first date. What Court would say if she could see me now, and in a dress, too.

Hand in hand, we walked through the moonlight to his house. I checked my phone again. I had less than twenty minutes to get home.

"Do you think your mom's back by now?" I asked.

"Yeah, she should be," he said. His voice was subdued, and I knew he was thinking about his dad.

"Will he get angry at her?"

"I don't know."

I didn't say anything else until we got to his house. His mother's SUV was in the driveway, and unfortunately, so was his father's car. Noah waved to me to wait for him as he went to the side of the front window. He peered around to look inside, then backed away.

"Well, he's not yelling at her. He's got the TV on, which usually means he's pretty chilled out." Noah fished his phone out of his pocket and typed on it. "I'm telling Mom I'm taking the SUV to get you home," he said. He finished and slipped the phone back into his pocket, pulling out his keys. "Ready?"

I glanced at his house. "Maybe you should stay over at my house. If your father's still mad…" I couldn't think of leaving him with that man.

"Thanks, but I better not. It just gets worse the longer I put it off."

"I don't want him to hurt you."

"I can tune him out. I'll just think of you instead." He grinned and held the door to the SUV open so I could slide in. The drive to my side of town took almost too long, since we had to wait for a train to cross over the tracks, but it did give me a chance to crawl into the back and change into my SmartMart outfit. Showing up in a dress wouldn't exactly be easy to explain to my parents.

It was three minutes to ten when we finally pulled into the driveway. The front porch light was on, but no one was standing in the window. I turned to him.

"Thanks for bringing me home."

"Thanks for coming over tonight. Maybe next time we can actually go on a real date."

"I had fun. Belle is great." I leaned over to give him a quick kiss. "Are you working tomorrow?"

"Yeah. You?"

"Nope. Saturday."

His fingers gently grazed my cheek. "Can you go out tomorrow night?"

"I wish. I'm grounded for staying out too late last night. But if I can figure a way out of it, I'll text you."

I kissed him again and slid out of the vehicle, turning to wave as he pulled out of the driveway. Considerate guy that he was, he waited until I was in the house before driving off.

I leaned against the door, my heart sinking to think of what he had to go home to. I really wished he could've stayed over, and screw what my parents would think. Noah and I hadn't even been out on a real date yet, but this relationship was already so much more *real* than the silly ones in my past.

Oh, Noah, there's a possibility that I could be in love with you. Deep down crazy serious love.

The thought was not as terrifying as I would have imagined.

CHAPTER
24

My parents didn't act any different than usual when I got home, which made me breathe easier and feel bad at the same time for deceiving them. I headed straight up to my room, the familiar pang stabbing me when I passed Grandma's room. She was already asleep. I returned Syd's frantic texts: *Are you out with Noah? Call me! Where are you?*

I typed: *Sorry. Yes I was out with Noah.*

Her return text was full of symbols that made me think she was either super angry or super excited. I guessed it was the latter.

Court's text was a little less subtle. *Did you guys do it?*

Her mind was always in the gutter. Which was exactly what I responded with. But I was glad to see it at the same time—at least she was getting used to the idea of Noah in my life.

My next text was to Noah, but it wasn't until I was pretty sure he was home. *You okay?*

I waited, staring at my phone until it buzzed. *Yeah.*

Yeah? That was all he had to say? I called him twice but he didn't answer. Another text from him: *Tomorrow.*

Tomorrow? He was working tomorrow, but I wasn't. I wanted to know that he really was okay. I heard how his dad yelled at him in Tallahassee. It still echoed through my head. I couldn't help feeling that I made it worse by being there tonight. It made total sense to me why Noah seemed so shy—maybe it wasn't shyness as much as low self-esteem. If I had been screamed at my whole life and told how worthless I was, eventually I'd start feeling that way myself.

I typed *Call me.*

I slid the phone into my pocket. If he didn't call me, I'd find a way to his house to check on him myself.

He didn't call me in the morning.

Or by noon.

Or by three.

No response to texts. No response to phone calls. I convinced my mother to drive me to SmartMart under the pretense that I needed emergency tampons. Noah wasn't working, though. Bessie told me he had called in sick.

Now I was starting to panic.

My mother had dinner prepared at six o'clock. She refused my requests to go out, even over to Syd's. I ate only a small piece of my meatloaf, too focused on how to get out of the house. I wished there was a big tree outside my second-story window. Maybe I could tie sheets together. If I got desperate enough, I might. I started having Rapunzel fantasies, but by seven o'clock, I'd had it. I texted Syd but she was out at a restaurant with her family, so I called Court to enlist her help. If anyone was an expert at figuring a way out, it was her.

Within a half hour, we were in her convertible, driving to Noah's neighborhood. It was surprisingly easy. My mother had a headache and went to bed early. My dad was engrossed in his computer. Rory was in her room playing her Xbox. I snuck out the back door and Court picked me up.

"Where the hell does this guy live?" Court complained, staring at the clumps of people standing around on street corners, staring at us as we passed.

"It's an old neighborhood, but it's not that bad," I reassured her.

"I hope not. I don't want to get carjacked."

We made a couple more right turns, then a left. Her GPS took us by the playground. It was only last night, but it felt like forever ago that Noah and I had been making out at the top of the slides.

"This one," I said, pointing to Noah's yellow house. His mother's SUV was in the driveway. His dad's car, I was relieved to see, was not.

I jumped out and slammed the door. "Thanks, Court," I said as she rolled down her window.

"Wait, are you leaving me here?" she asked, looking around like she expected to get mugged at any moment.

I threw a dirty look at her. She pouted. "Okay, okay, I'll

wait for you, but don't be too long."

"Actually, as soon as that door opens, drive away."

"And leave you *here*?"

"I'll be okay. Keep your cell phone on and I'll call you if you need to come back. And don't say anything to Bryce."

She sighed heavily. "All right."

"Thanks Court." I ran up to his front door and hesitated. Should I knock? Ring the doorbell? It was after eight o'clock, so Belle would be in bed, but what about Noah's mother? She seemed cool, though.

I rapped my knuckles against the door. I could hear talking inside and saw the blinds shift in the dining room window. I waited.

Mrs. Grayson pulled the door open. She looked tired, her normally tight bun falling out of its pins. "Lex, *mon dieu!*" Her eyes darted around. "It is late."

I could hear Court pulling out of the driveway. "I know. I'm sorry. Is Noah home, Mrs. Grayson?"

She glanced over her shoulder, then back to me. "Noah is not well right now. Call him tomorrow?"

She started to close the door, but I put my shoe in the way. "My ride just dropped me off. I don't have a way of getting home now. I know he's there. Please, can I just come in and talk to him?"

She looked at me for a moment, considering that. Then she sighed. "Okay. You are maybe what he needs right now."

That sent my stomach spiraling. She opened the door back up and beckoned me in. I looked over to the hallway where Noah stood with his arms folded in front of him.

He had a ball cap on, pulled down over his forehead, but otherwise he looked normal.

"Why haven't you answered my calls or anything?" I stepped toward him but he moved back farther into the shadow of the hall. "What is the problem, Noah?"

"Go home, Lex."

My heart sank. He did blame me. His father screamed at him for having a girl over and for letting her push him around, and now Noah blamed me for it. It might have been my fault. Maybe I shouldn't have insisted Noah take me home. Maybe we shouldn't have stayed at the playground so late.

No, that couldn't be it. That didn't sound like Noah.

I glanced over my shoulder, but Mrs. Grayson had disappeared. "Noah, I'm sorry. I didn't mean to get you into trouble." I knew my voice was cracking. The idea that he might actually be mad at me hurt.

He took a deep breath. "It wasn't your fault."

His voice sounded strange. Like it was coming from someone else. Something was on his face. I reached up to touch his cheek but he jerked his head back, offering me a glance at the other side of his face.

Holy crap.

"Noah," I whispered. "Oh my God."

He grabbed my hand and pulled me back to his room. His desk lamp provided the room's only illumination, so I was barely able to see the cut on his lip and what looked like a bruise along his jaw. He sat on the bed and I sank down by his side.

"What…why? It was me, wasn't it?" My heart hurt so badly it felt like someone had a fist around it, squeezing it like a water balloon.

"No, it wasn't you at all. It was the money. I refused to give him what I'd made. We have too many bills due for me to hand over our cash. We got into a fight about it, I told him he sucked as a father, and he hit me. That's what set him off. Not you. This wasn't your fault."

I touched his jaw with a very light finger, but he flinched. "Do you believe this is *your* fault?" I asked.

He shrugged. "No. Not really." He tried to smile but winced, touching the side of his face. "The one good thing that has come of this is that my mother kicked him out of the house, and I think for good this time."

"Oh, joy," I said drily. "I'm glad she didn't wait until you were dead."

He pinched his eyebrows together. "It hasn't been easy for her, either, Lex. She couldn't leave him because she was still trying to get her citizenship and she needed his insurance. It's also why I've been working so hard with two jobs."

"So what's changed?"

He grinned, then flinched again, touching his lip. "She got a full-time job. That's where she was when you were here last night. They offered it to her and she had to go fill out the paperwork. She wanted to surprise me with it."

"At night? Where is she working?"

"She's a night manager at Busch Gardens. She had a job like that in Canada, so she had the experience. It's actually cool because we get free park tickets and all. And I'll be home with Belle at night. Mr. Hanson said he'd make sure I'm off by seven o'clock so she can make it to work."

"What about Cooper's?" The thought of that disgusting guy who hit on me crawled over me like a bug. Ugh.

"I'm keeping it through the summer, then I'll quit. That way we won't have a break between her paycheck and what we make now."

He had it all figured out. I relaxed against his shoulder and he wrapped his arm around my waist, nestling his cheek in my hair. "I'm really glad for you all," I said.

"Yeah," he replied. "She was going to surprise me with the news when she got home, but he was here so she didn't get the chance. She lost it when he hit me—started beating him back, screaming that she was done. He left after that."

"Are you sure he's gone for good?"

Noah's arm tightened slightly around me. "I hope so," he said. He didn't sound certain. I wondered how many times his mom had kicked Tom out of the house just for him to work his way back in. *Please, don't let him back in this time.*

I touched his lip gently with one finger. "Have you put anything on this?"

"I put ice on it," he said.

"It'll be hard not to kiss you until it heals."

He took my face between his hands, his eyes soft. "I'll live through the pain. Trust me."

His lips found mine, soft as a feather.

He lived. We both did.

CHAPTER
25

Funny how much more tolerable SmartMart was now that Noah and I were together. I moved about the store the next couple of weeks in a happy daze—shelving, bagging, checking out, and even greeting with a smile on my face. A few times we sneaked into the stockroom and made out for a few minutes. It was totally hot and the only real time I could spend with him, since I was still grounded.

At home, things weren't so great. Almost every day I confided in my grandma, telling her about Noah, promising to bring him over so she could meet him. At first, Grandma would smile and ask questions, but then she'd ask me the same questions and forget who I was talking about. I just answered her again and kept talking. I did figure out that she remembered a lot more things from when she was younger, so sometimes if I didn't want to think about her forgetting stuff, I'd talk to her about when she was a kid. She told me lively stories about her and her sisters.

Grandma wasn't the same physically, either. Dr. Ahmed said the pneumonia most likely escalated her troubles. She never went anywhere now without a family member or the Willy Wonka nurse escorting her. Dr. Ahmed told us most Alzheimer's patients don't know they're declining, but Grandma knew. Some days she'd sit in her chair in her room and stare out the window, not even wanting to go for a walk around the nearby park, which used to be her favorite thing to do. On those days, she'd barely acknowledge me when I visited her, and each time, the tiny fissures in my heart stretched further. She knew I was there and she chose not to talk to me. And she was declining so fast, part of me wanted to scream at Dr. Ahmed that the medicine was making it worse, though I really had no clue.

Grandma became the topic of many arguments with my dad, too. I knew my anger toward him was a result of her not responding to me, and I knew he couldn't deal with it. Even though it was obvious that he was hurt, I'd still yell at him that he wasn't spending as much time with her as he used to. I even overheard my mother tell him one evening, "Jackson, she's right. You need to visit with your mother now more than ever. You'll regret it if you don't."

I finally told Noah about my grandma, and he was everything he should be—caring, warm, understanding. He was perfect about everything—or at least until Bryce decided to show up at SmartMart.

With just a half hour left in my shift one afternoon, I was

organizing produce—and why the hell was that guy holding up a banana to his pants—when I heard Bryce's familiar loud voice asking Ruthie where I was. I dropped the grapes back in their bin and ran to the front. Court was next to him, her arm tucked loosely through his. Ruthie went off to greet another customer as I glanced around to make sure Noah wasn't nearby.

"What are you doing here?" I asked, giving them each a quick hug.

"Court needed some girl thing so we thought we'd come pick you up." He kissed Court as she pulled away from him.

"'Girl thing' means tampons," she said to me, winking.

Bryce put his hands over his ears. "I did *not* need to hear that, Court!" he yelled as she walked away, giggling wickedly. "Seriously, sometimes I wonder how I put up with her."

I smacked his arm as Ruthie walked back over.

"Oh, Ruthie, this is my friend Bryce."

Bryce smiled and said hello as Ruthie looked from him to me, her face confused.

"Lexus, you're dating Noah *and* this boy?"

My heart dropped into my shoes.

"Noah?" Bryce asked, frowning at me.

"No," I said quickly. "Ruthie doesn't know what she's talking about." *Damn it, Ruthie.* "So it looks like it's going to rain," I said, nodding at the slight darkening outside.

Bryce kept his eyes on me, his expression still.

"Is it going to storm?" I asked again, knowing how lame I sounded. When did I ever care about the weather?

"There's some tornado watch or something," Bryce said,

still frowning. "So Noah—"

"Tornado?" Ruthie asked, her face going pale. She breathed heavily as she backed away. "Tornado! No!" She started to scream and pivot around in circles, grasping her head and yelling, "Tornado!" at the top of her lungs.

I tried calming her down, talking softly, telling her there was no tornado, that it wasn't even raining, but she was too panicked to hear me. Thankfully, there weren't many customers at the front right now.

"What's with her?" Bryce asked. At least he was distracted now.

"I don't know. I guess she's just freaked by tornadoes." I cursed at myself as Ruthie started up with her wailing again. "Just go outside," I told Bryce, grabbing his arm to push him toward the door. "I'll clock out and meet you at your car."

"Okay, fine, I'll text Court and…" He hesitated as he noticed the people running our way—Mr. Hanson and, *oh crap,* Noah. I felt his arm muscles shift as his fists clenched. Noah also stopped as he saw Bryce staring at him. I dropped my hands quickly.

"What's going on?" Mr. Hanson asked as he reached us.

"Someone mentioned something about a tornado, and Ruthie got upset. Of course, there is *no* tornado," I added as Ruthie clutched her head again. "It's a beautiful day. Look—you can see the sun, Ruthie."

"That's right, it's a beautiful, calm day," Mr. Hanson said soothingly to Ruthie as he ushered her away toward the employee area.

Noah's eyes were narrowed as he faced off with Bryce.

The air was so sharp with tension between the two, I could almost see the sparks flickering. All they needed were hands on holsters and we'd have a Wild West showdown. "Calm down," I told Bryce quietly. I could see Carolyn looking at us from a few aisles over. "Don't start anything."

"Ruthie doesn't know what she's talking about, huh?" Bryce repeated in a sarcastic tone, turning his accusing gaze to me. "When I asked, you told me you just worked together and you weren't even friends. Is she right? Are you going out with him?"

I opened my mouth, but nothing came out. The look in Bryce's eyes was a mix of shock, anger, and hurt. Dating his enemy behind his back was the worst thing I could've done to him.

A real friend would've told him a long time ago.

My silence was enough confirmation for Bryce. He shook his head. "I can't believe it."

"I'm sorry," I said softly, keeping my eyes on him mostly so I wouldn't have to see the hurt that I knew was also on Noah's face.

"So you couldn't even tell me to my face?" Bryce turned his glare on Noah. "This whole time you've been screwing this asshole and you didn't have the decency to tell me."

Noah stepped forward then, scowling and clenching his fists, but I got between them. "He's *not* an asshole, and—"

Whatever else I was going to say was lost as Carolyn appeared. "What's going on?" she rasped in her smoky voice.

"Nothing," I said quickly, trying to keep my expression calm, like we were just having a pleasant conversation.

She looked between the two boys and then at me. "Back to work," she told me before moving away.

"Go before you get me in trouble," I whispered to Bryce. "I'll meet you outside."

"Don't bother," he said. "I'm sure you can find another way home." His nose flared as he glared at Noah, then he left.

I turned around. "Noah—"

But Noah pivoted on his heel and walked away, leaving me alone.

"Hey girl," Court said softly as she came up to me, a plastic bag threaded through her arm. "I saw what happened. You okay?"

I nodded, biting back the tears. She reached out to pull me into a hug. "I told you it was gonna blow up in your face," she said, which I guess was her way of comforting me.

"I know," I said, my voice muffled in her shoulder. I pulled away and rubbed the heel of my hand at my wet cheek. "This sucks."

"Yeah, I know. He'll get over it, eventually." I knew she was talking about Bryce, but it was Noah I was worried about now. Would he?

"I have to go," Court said, glancing at the doors. "Now I've got to pretend I didn't know anything about it. I can't stand lying to him." She sighed, then smiled at me. "Don't worry, it'll be okay."

She promised to call me later and left. Ruthie came back to the front a few minutes later, looking completely composed like nothing had happened. The clock over the door said I had twelve minutes left, but I told Ruthie I was leaving early. She smiled and said good night, happily oblivious to the scene that just happened. I wished I could be as oblivious. Instead, I felt sick to my stomach.

Noah was at the time clock when I got there, his arms crossed.

"Hey," I said quietly. "I'm *really* sorry about that."

"About what?" he asked, the scowl creasing his face in a way I hadn't seen before. Noah's anger actually aimed at me hurt like nothing I'd ever felt, but I deserved it. "About the fact that your jerk of a friend tried to scare Ruthie?"

"He didn't do that on purpose," I cut in. "He didn't know—"

"Or about the fact that you said we just worked together. Or that you were so embarrassed of me that you couldn't bring yourself to tell him we're together?"

"I'm not embarrassed of you. I've been afraid to tell him because I knew he'd react like that." I waved a hand toward the store entrance. "And I knew he'd make it worse for you."

"Yeah. For *me*. That's why." He shook his head as I reached for him. "I have to get back to work. You know, to my job where I'm your manager and apparently nothing else."

He turned around and walked away.

I should've called out to him to apologize again, but the words stuck in my throat. I sucked as a friend on both sides. This whole time I'd thought to be friends with Bryce meant I had to despise the guy he hated. To be with Noah meant I had to turn my back on my best friend.

And now I had neither.

CHAPTER 26

I texted both Bryce and Noah over the next few days, but neither one responded. And the days Noah was at work, he said very little to me. He was polite, because I didn't think Noah knew how to not be polite, but so cold that he made Roxanne look like the cuddly Charmin bear in comparison. Syd told me to stop trying so hard.

"He'll come around when he's ready," she said as we practiced at the batting cages.

I smacked the bat against the softball as hard as I could, the resounding *whack* not as satisfying as I'd hoped. "I don't know. He's really mad, and I can't blame him."

"Yeah, well…"

And she left it at that. She, like Court, had warned me, but I appreciated her not rubbing it in my face.

"What about Bryce?" she asked. "How are you going to

fix things with him?"

I smacked the next ball. "I don't know. I should've been honest with him, but he wouldn't have understood if I'd told him earlier, either."

"Yeah, I think you're right. I know you should've told him, but enough's enough. He's got to get over hating Noah one of these days."

"I know." At least I had Syd. And Court, too. I wanted to trust that my friendship with Bryce was as important to him as it was to me, but at this point, considering he thought I was a traitor, I didn't have much hope.

My days quickly went from being awesome and in love to sucking big time. Then came the strangest day—the day Noah's friend Miller showed up to check me out, which was the only reason I could think of for that visit. He found me in the toy aisle, sorting out the chaos of puzzles, games, and Legos that never seemed to stay organized. A scrawny guy with glasses walked down the aisle, his eyes landing on my nametag. "You're Lex, right?" he asked lightly.

I nodded. "Aren't you…?"

"Miller." His smile dropped. "I'm a friend of Noah's."

"Oh. Yeah, I remember you from school."

He snorted. "Right. I'm sure you would."

I'd read the word "nonplussed" in books before, but this was the first time I'd actually experienced it. This guy had it in for me. I wondered if Noah told him what happened and now he was here to have his back. "Did I do something to—"

"Yeah, you and your friend Bryce," he cut in. "I know

what you're doing, and you can just stop right now."

"What I'm—"

"What happened was two years ago. When are you assholes going to stop punishing him?"

I crossed my arms and frowned. "Stop calling me an asshole, okay, and explain yourself. I'm not punishing him."

He snorted. "Oh, yeah. So you think I'm supposed to believe you really like Noah after what he supposedly did to Bryce? Well, let me tell you something. You don't know shit about him. Noah's the best person I know. The *best*. You walk around with your friends acting like you're so cool at school, when you are nothing but fake. That's fine, but I'm not going to let him think he's in love with someone who's out to get him. Especially not when he's done so much for me. Got it?"

What the... "Whoa, Miller, stop. First of all, you come here accusing me of using Noah, which is crap. I'm not using him. I actually like the guy, and whether you believe me or not is up to you. I don't really give a shit." Although I had to admit, the fact that he apparently didn't know what happened the other day was a relief. Noah wasn't a talker.

"I don't believe you."

"Like I said, I don't care." Normally, I'd appreciate the whole "best friend" confrontation—I know I'd appreciate Syd doing this for me. But I lost respect for someone who called me an asshole. Screw that. "I get that you're his friend and that you care about him, but—"

"Friend?" His voice reached squeaky registers as he took off his glasses and stared at me, like that was going to intimidate me. "You don't get anything. Noah is like a brother to me. Bryce already did damage to him for something he didn't do. And if you hurt him, too, you'll regret it. I won't let him go through hell again."

My stomach dropped. "Wait a second. What do you mean, something he didn't do? What are you talking about?"

He studied me for a moment, his chin jutted out like he was in deep thought. "Miller, what didn't he do?"

"You really don't know?" he asked, raising his eyebrow like he didn't believe me.

"Know what?"

"He didn't say anything to you?"

"Miller, I'm going to ram this light saber down your throat if you don't tell me."

He stared at the floor, losing his menacing posture. Now he just looked like a nervous kid. "Noah didn't rat on Bryce, did he?" I asked.

Miller's eyes stayed on the ground, but he shook his head.

"It was you?"

"Yeah." His voice was raspy and quiet. His gaze finally raised to meet mine, his eyes tortured. Clearly the truth had been plaguing this guy for two years.

"But why? Why did Noah say it was him?"

"Bryce didn't see me in the shadows. But I saw him spray paint all over the other school's sign, and it made me mad. Bryce always thought he had the right to do whatever he wanted. He was a jerk in middle school, and I knew things hadn't changed when he got to high school. I wanted to out him for the slimeball that he was, but it backfired." He winced at the last words slightly as he placed the glasses back on his face.

"And you let Noah take the blame." I swallowed over the lump in my throat.

"I didn't want him to," he said quickly. "I was going to tell everyone it was me, but Noah wouldn't let me because they already thought it was him. He said Bryce and his friends would be harder on me because I'm so…well, I'm much smaller than him."

"So instead of telling Bryce like a real friend would, you let Noah be tortured for two years. *Two years*!" I swallowed over the lump that had formed in my throat. This was definitely not the time for tears, though it hurt like hell to think back on what Noah went through for his friend. "You watched while they called him names and hated him, all because you were afraid. And you tell me we're fake? You're the fakest of them all."

"I know," he said miserably. "I hate myself for letting that happen to him. I…I want to make it right, no matter what he says. But I don't want him to get hurt." His expression became pained. "Please promise me you won't hurt him."

I stood tall and glared at him. "I don't need to promise you anything. I don't owe you, but you owe Noah, and a whole lot more than just coming in here and making threats to me because you feel guilty. You need to tell everyone the truth."

"I know," he said again. "I will."

"You can leave now," I said, pointing over his shoulder

and watching him walk back the way he came.

I set the light saber down and leaned against the shelves. All this time I believed, like everyone else, that Noah ratted on Bryce, when all he did was cover for his friend. Knowing Noah like I did now, that didn't surprise me at all. But to be completely ostracized from the school because of something he didn't even do—I couldn't imagine anyone doing that for me.

Then I remembered that Noah did exactly that for me, when he told Mr. Hanson he was responsible for that Coupon Queen's complaint after I'd annoyed her. Guilt flooded over me. I hadn't said anything that day, either. I could've told Mr. Hanson the truth like Miller could've told Bryce. Noah deserved better friends than us.

And he also deserved better than a girl who was too afraid to tell her best friend that she was in love with his enemy. An enemy that wasn't even real.

I sought out the floor manager and got relieved for break. My first stop was at my locker. Noah's shift today didn't start until three, close to when I'd be leaving, and he was working too late for me to talk to him. I pulled out my cell and texted him as I sat in the break room.

I know you're mad at me. I know you hate me because I didn't have the guts to tell Bryce about us. U R right, and I don't deserve you. But I still

My thumb accidentally hit the send button before I could complete that sentence. Then again, what was I going to say? I still love you? I never said it to him before. I should have. I'd loved him for the longest time now. What Miller said didn't change that at all, but would Noah believe me?

The world: 1, Lex: 0

My thumb hovered over the heart emoticon that I'd never used because I thought it'd be too sappy. I remembered the set look on Noah's face when he came out of that meeting with Mr. Hanson, the man whose opinion of him mattered more than his own father's. And I thought of the look on Miller's face—that tortured look that spoke volumes about what he watched Noah put up with the past two years.

I touched the heart emoticon, sending that instead of the words.

"I love you," I whispered aloud.

CHAPTER
27

Noah didn't respond to my text, but I didn't expect him to. I'd gotten used to radio silence by now. The day after, I went in to SmartMart for my afternoon shift in a torrential downpour. Grandma had perked up that morning, again telling us that it was going to be a bad storm season. I didn't mind the rain. The pretty days were the hardest to work, since it sucked being stuck inside chilly SmartMart when my friends were hanging out at the beach. Not that I really hung out with them lately. Syd was on vacation with her family, and since Court was with Bryce most of the time and he wanted nothing to do with me, I didn't get to see her much, either.

Today I was on greeter shift with Ruthie, who had started to get on my nerves again. For some reason, Mr. Hanson had scheduled the last three days with me as greeter. Not only did I have to put up with Ruthie's cart games, but I didn't see Noah much, which made me wonder if Mr. Hanson was catching on and giving us less opportunity to be together. Of course, considering Mr. Hanson was the one who encouraged Jake's pranks, I somehow doubted it.

"Look at me, Lexus," Ruthie said, swinging around and around on the cart like we were at Disney World. "Look at meeeee...."

I smiled tolerantly, but I was tempted to push the cart out the door into the rain. I liked Ruthie—at least I didn't feel like rolling my eyes all the time at her anymore—but sometimes she drove me bananas. She loved the Dreadful Greeter Position and always greeted every customer like they were the most important people in the world. It probably made them feel good, but I was going to stick with my boring "hello."

The customers that day were an oddball mix—was the rain sending in all the crazies at one time or was it a full moon? And I meant that literally, considering one woman came in with pants that had slipped halfway down her butt. It didn't look like she was wearing underwear. I did notice that her top was probably three sizes too small. Did people not have mirrors?

A guy dressed in hunting attire walked in with an umbrella, which didn't strike me as strange until he shook the umbrella out and I noticed it had a pink bunny rabbit print on it. I laughed, and even Ruthie thought it was funny. "Hippity hop, hippity hop," she said, jumping up and down with hands perched in front of her. The guy gave a backward look at her like she was the weird one. Which made me laugh harder. It was the first time I'd laughed in a few days, and I was grateful to Ruthie for it.

Noah was working the floor today. He stopped by once to see how we were doing, though he addressed Ruthie more than me. The fact that he stood near me without scowling now made me feel a spark of hope.

Every time he walked up, Roxanne, who spent most of her time wandering around the produce section, would stare at us with her pinched face, just waiting for us to "get out of line." Clearly, she didn't notice that things had changed now, although she did still intimidate me. I was so afraid she might do something to jeopardize Noah's job that I just kept my eyes averted. At the same time, I felt kind of bad for her. Noah protected Miller from getting bullied by covering for him with Bryce, and though I didn't know what happened with Roxanne in high school, I had a feeling no one ever covered for her. I wondered what she'd be like today if someone had.

"Storm's getting worse," Noah said as he stood next to me to stare out at the darkening sky. My heartbeat quickened at his voice. It'd been too long since he'd spoken to me.

"I know. Looks bad."

And that was the end to our fascinating conversation as he nodded and walked away without looking at me. Still— progress.

"He likes you. A lot," Ruthie said loudly behind me. I jumped.

"Ruthie, he likes you, too."

She giggled. "Not as much as he likes you. Did you do it yet?"

My mouth dropped open. I could not have heard her just say that. "No, Ruthie." Time to change the subject. "Want to play cart coaster?"

"Yes!" She jumped up and down and clapped her hands. So for the next hour, we went around and around on the carts. I would never admit this to anyone if they'd asked, but it was kind of fun. And it kept her from asking if Noah and I had "done it."

The thunderstorm raged around us, and by four o'clock Ruthie and I had discontinued the cart game to just stare at the doors. It even hailed, sounding like a hundred giants tap-dancing on the roof. Ruthie put her hands over her ears as the crack of thunder announced each blast of lightning. Nobody was coming in the store now, and most customers were standing near the doors with their loaded carts, waiting for the storm to calm.

"Ahhh, Lexus," she groaned, holding her ears as another snap of lightning hit nearby.

Noah walked up and put an arm around her shoulders. "It's okay, Ruthie. It's just the thunder laughing at a joke the lightning said."

Ruthie nodded, but she still kept her hands over her ears.

"See? It's just an afternoon thunderstorm," Noah said. I wasn't sure about that. It was getting so dark outside that it looked like evening instead of afternoon, and there was an eerie greenish tint to the sky.

"It's getting really nasty out there," Mr. Hanson said, joining us. The winds were gusting now. It was hurricane season, but we would've known days ago if one was coming. "We're under a...um..." He glanced at Ruthie. "A T-warning."

"We're always under a T-warning," I said. It was true — Florida was known for eccentric summer weather. Tornado watches weren't that unusual, though we usually didn't get anything more than crazy wind and rain and the occasional waterspout. I wasn't worried.

Until, of course, the shopping carts started sailing across the parking lot and ramming into cars. At the same time, a lightning bolt sliced into a pole across the street, causing the wires to fall and spark. The lights in the store flickered. Noah and I backed away from the door with Ruthie following us, moaning and holding her head.

Mr. Hanson stopped a woman as she was pushing her cart full of bags toward the door, attempting to open her umbrella. "Excuse me, ma'am. The weather's getting really bad, so we're going to keep everyone in the store for now, just in case."

The lights flickered again, then went off, leaving us in near darkness. Soon, though, the lights flickered again and came on, dimmer than before. My pulse started racing — now I was starting to freak out. Without thinking, I reached for Noah's hand. His fingers wrapped around mine, and it was comforting more than anything.

Mr. Hanson escorted the woman with the cart toward the employee area, throwing orders over his shoulder. "Noah, comb the back of the store. Get everyone into the restrooms in the back. Bessie, get the cashiers and customers up front into the employee hallway."

Noah nodded. "Go with Hanson to the hallway," he said gruffly. He squeezed my hand once, then let it go. "It's smaller and a lot safer, I think." He patted Ruthie's shoulder. "Everything will be okay." She didn't pay attention to him, just rocked back and forth on the balls of her feet.

Noah started jogging toward the back of the store, yelling at customers here and there to follow him.

"Come on, Ruthie, let's go," I said, fully intending on joining Noah instead of heading to the hall like I was supposed to. If we were going to get hit with seriously bad weather, I'd rather be with him, regardless of how he felt about me.

"Noooo…" Ruthie was keening, holding her hands over her ears as lightning cracked loudly over the store.

"Ruthie! Ruthie, let's go!" I tried tugging on her arm, but she was solid, unmoving. "Ruthie! There's a tornado coming!"

As soon as the words left my mouth, I realized my mistake. Ruthie fell to her knees and started rocking. "Noooo…" she cried loudly. "Noooo…"

I pulled on her arm, but she wouldn't budge. "Ruthie!" I looked around quickly. Everyone was already moving. I shouted out to Roxanne, but she was already running. I didn't know if she could hear me.

Ruthie screamed as lightning crackled over the store. I could see stragglers pushing their way into the employee area several feet away.

"Help!" I screamed, but my voice seemed to go nowhere. My instincts cursed at me and told me to get the hell out of there, but I couldn't leave Ruthie. "Come on, Ruthie!"

"Lex." Bessie was next to me, taking my arm calmly and pulling me away. "Let me." She nodded toward the last of the people heading through the employee door. "Go."

I backed away, relieved, as Bessie crouched next to Ruthie. "Ruthie, it's okay. This isn't so bad. It's a game, Ruthie. Just a game."

"Nooo…" Ruthie howled. "Noooo…tornado."

Bessie kept crooning to her, but Ruthie refused to move. I hesitated, looking through the outside doors, into the blue-gray of the storm. Boxes, plants, and leaves were all blowing sideways. Palm trees were bent almost in half. And the sky— "Bessie!" I shouted.

Bessie looked up at me, then followed my gaze to the angrily swirling clouds. Her face paled. She started pulling on Ruthie's arm urgently, but I knew that wouldn't do any good. I joined her, but Ruthie was really freaking out now, holding her head and yelling. The sound changed from a whistling wind to an unmistakable roar. For a split second, I was in shock myself. I knew what that sound meant from those tornado chaser shows my dad liked to watch.

I shoved my fear away. We had very little time, and I knew the only way to move Ruthie was to make her think this was fun. "Ruthie, we're going to play cart coaster, okay?" Keeping my voice steady was the hardest thing I had ever done in my life. I grabbed a cart, ignoring the palm fronds that were hitting the windows, and rolled it to her as fast as I could. Bessie was repeating my game idea to her.

Ruthie slowly released her ears. "Cart coaster?" she asked hopefully.

I was shaking now, so hard that my hands barely managed to grasp her arm. "Yes! Come on, Ruthie. Cart coaster. It'll be fun!" Inside my head, I was praying as hard as I could. I thought Bessie was, too, her wide eyes staring at the door behind me. "Lex," she said, her voice enough of a warning that I didn't even turn around to see what was happening.

The building seemed to shake, or at least that's what it felt like to me. I got Ruthie to latch onto the cart, and as soon as she stepped off the ground, I started running as hard as I could, adrenaline kicking in.

Glass smashed behind me. I looked over my shoulder to see the entrance doors blow in. Shards of glass hit my back, and I could hear Bessie yelping. The cart skittered over the glass and Ruthie started howling.

"Hang on, Ruthie," I yelled, shoving the cart through the glass. Something swiped the side of my face that felt like palm fronds.

We turned down the frozen food aisle to get away from the blast of wind, making a left at the end of the aisle, running as fast as we could to the back of the store where I knew there was at least a walk-in freezer to hide in. We weren't even halfway to the back when a large shelf display crashed to the ground in front of us. I skidded to a halt, almost dumping Ruthie, who struggled to keep her clutch on the cart.

"Bessie, in here!" I said, pushing the cart through the door to the bakery. I turned around, but Bessie wasn't behind me.

"Bessie!" I screamed again and again. I thought my heart was going to explode. Behind me, Ruthie howled. I could hear a strange ripping sound somewhere. "Ruthie, get off the cart and under that table," I shouted, pointing toward a large metal cake table. "Now!"

I ran back through the door amidst the chaos of wind and rain that had found its way inside. Bessie was lying on the ground, the boxes and cans that fell off a nearby shelf surrounding her. "Bessie!" I climbed over the stuff to crouch next to her. She was conscious but bleeding on her face and arm.

"I think I broke something," she moaned. She was holding her side.

"We need to get out of here! Come on, we're just steps away from where Ruthie is. Ruthie needs you. Come on, Bessie." I was shouting as the wind whipped around me, pelting me with rain and leaves and boxes, and cans rolled everywhere, but she was in so much pain I wasn't sure she could hear me. I screamed as plaster tiles fell around us. The roaring from outside was moving inside. "Bessie, please, I don't want to die and I don't want you to die."

She nodded, letting me help her into a standing position, or a crouching position, really, as she was holding her side. I helped her limp forward, almost dragging her, ignoring her cries of pain as my eyes fixed on the square window of the bakery door. Something hit me in the back, but I kept moving. Five feet. Four. Three—something smacked the top of my head—two. One.

We pushed through and the door closed behind us. It was a little calmer in here. We could still hear everything crashing and shaking, but at least nothing was flying at us now. I tried to help Bessie get as comfortable as she could under the big table, next to Ruthie, but she was fading out of consciousness.

"Bessie, stay with us, it'll be over soon," I said. I had never been in the middle of a tornado—was it normal for them to last this long? I grabbed a couple of cake pans from the shelf next to us, handing one to Ruthie. "Hold this in front of you if anything flies at us." She nodded and grabbed the pan, holding it over her face like a mask.

A crash hit just outside the doors, like a huge wrecking ball was smashing the store. Then came the wind, blasting again. The door to the bakery flew open and debris swept through.

"Ruthie, protect your face," I yelled, holding up the pan in front of my face.

Ruthie screamed and Bessie passed out. Ruthie and I held hands as tightly as we could, arms over Bessie as if we could protect her. I said prayers over and over in my head that the storm would go away and leave us alone. I prayed that Noah was safe, that Mr. Hanson and Roxanne and Larry and Jake and the customers were safe.

Another crash—this one close to us. Everything fell down around us—plaster and foam and white and tile. I screamed, then started coughing as my lungs filled with dust that floated in the air. I pulled my legs in as tight as I could and Ruthie did the same. More smashing sounds, this time over our heads.

We were being buried alive.

I pulled Bessie's legs around so the metal table protected them. The table was pressing down on our heads, dented by the falling debris.

We were going to die.

For the first time, I felt calm, eerily relaxed. It was like I couldn't run any further, so my mind was giving up. I shook my head and cuddled closer to Bessie as Ruthie grabbed my hand.

I couldn't give up.

Then the crashing stopped.

CHAPTER
28

Silence.

Eerie silence, like standing in a cemetery at midnight. I sank back and closed my eyes. We survived. With some scrapes and bruises and whatever, but we were still alive. I hoped Noah and everyone else was safe. And my family. I had no idea where this tornado was headed.

I coughed and coughed and retched over powder that filled the air. Ruthie was coughing, too. "You okay?" I croaked to her shadow in the quiet darkness.

Pinpoints of light from around the sides of the rubble illuminated the tiny space enough for me to see that Ruthie's eyes were wide and frightened, but she nodded. "Is it over?" Ruthie asked, her voice shaking hard.

"I think so. Bessie?"

Bessie was still passed out. I placed a finger on the side

of her throat and found her pulse. "She's okay, Ruthie. She's breathing. But, I don't know. I think she's got broken ribs or something. We probably shouldn't move her too much."

I glanced around. There were blocks and tiles and broken tables and who knows what piled around us. There was very little room under our small table, which had seemed so big before. I kissed my dirty hand and touched it to the metal table leg. "Thank you, table."

Ruthie giggled, which made me giggle, too. "What is wrong with us, Ruthie?" I asked.

"I guess all the scary was pushed out of us and the only thing left is the funny," she said, giggling again. Strange thing to say, but accurate, I guess.

"What is all this stuff?" I asked, brushing the powder off my pants.

Ruthie stuck her finger in her mouth. "Flour!"

At least that made sense, considering we were in the bakery. "We need to get out of here," I said. I slipped my hand into my pocket, then remembered that my phone was in my bag in the locker. *Crap.* I tried shoving at the wall of ceiling tiles and plaster, but all that accomplished was to cause a small avalanche of debris.

"Do we scream for help?" Ruthie asked.

"I guess so."

So we did. We yelled, "Help," and, "We're here," and various versions of that, but nobody answered. Our voices swirled around in this tiny space without going farther, but we still yelled until our throats and ears were sore. Every once in a while we stopped and listened, but the silence around us was unchanged.

I rested my head back against the wall. "It's okay, Ruthie." My voice was hoarse. "They'll come find us. The fire trucks will be here and they'll come in after us. We just need to sit tight."

"Oooh, fire trucks? With the sirens and everything?"

I nodded, suddenly so incredibly tired. My body ached from my neck down. "Sirens and everything." I closed my eyes. "Listen for them."

I opened my eyes at some point. Had I fallen asleep? My head was aching. I tried to shift a bit but my back was too sore. Ruthie was stroking Bessie's hair and talking to her. Bessie was staring up at the ceiling of the table, her face scrunched up in pain. I wished I could do something for her.

"Bessie!" I adjusted my position to face her. "Are you okay?"

"I'm fine," she said in a strained whisper.

I took her hand. "Is there anything I can do?"

She jerked her head slightly to indicate no. I wrung my hands, wanting to help her. "I know it hurts, but…" I didn't know what else to say.

"It's okay, Bessie," Ruthie crooned. "I can hear someone right now. Someone is telling us we are going to be okay. They're trying to get in here now, but there's lots of stuff they have to pull away to get to us."

I glanced at her sharply. There was no one. What made

her think someone was going to rescue us soon? No one could hear us. No one knew we were even here. But Bessie's eyes were fixed on Ruthie as if every word was a lifeline.

I dropped her hand and sank back on my heels, wrapping my arms around my knees. I wondered how much of the store got hit—and if anyone else was hurt. And where was Noah? Did he make it? My imagination took hold and I started imagining him struck in the head with flying debris or maybe even carried out of the store with the force of the winds.

Noah—I never made things right with him or Bryce. Why didn't I just tell Bryce how I felt earlier? He could've dealt with it. He at least would've appreciated that I told him rather than finding out accidentally from Ruthie. Noah thought I was embarrassed of him. Bryce thought I was a traitor.

The tears burned a path down my floured cheeks. I buried my head in my arms. Bessie stirred next to me, and it occurred to me that I didn't know much about her family at all. Were they aware she was in trouble? When my grandma disappeared, we knew immediately. Did Bessie's kids or grandkids look out for her?

I felt a hand pat my arm. "It's okay, Lexus. It'll be okay. They'll find us. They're out there right now, trying to get in."

I lifted my head to stare at Ruthie's faint silhouette. If I wasn't so depressed, I'd have laughed at us: Ruthie crooning to me and Bessie about people coming to save us, Bessie savoring each of Ruthie's words, and me crying my eyes out like a baby. I sniffed. Of the three of us, Ruthie was the only one holding it together.

"Yeah, you're right, Ruthie. They'll come for us. They have to."

Time passed so slowly. I wished I had a watch so I could see if it had been minutes or hours that we were stuck here. Why did none of us have a watch? Ruthie fell asleep, as did Bessie. I envied them. All I could do was sit here and think about the terrible possibilities. I thought I could hear sirens, but it was muted.

Again, I tried to push and pull some of the tiles and crap blocking us to see if I could work our way free, but that only caused rubble to fall into our space. It was the most frustrating thing—there could've been only a few inches separating us from fresh air, but there was nothing we could do about it.

Ruthie eventually woke up. Even though my dry throat hurt, I talked with her to pass the time. She started telling me about her dad. "When did you see him last?" I asked.

Her face clouded. "A while ago." She dropped her head and I felt bad for bringing it up in the first place.

"I'm sure he loves you."

She nodded. "He does. He says that..." She broke off, frowning. "He did say that."

"So where do you go to school?" I asked to change the subject.

She laughed out loud. "I went to school when I was little, but I am twenty-six now."

Twenty-six? I had no idea. I thought she wasn't much older than me. "Where do you live?"

The minutes and hours dragged on. I was so hot and thirsty that all I could think about was the fact that a sink with water was only a few feet away, and we couldn't get to it. We tried shouting for help every so often. I took turns with Ruthie so we could limit the use of our voices. Bessie even tried once, but the effort was too much for her. We heard motors and sirens, and occasionally what sounded like voices, though I wasn't sure about that.

I started making promises in my head. *I promise I'll be nicer to Rory. I promise I'll be more respectful to my mother. I promise I won't be mean to anyone anymore, even bitchy Roxanne. I promise... I promise...*

Ruthie and I stopped talking altogether, even to shout for help. She looked dazed, unable to even stroke Bessie's hair anymore. Bessie couldn't stay awake. It didn't help that it was so hot in the small space, the air so thick I might've been able to see it if it were brighter. My head was aching now and my throat was dry as a desert.

It must have been hours now since the tornado. It was darker now—the little pinpoints of light just a faint haze. It didn't get dark until almost nine o'clock, so I knew we had been in here for several hours. The air was getting too thick; we needed more than just little holes to produce oxygen, but I was afraid to try to move any of the rubble again.

I had my eyes closed, on the verge of sleep, when a sound like bricks being smashed startled me awake. I held my breath, listening. Another smash, then a rustling noise.

"Ruthie!" I poked her, jostling her awake. "What's that sound?"

She rubbed at her dirty face and tilted her head to listen. "Help!" I shouted hoarsely. Ruthie joined in. "Help! Help!"

I could hear voices for sure now—men shouting, though I couldn't understand what they were saying.

Bessie was still out of it. I put a finger against her neck and could feel a faint, throbbing pulse. We doubled our efforts. "Help! We're stuck in here!"

I was sure they could hear us now. A man's deep voice said something, but I couldn't understand anything other than "out."

It was the only word I needed to hear. The sounds were definitely of people pulling rubble away. Lots of people. I wanted to cry in relief, but it would take too much energy. "Ruthie, they're coming to rescue us."

Ruthie took my hand and held it up like we were champions. "We're okay!" she sang in a scratchy voice. I could've hugged her.

"Yes, we're okay!"

We could tell they were close when the space suddenly got less dark, and the light began to find its way to us. It was all I could do not to push myself out of the remaining wreckage.

Ruthie didn't feel such restraint. When it was clear there was only a few inches separating us from our rescuers, she pushed against the rubble again and again. I blinked hard and held an arm up to cover my eyes as a bright light shone in on us.

"Oh my God, there they are." I recognized Mr. Hanson's voice and others yelling. Some crying, some sobbing, some cheering. I couldn't see anything for the light shining in. Ruthie wouldn't climb out.

"Go on, Ruthie," I said to her. "They're waiting for you."

"No, Bessie first."

Of course Ruthie wouldn't leave Bessie. I wouldn't, either, but the fact that she stayed behind until Bessie was rescued made me want to hug her.

It took a while for the rescue crew to clear enough rubble and crawl over to us. I could hear my dad yelling at me that he loved me, Ruthie's mom shouting the same to her. I didn't hear anyone calling for Bessie.

"Bessie," I said as the rescue workers climbed over the rubble to get to us. "You'll be fine now. They're going to take you to the hospital and get you all better. We'll be there for you."

Ruthie held Bessie's hand and patted her hair. "You're safe now, Bessie. I love you, Bessie." She started crying. I wondered how she had any tears to cry, but I put my arms around her as the rescue workers carefully lifted Bessie onto a stretcher and carried her away. A couple firemen held their hands out to us and helped us crawl out of our little shelter. I peered painfully around in the light and my jaw dropped to see the wreckage. Nothing but what looked like rocks and cement blocks and tile everywhere. I looked back at the little table that had protected us for so many hours. I felt this weird love for it. I was losing my mind.

My mind was such a blur as the firemen steadied me, my eyes blinded by work lights, that all I could do was count hands.

Four hands to pull me up and out of the wreckage.

Six hands to embrace me as soon as my feet touched the solid ground. Arms circled around me. I recognized my mother's heavy perfume, my sister's smooth hair, my father's deep voice.

And two hands—two hands I'd thought about the most.

Noah pulled me to him, his arms shaking. I stared up at him, blinking. His eyes were red—were those tears? He never cried. Not even when his father screamed at him.

"Lex, I'm so… I'm sorry, and I…"

He couldn't finish his sentence, just pulled me to him in a tight hug. I could see my dad raising an eyebrow and my mother whispering something to him. It didn't matter that we had an audience. I was in Noah's arms. He still cared about me. After a while he finally released me, brushing my hair over my ears. Then he opened his mouth to speak the words I'd been waiting to hear.

"You look like shit."

I laughed, then coughed. Immediately, a bottle of water was thrust into my hand. I took a long drink. "I've looked better."

He touched my cheek with his fingers. "I was in shock when I found out you never made it to the safe side of the store. When I saw that this entire right side was demolished, the exact place I'd last seen you…everything went black in my mind and…and I should've made sure you got where you were supposed to… I shouldn't have…"

He pulled me tight against him. I closed my eyes and enjoyed the feeling of being alive. The world was right-side-up again.

CHAPTER
29

Half of the store was demolished—the rest was almost untouched. I stared around, shocked that we could have survived this under nothing but a bakery table.

The rescue team took me to the hospital, though I told them I was okay. My mother rode in the ambulance with me, which wasn't my choice, but at least she didn't nag at me for this or that. Mostly, she held my hand and stroked my hair. That part wasn't so bad, I guess. My dad and Rory followed behind in their car, and Noah behind them. Ruthie was in a separate ambulance. It was embarrassing to be rushed to the hospital like I was a heart attack victim or something—lights and sirens and everything.

"Oh, stop it, Alexis," my mother said when I commented about how unnecessary it all was. "Just let them do their job."

In the emergency room, doctors examined me. I thought

I only had some scrapes and bruises, but they disagreed. Apparently I was dehydrated, in shock, and had a possible concussion. My mother helped me take a shower, which made me feel much better, though a little sleepier.

The only, and I mean *only,* upside to all this was that Noah stayed with me all night. Mom had offered, but I convinced her to go home. "I'll be fine. I don't even know why they're forcing me to be here."

"Don't you want me to stay and get you things?" she asked.

"No, I just want to sleep. But I'll have a hard time sleeping if I know you're uncomfortable sitting on that chair."

She glanced at the ugly blue vinyl chair. This room was not equipped for overnight guests. "Well, if you think you'll sleep better," she said.

I smiled at her. "I do." I yawned, surprised to find that I actually was tired. But then, it was almost midnight. "I'll see you tomorrow."

"I'll be here early."

"Not too early, please. I'll probably sleep in."

She kissed my forehead and held my hand to her chest, over her heart. "I am so glad you're okay, sweetheart," she whispered. She kissed me again and left.

It took all of one minute for Noah to come in after she left. I shifted my body on the bed so he could sit next to me. The nurse came in and adjusted my IV bag, looking at Noah, then me, with eyebrows raised.

"Please," I said to her, "let him stay." She was young. I hoped she would understand.

The nurse twisted her mouth to ponder that, then nodded shortly. "But no funny business. And first thing in the morning, he goes."

I thanked her and she left, closing the door softly behind her.

I scooted over on the bed, toward the IV stand, so Noah could lie down next to me. He kicked off his shoes and pulled off his shirt. The room was darkened, but there was enough light that I could see the broad outline of his shoulders.

"Nice," I said.

"I can't sleep with a shirt on. It feels like I'm tangled up."

I batted my eyes at him. "I hope you can sleep with pants on."

He laughed and lay down next to me, kissing the top of my hair. I snuggled up into his arms, against his chest, his body warm in the frigid room. He pulled the blanket over us. It was like none of the events with Bryce had happened. I had my Noah back.

"Noah," I said quietly.

"Yeah?"

"How do your friends feel about us?" It was something that'd been on my mind since Miller's visit. We'd always talked about my friends, but I never asked him about his.

His cheek brushed against my hair. "About how your friends feel, I guess."

I sighed. "It's just Bryce. Syd and Court are fine with us. But what I really want to know is how does Miller feel?"

He sighed. "I was wondering when you were going to get to that. He told me he came to talk to you."

"Yeah. I don't think it ended up like he planned." I propped myself on the arm that didn't have a needle stuck in it. "Why didn't you tell me what really happened that night? Why didn't you tell me it wasn't you?"

"Why should I have to?"

"Because—because you know I thought you had told on Bryce. This whole time, I thought it was you. Why would you let people think something like that about you?"

His eyes pinched slightly at the corners. "Maybe I don't care as much as you do what everyone else thinks. Miller is a sensitive guy who was bullied nonstop in middle school. Do you think I should've let him take crap for this? All he was doing was getting back at one of them."

I didn't like the way he said "them." *They* were still my friends. "I know you don't think much of the friends I hang out with. Why would you ever want to go out with me in the first place?"

He touched my face with his finger, trailing it down to my chin, then down my neck. Electricity shot through my body at his touch. He stopped at the V of my neckline. "I used to think you were like the rest of them, you know. Beautiful, popular, and couldn't see past your own clique. Plus you were friends with that…with Bryce."

"So what changed?"

"You came to SmartMart." He smiled at me. "You—perfect, popular, beautiful Lex—I was so sure you wouldn't last the week." He chuckled as I poked him in his side. "It's true. I knew you were forced into the job. We all did, which is probably why Roxanne hated you from day one. But I saw you laughing with Ruthie—not at her—and playing her cart game, which no one ever did. I overheard Bessie telling Mr. Hanson how kind you were, how sweet." He curled my hair over my ear. "It's like I needed to see you through their eyes before I could finally see you through mine."

"Wow," I said softly. This guy knew how to talk to a girl for sure. And the best part was that it was one hundred percent genuine Noah. "And here all I was shooting for was that you liked how my butt looked in my awesome SmartMart pants."

He laughed so hard at that I thought he was going to fall off the bed. I put my finger over his lips, glancing at the door and hoping the nurse wouldn't come in to break us apart. He took my finger and kissed it. "You know I love you, don't you?"

I stared at him. "You do?"

"*Je t'aime*, Lex."

He loved me, and the words were like tiny sparks shooting through my body.

"*Je t'aime*, Noah. I love you, too." I told him, the words coming so naturally, I wondered why I didn't say them to Noah before. Sliding my hand down to his bare chest, I could feel his heartbeat thumping along with the rhythm of mine. Matching heartbeats, just like Grandma said.

"And I loved you long before I found out you didn't tell on Bryce," I added. It seemed important to tell him. "What Miller said didn't change that at all for me."

He smiled as he pulled me in for a serious, heart-melting kiss.

CHAPTER
30

I slept better than I had in a long time in Noah's arms. We tried to stay up talking but I was exhausted. I didn't even realize I had fallen asleep until the same young nurse came in at the end of her shift to oust Noah from my room. Poor guy barely had time to slip his shirt back on before she was ushering him out. It was only seven a.m., so after she took my vitals, I fell back asleep.

Before my mother arrived to take me home, I visited Ruthie with the flowers my parents had brought to me. Her mother was in the room. She was all smiles and appreciation for the flowers, for saving Ruthie, for everything. Ruthie was herself, vibrant and chatty as usual. She was thrilled about the hospital food, especially the generic plastic tub of cherry gelatin, so I gave her mine, too.

"You're going to work with me at SmartMart again,

right, Lexus?" she asked.

I smiled at her. "I'm sure I will, Ruthie. You're my cart coaster buddy, right?"

She grinned at that. Ruthie was okay, and more than okay. She held it together when we were under that table. In so many ways, she was stronger than me. I smiled as she dove into her food. Maybe I could send a basket of real Jell-O to her house later. I knew she'd like that.

Bessie had more problems than Ruthie and me, which was worse still because of her age. She suffered severe dehydration, two cracked ribs, and a mild concussion, not to mention several scrapes and bruises. She had to stay a few days longer, but she was coherent when I went to her room to visit. My heart hurt to see her looking so wilted and old in the hospital bed. The nurse assured me that she would make a full recovery. Her son and grandson were next to her, both of them profusely thanking me for saving Bessie's life. I asked them to please stop by Ruthie's room, too, since she was also responsible for saving Bessie. They promised they would.

The hospital released me at ten o'clock with a list of things to watch out for. Though they clearly thought I was fine, my mother pretty much jailed me at home to "recoup." I just thought she wanted to keep me close, since for a while she thought I had died. She was uncomfortably attentive, bringing me chicken noodle soup—it wasn't like I had a cold—and brushing my hair for some reason. The upside was that I could read and watch TV without any interruptions. Rory was even nice and thought of someone other than herself for once. Well, at least one time, when she unloaded the dishwasher for me. But that was the highest degree of unselfishness for her. I spent a lot of time hanging out with Grandma in her room—so much so that my parents let the Willy Wonka nurse take time off.

Syd and Court were in tears when they heard what happened at SmartMart. They came over to the house as soon as I got home and cried and apologized—for what, I didn't know, and I didn't think they did either. But it was a nice reunion, anyway, and very much like the old days, sitting outside on the patio and talking about relationship things.

"Have you been hanging out with Cole or Ryan?" I asked Syd. She had been dead set on going out with one of the obnoxious twins as soon as they came back to town, but she hadn't said anything much about them lately.

She gave me a look that clearly said *What the hell?* "Those guys are jerks. Why would I want to hang out with either of them?"

Ah, translated: they were jerks to *her.* But at least she finally realized they weren't good enough for her. "Need me to kick their asses for you?" I asked at the same time that Court said about the same thing.

"No. I'm over them."

"You'll find someone," Court piped up. "Someone who deserves you."

Syd winked at her. "Hey, I'm good being single. Being single leaves me free to mingle." She waggled her eyebrows, making Court and me laugh.

Noah ignored my mother's warning that I needed rest when he showed up the second day with flowers—yellow roses, which were beautiful—and plenty of kisses, which I loved most. I think he made her uncomfortable, which was awesome. I introduced him to my grandma, too. She loved meeting him, though I knew her memory of him would last until he walked out the door. I'd remind her a thousand times if that's what it took, though.

Noah refused to let Miller tell anyone what happened two years ago. When I asked him about it, he said, "It's between me and him, and it's been a long time now. Why would I throw my best friend under the bus?"

Some best friend, I wanted to say, but I didn't say anything. If Noah wanted to keep quiet, I couldn't force him, and deep down I understood where Miller was coming from. After all, I let Noah take the blame for that awful customer with Mr. Hanson. I had no room to talk, even though the repercussions of what happened with Miller were worse. And though a part of me still had hope that Miller would tell Bryce, maybe Noah was right. Maybe it wouldn't help at all for Miller to own up to it. After two years of holding a grudge, I doubted it would be easy for Bryce to redirect his anger to someone else.

Bryce finally stopped by a couple days later, full of apologies, but he hadn't put everything behind him like I'd hoped.

"I still can't believe you're dating that guy," Bryce said as we sat by the pool.

It took everything in me not to shove him into the

water. How long was he going to keep this stupid grudge? "It happened two years ago," I said. "You treated Noah like shit for two years, and to be honest, if you want to continue acting like that then we can't be friends."

He gaped at me. I continued. "Noah and I are dating. Serious dating. I didn't tell you because I knew you'd freak. You've been my best friend for years. But if you can't accept him, then I can't accept you."

Bryce stared out over the pool for a long time without speaking. I sipped my Diet Coke and waited. I hated giving him an ultimatum like that. Bryce was like my brother, and it killed me to think of not having him in my life. Whatever he decided I'd have to stick to, though. There was no way I could let Noah keep going through hell, whether Miller told the truth or not. I was determined to protect him from Bryce, Holly, and anyone else who tried to keep making his life a living hell.

"Fine. I'll accept that you like him," he said gruffly. "Maybe he *has* changed. But don't expect me to double-date with you guys anytime soon."

My heart ached to hear those words. Really, it didn't sound too much better than things were now, but I knew it was the best he could do right now. "Okay." Maybe Bryce would get that baseball scholarship he wanted so bad and would put all this behind him. I had to hope.

SmartMart was a mess. It would take a couple months to rebuild before the store could open again, which meant I was out of a job. I was fine with that, since my dad convinced my mother to help me out with the car. It wasn't like I got fired or quit. Half the damn store was gone. I wanted to take Noah with me on the car-shopping trip, but my dad told me not to push my luck. All in all, I was thrilled with the Honda Civic they bought me. I got to pick my color—red—which made my mother frown. "It's a car for safety, not for hot-rodding," she said grumpily. That made all of us laugh. Hot-rodding in a Civic.

Mr. Hanson offered me a part-time job whenever the store reopened. It was on the tip of my tongue to politely decline. I had my car and my parents would pay insurance and gas until I went to college. And I played softball, though that wasn't until spring and Mr. Hanson said he'd work with my schedule. But then I thought about Noah working his ass off for college. Not a bad idea for me, too, since I didn't want to live in my parents' pockets forever. So I accepted.

What could I say? I was on a high. I could handle it all—Roxanne, crazy customers, and Ruthie. I did ask to be relieved from bathroom duty, which he agreed to. Noah even owned up to our relationship. Mr. Hanson simply shrugged and said we were teens and he couldn't expect much else, so we took that as a good sign. Roxanne would be shocked.

I looked forward to telling her.

The rest of my summer until I had to leave for my weeklong softball camp revolved around Noah, and since he was only working at Cooper's three nights a week, we had plenty of time together. My mother and even my dad commented on occasion that it was unhealthy how much time I was spending with him, but I ignored them.

I got to meet another friend of Noah's, Steve, who

apparently was a math genius as well as a master at gaming. Steve was friendly and very funny—the kind of guy who cracked jokes with a totally straight face so you weren't sure if he was kidding or not. We got along great.

I told Noah I didn't want to hang out with Miller—I still had a bad taste in my mouth for what he'd done. But it seemed to hurt Noah's feelings that I couldn't stand one of his friends, so I agreed to go to a movie with a large group of friends on both sides—minus Bryce, of course. Miller and I said hello but that was pretty much it. I talked to Steve most of the time. I noticed Syd had her eye on him, too. By the end of the night, they'd pretty much tuned out everyone else but each other. A couple days later they were meeting up for pizza. I guess Syd was rethinking the whole single/mingle thing.

Noah's mom was always happy to see me when I'd come over. Noah said she was just glad he was dating "like a normal kid." She asked him to keep his door open when we were in his room, though, to his total embarrassment. Guess she didn't trust us that much.

The time I wasn't with Noah and my friends I was at home, reading magazines to my grandma or talking to her about this or that. Most days she'd stare out the window, talking very rarely. She didn't even want to go outside for walks. Whatever happened with that stupid pneumonia did a number on her, and she wasn't the same. I still watched shows with her and talked with her, and on her best days she'd talk back, even exchanging sarcastic comments with me like old times.

I wished I could bottle up those moments and save them for the days when she looked at me like she wasn't sure who I was.

One unexpected side effect of Grandma's decline was that my mother and I spent more time together. I had a feeling my dad was trying to convince her to spend more time with me, especially with Grandma so distant these days. He'd give her one of those looks that parents did when they thought their kids weren't looking, the expression that plainly said, *This is your chance.* So when he asked me what I was doing and I said probably just working on my summer math, out came the look and suddenly my mother would get the urge to play Spades with me.

The funniest thing was that I didn't mind. I didn't know if it was because I was craving attention, or because I actually appreciated that she was making any effort at all that didn't involve pointless shopping trips. She'd even ask me about softball, what I hoped to get out of softball camp, stuff like that. I gave her basic answers, since I still got the feeling she didn't understand it. She did ask what I planned to do in the future but I gave her a vague response about just focusing on high school right now. Maybe someday I could tell her, but I didn't want to set our relationship back again. I liked that she was trying.

Sometimes we played cards alone, and sometimes we'd get Grandma to join us. Those times were my favorite, especially when Grandma was having a "good" day, laughing and poking fun at me like the old days. I could almost pretend like things were back to normal—well, a normal that included a mother who actually wanted to be around me.

During a game one day, Mom asked if I regretted taking that lipstick two months ago.

"Of course I do," I told her.

"Really?"

She tilted her head, a tiny smile playing on her lips as she winked at my grandma. Oh, I got it. If I hadn't taken the lipstick, I wouldn't have ended up working at SmartMart, and more than likely Noah would've remained the shy, reclusive kid at school who I never would have noticed.

Grandma laid a spade on top of mine as Mom asked, "So what'll happen when you return to school?"

I sighed. "Well, let's just say I don't think my prospects look good for Homecoming Queen."

Honestly, I didn't care about me—it was Noah I worried about. He might have been better off being left alone. But I'd do everything I could to keep them from hurting him. Maybe Bryce would come around and try to get to know Noah. And maybe eventually his friend Miller would confess to telling on Bryce so long ago and everyone could just let it go.

Grandma touched my knee with her thin hand. "Don't forget, you're not in a cage. You're free to be yourself, even if it means being alone."

I smiled at her. "I won't be alone, Grandma. I'll have my boyfriend, Noah." I always said "boyfriend" to clue her in when I mentioned Noah. It seemed to help, at least as far as I was concerned.

She nodded. "Ah, and if he can't take the pressure? You

will still need to be strong for yourself. Not for anyone else."

Her words didn't bother me. She didn't know Noah. He'd made it clear he wasn't going anywhere. His text later confirmed it for me.

Hey.

Hey.

I love you.

I love you too.

I smiled. Those words were all I needed. He and I could get through this next year. We'd handle any of the crap people threw at us.

Together.

ACKNOWLEDGMENTS

I will forever acknowledge first how important my wonderful children are to this process. Whether it's bouncing story ideas around, making me laugh, dealing with my cray-cray self when I'm on a deadline, or helping me come up with awesome names (thank you, AJ, for SmartMart!), their support has been extraordinary. Jack, AJ, and Elaine, I love you all the way to the moon and back.

To Agent P—Pam van Hylckama Vlieg—thank you for tirelessly cheerleading all my stories. You put your go-get-'em skillz to work like nobody's business, and I greatly appreciate it!

Eternal gratitude to Stacy Abrams for lifting the rug under which I try to sweep everything and helping me identify holes. You are an amazing editor, and I'm grateful for you "getting" my vision, even if I take issue with the fact that you haven't watched enough Disney movies. One day I shall buy you a $1.50 cup of tea just to laugh as you roll your eyes. And to Tara Quigley, my butt-chair pal, you're the sweetest savvy editor. Thank you for working on this project and appreciating my goofy sense of humor.

Heather Riccio, I adore the fabulousness that is you. You always go above and beyond the normal call of a publicist to make your clients feel special. Sometimes I wonder if you even sleep.

My beautiful book covers have been more than I could ever imagine, and for that I have Kelley York to thank. You are ridiculously talented, and I'm grateful that you once again agreed to be my cover designer. And to the Entangled and Macmillan teams, thank you for again making my dreams come true and helping me see *Paper or Plastic* to fruition.

Thank you to the early readers of this book—my mother, Pat Harris (playwright extraordinaire); Peggy Jackson (for the many ideas generated from our nightly walks to Starbucks); Lindsey Jackson (for helping me keep it real); Leslie Fillip (you're like a boss—and I still can't get it right!); Marlana Antifit (talented and fearless leader); Jen Woods (you are so fetch); and Patricia Ivanushka Taylor (Puma? Puma!).

To my fellow ChicksTracey Smith, Eva Griffin, and Peggy Jackson—you support me, inspire me, and a-MUSE me, and I love you all!

I have enormous appreciation and respect for my talented critique partners who saw me through all my crazy—Kristen Lippert-Martin, Tara Kelly, Julie Bourbeau,

Marlana Antifit, Peggy Jackson, Joe Iriarte, Dennis Cooper, Christy Koehnlein, Rina Heisel, Stephanie Spier, Jennye Kamin, Tori Kelley, and Lauren Vandivier. Special thanks to the OWLS for plenty of laughter and good times during our meetings and SCBWI conferences.

The past couple of years would've been much more challenging without the support of the fantastic writers who make up OneFour KidLit. I love you all! And thank you to the Florida SCBWI organization—Linda, Curtis, and Gaby, you have helped make this group feel like "home" to me. And to all the bloggers, librarians, booksellers, and readers, you keep writers' dreams alive. Thank you from the bottom of my heart for your support.

Enormous gratitude to all those who shared their expertise, especially Jeanette Pulgarin and Trey Tatum. And to my fellow YA Chicks Kickin' It gals, Amy Christine Parker and Christina Farley, I'd go on road trips with you guys any time!

To Emily and Grace, you girls are special even beyond your lovely names! Thank you for being a part of this process.

I am truly grateful to the entire Food & Beverage/ Merchandise Line of Business team for making me laugh and keeping me sane during this process. You make the "day job" a true pleasure.

And to my greatest love and best friend, David, thank you for helping me keep it real, for identifying the holes, and for your never-ending support. Our love story inspires my stories.

Don't miss Vivi Barnes's thrilling and romantic debut, OLIVIA TWISTED

Oᴌɪᴠɪᴀ

He tilts my chin up so my eyes meet his, his thumb brushing lightly across my lips. I close my eyes. I know Z is trouble. I know that being with him is going to get me into trouble. I don't care.

At least at this moment, I don't care.

Tossed from foster home to foster home, Olivia's seen a lot in her sixteen years. She's hardened, sure, though mostly just wants to fly under the radar until graduation. But her natural ability with computers catches the eye of Z, a mysterious guy at her new school. Soon, Z has brought Liv into his team of hacker elite—break into a few bank accounts, and voila, he drives a motorcycle. Follow his lead, and Liv might even be able to escape from her oppressive foster parents. As Liv and Z grow closer, though, so does the watchful eye of Bill Sykes, Z's boss. And he's got bigger plans for Liv…

Z

I can picture Liv's face: wide-eyed, trusting. Her smooth lips that taste like strawberry Fanta.

It was just a kiss. That's all. She's just like any other girl.

Except that she's not.

Thanks to Z, Olivia's about to get twisted.

Available now!

Check out more of Entangled Teen's hottest reads...

CINDERELLA'S DRESS by Shonna Slayton

Kate simply wants to create window displays at the department store where she's working, trying to help out with the war effort. But when long-lost relatives from Poland arrive with a steamer trunk they claim holds *the* Cinderella's dresses, life gets complicated. Now, with a father missing in action, her new sweetheart, Johnny, stuck in the middle of battle, and her great aunt losing her wits, Kate has to unravel the mystery before it's too late. After all, the descendants of the wicked stepsisters will stop at nothing to get what they think they deserve.

WHATEVER LIFE THROWS AT YOU by Julie Cross

When seventeen-year-old track star Annie Lucas's dad starts mentoring nineteen-year-old baseball rookie phenom, Jason Brody, Annie's convinced she knows his type—arrogant, bossy, and most likely not into high school girls. But as Brody and her father grow closer, Annie starts to see through his façade to the lonely boy in over his head. When opening day comes around and her dad—and Brody's—job is on the line, she's reminded why he's off-limits. But Brody needs her, and staying away isn't an option.

LOVE AND OTHER UNKNOWN VARIABLES
By Shannon Lee Alexander

Charlie Hanson has a clear vision of his future. A senior at Brighton School of Mathematics and Science, he knows he'll graduate, go to MIT, and inevitably discover the solutions to the universe's greatest unanswerable problems. But for Charlotte Finch, the future has never seemed very kind. Charlie's future blurs the moment he meets Charlotte, but by the time he learns Charlotte is ill, her gravitational pull on him is too great to overcome. Soon he must choose between the familiar formulas he's always relied on or the girl he's falling for.